Honored

by

Rose Thorgaard

A Dark Mafia Romance, Book Two

This is a work of fiction. Names, characters, places, and incidents are either the product of the author's imagination or are used fictitiously, and any resemblance to actual persons living or dead, business establishments, events, or locales, is entirely coincidental.

Honored

Cover Art by *The Wild Rose Press, Inc.*

The Wild Rose Press, Inc.
PO Box 708
Adams Basin, NY 14410-0708
Visit us at www.thewildrosepress.com

Publishing History
First Edition, 2024
Trade Paperback ISBN 978-1-5092-5305-0
Digital ISBN 978-1-5092-5306-7

A Dark Mafia Romance, Book Two
Published in the United States of America

Dedication

For those who truly believe love conquers all

Chapter One

Livia

My vision went blurry as I watched the city zoom past the car window. People rushed to their jobs or to the café, just doing ordinary things. I missed ordinary things. A few months ago, my direst concern was getting to classes on time because I hated waking up early and consistently slept through my alarms. Going to the art studio, cooking, hanging out with my friend and confidante, Eric Walsh—those were all normal things I used to do. Even Dante Castellano's presence in California became ordinary to me, in a way.

Now, as he sat beside me, he seemed just as lost for words as I. Spending the past week in denial only postponed the shock, which hit me like a freight train the moment I woke up this morning. I was never going to see my uncle again.

Dante had showered me with nothing but love and affection for the past week, but it hadn't covered his misery.

When I lived at home, he'd been a regular fixture, but I didn't know until after Uncle Michael was gone that Dante had become like a son to him. Knowing now how much their bond meant to them, it hurt even more to see the betrayal on my uncle's face when he realized the truth of our relationship. It was akin to seeing your beloved child break your most prized possession.

But why couldn't he have seen that Dante didn't break me?

I told myself if I refused to think about my uncle's death, I could support Dante—just as I suspected he was doing for me. I couldn't decide whether it was worse to lose blood family or chosen family, who you came to love without the familial obligation. Judging from his reaction, I had to say it was easily comparable to my pain. The storm raged behind his eyes, but it was obviously about more than my uncle. Part of his turmoil was about the giant pink elephant in the room. *Not the time. Don't think about it.*

While I wallowed in grief, I couldn't help but lose myself in my worries about our future. I should have been thinking of nothing but the funeral ahead, but I couldn't ignore the fear that I'd soon be mourning Dante. Maybe I had been in denial or blocked it out, but I knew what I heard before I passed out that night. He was expected to take my uncle's place, and I didn't know what to do with the information.

Selfish girl. My uncle was gone, yet I was scared out of my mind, thinking how little I knew about how things ran and the line of succession. I'd been under the impression that Dante was only a bodyguard or a soldier, low enough in the ranks that he wouldn't be expected to take a position of power. To a degree, I could reconcile his occupation with myself. But this? Some women craved powerful men and the authority they commanded, but that was something I'd never thought about before.

I assumed my uncle would always be there to run things, but I should have realized how stupid that was. Everyone else I loved was gone. Why did I think he was immune to death? And now being forced to watch Dante follow the same path…

What was the alternative? Go back to my solitary life, pretending anyone who came after Dante could ever compare? It was an impossible task. He'd awakened something dormant in me that couldn't be neatly tucked away. I craved him, and not just sexually. His tenderness, strength, and his brilliant mind. A shiver ran through me when I pictured the raw emotion that came from him when he played his violin for me.

Dante must have felt me trembling because he gently stroked my hair to get my attention. "We're here, baby."

I jolted, coming back to the present, and turned to look out the window. The opulent church came into view as we pulled up in front, with its steeple reaching to the cloudy sky. Dante halted me before I could open the door. Instead, he exited on his side to swing around the back of the car. He practically carried me out of the backseat.

"Don't treat me like I'm made of glass. I'm fine."

The heat emanating from his hand seared my wrist where he tightened his grip. "I promised I wasn't leaving your side today, and all I'm doing is fulfilling that promise."

In many ways, I resented him for putting me in the uncomfortable position of having to bend my morals for him. It wasn't as if I didn't know he'd committed crimes; his being head of the family made him more culpable. Nothing went down without the Don's approval. If Dante was the boss, the target on his back enlarged exponentially. Frustration got the better of me. "I don't need to be coddled."

Till now, he'd exhibited the patience of a saint with me, but he looked close to his limit. He bent down, holding my chin firmly in his hand. His eyes flashed with irritation and a little pain too. "Maybe *I* need you near me for comfort. Did you think of that, Livia?"

Guilt stabbed me in the chest. "I'm sorry…I didn't mean it that way. I don't know what I'm saying."

His eyes softened, and he laid a gentle kiss on my forehead. "I know. We're going to get through this together, okay? I know you've been trying to keep us afloat, but let me take over for today, at least."

I buried my face in his chest. Every time he saw my reddened eyes, he broke a little more. I couldn't even appreciate how handsome he looked in his bespoke suit. Getting tears and the minimal makeup I wore all over it would only make matters worse. "Okay…I love you so much."

He curled his arms around me. "I love you more. I'm here for you, baby."

We didn't speak again as he ushered me inside. Some hushed conversations from the pews halted abruptly as we entered through the huge double doors. Every pair of eyes in the room seemed to gravitate toward us. It felt like we were being penetrated by a thousand tiny needles. I focused on the beautiful stained-glass windows gracing every wall of the church. The bright blues and deep reds shining with what little sunlight streamed in felt significant, a shred of light on a cloudy day.

This was the same church where my parents had been waked and the memories became too much for me to handle. I'd only been ten at the time, and I felt like I was ten years old all over again. A meek, whimpering mess in the front pew—surrounded by my father's men on one side, and my uncle on the other. I remembered being grateful at the time that at least I still had him.

As my steps faltered, Dante slid an arm around my waist. We increased our pace to the front set of pews, but when he nudged me to sit down, I refused. No matter how distraught I was, I refused to disrespect my uncle's memory. Walking back toward the font of holy water, I anointed myself before I took my position next to Dante, who had ignored the tradition himself.

Does he think he's going to burst into flames if he touches the holy water?

The priest arrived and the mass began. I squeezed the hell out of Dante's hand while trying not to cry in front of all the intimidating gangsters and their wives occupying the rows behind us. A few familiar faces stood out from the crowd, but after all the years I spent away, they felt like strangers. I was sure they didn't truly know my uncle either, most of them being business associates. They had the nerve to insult me by sitting in those pews, feigning grief, acting like his death was anything but a byproduct of their business. Maybe some had even been in on his murder. Was I the only one who saw that?

I'd agonized over the eulogy I wrote for my uncle, but I didn't know if I could get through it without crying. I truly didn't think any of the people here deserved to hear it. Somehow, I hoped Uncle Michael would.

I needed to do this. The last time we were together, we'd spoken harshly to each other. He looked at me with such disappointment. Somehow, I would have preferred that to be the last time I saw him, instead of what happened after. I could hardly bear to think about it.

The images flashed before my eyes like some sort of

twisted scrapbook. His last words were an angry curse at the man who had kidnapped me, and his last movements had been to protect me. As soon as I squeezed my eyes shut, I heard the gunshot, then the dull thud of his body hitting the ground.

I inhaled a shaky breath to calm myself.

Dante nudged me back to reality when I still hadn't moved from my place beside him. "You don't have to go up there. I'll read it for you."

I blinked away the tears. "No. I have to tell my uncle I love him before we put him to rest."

After smoothing down my dress, I rose from the pew, willing my knees to stop wobbling as I made my way to the pulpit. When I stepped behind it, I met Dante's eyes and he gave me a nod of encouragement. The little piece of paper I had scrawled on the night before shook in my hands. It was only then I managed to get through it without completely breaking down. Some of the ink was smudged, but luckily, it was still legible.

I cleared my throat a few times and avoided all the eyes staring back at me. There were at least a hundred people here, only a few who I knew by name. Instead, I focused on the stained glass above the heads of all the strangers I saw as intruders on my private grief. "Michael Rossi was more than just my uncle; he was my guardian angel. After my parents died, he welcomed me with open arms into his home and his life. As you all know, he was a busy man, but he always made me a priority, even for silly things, like coming to watch me dressed as a tree in a middle school play." A few light chuckles sounded from the crowd before I went on. "He was a constant source of love and support in my life, even from behind prison bars."

One of my last happy memories with him came to mind, as we strolled around in Times Square, before the ultimate events that sent my life skidding out of control—my uncle's arrest, and the incident at Augustine's. Tears welled up when I thought of the man who murdered my uncle. My throat tightened.

"He protected me while supporting my dreams and ambitions. He was a kind and fair man, even if he could be stubborn at times. But his influence will stay with me, and I'll always feel his presence watching over me." I willed my voice not to crack as I uttered, "I love you, Uncle Michael."

Unable to hold the tears back anymore, I let them trickle out as I folded up the paper again and turned my back on the crowd. The casket holding my uncle's body was in front of me now. There was no more avoiding this. *He's gone, Liv. You're alone.*

Right then, I didn't give a damn. I slowly lowered to my knees in front of the casket, resting my forehead against the smooth wooden lid. "I'm sorry for being ungrateful. I just hope you can be proud of me someday, and that you'll be watching me still. I miss you so much already."

In my head, I swore I could hear him saying, *I miss you too, sweetie.*

The heat from Dante's hand on my back grounded me in a way I had never felt before. I sensed it was him without needing to turn. A moment later he was on his knees beside me. It was deadly quiet, but I heard the distinct sniffling of a few people watching our private moment. He wrapped his arms around me with no regard for anyone else.

Instead of speaking to me, he followed my lead and

addressed my uncle. "Michael, I'll never be able to pay back everything you've done for me. You saved my life more than once, and I'll make sure I do everything I can to deserve the chance you gave me."

He turned his tearful gaze to me before he continued. "You left me with a precious gift, and I swear to you, I'm going to spend the rest of my life guarding and cherishing it." He laid his palm on the casket for a moment before he stood up, pulling me with him.

He held me to his side with his arm around my shoulders as he led me back to the pew, shielding me from the sympathetic gazes of everyone around us. I clung to Dante's side, focusing on his thumb stroking the back of my hand as we listened to a bunch of people say kind things about my uncle.

Everyone would talk about the don's niece having a meltdown at the mass. Sometimes I forgot how small this island could be.

The only time Dante left my side was to help carry my uncle's casket with the other pallbearers before we left for the cemetery. I followed behind them as they carried my uncle to the hearse, staring down at my feet as I walked. I could barely stand to even look at the wooden box, knowing my uncle's body was in there and he would never get up again. For a brief moment, I almost wished I was religious. At least I would feel better, believing his soul was in Heaven, looking down on me. I couldn't decide whether that would be better or worse. Would he be disappointed in me as he watched me going down a road he vehemently disapproved of, while being completely unable to stop it?

****

The burial was difficult to watch, but knowing there

were fewer people to witness my constant stream of tears and choked sobs, it became easier to let my guard down. Dante stood at my side, clasping my hand.

To my left stood Giovanni Gallo. I hadn't seen him in four years, but I'd known him since I was a child. Well, *known* was a strong word. I had known *of* him and seen him around at the house, more so after my uncle went to prison. He still looked the same though slightly older. The silver hairs sprouting near his temples were a stark contrast to the thick jet-black mane covering the rest of his head. Every time he smiled, it pronounced the fine lines around his kind eyes.

I wondered if he still considered me a wild child. He knew more about me than I did about him. I didn't even know what position he held in my uncle's crew, nor any of the other men who surrounded us. At least I found comfort in the familiar faces, even if they stayed mute and stoic. *Déjà vu?*

Dante's face remained as expressionless as the rest of the men's. He was much better at masking his emotions than me, and while I usually saw it as a negative thing, today I was grateful for it. If I saw his tears again, I would lose it. I squeezed his hand, hoping the small gesture would comfort him a little. When I shivered in the harsh winter air, he didn't waste a second slipping off his jacket and placing it over my shoulders.

Once the hardest part was over, then came the obligatory train of condolences from the men who had been my uncle's partners in crime, probably longer than I'd been alive.

Giovanni turned to me, and even in my grief, I found it slightly humorous when I realized this was probably the first time he ever addressed me directly. "Livia, I'm so sorry for your loss. Michael was a good man, and he loved you like his own. We all care for you, and we'll continue to be there for you. We know where our loyalties lie." He spoke calmly, but with determination as he gestured to the other suited men, who nodded in agreement.

I closed my eyes for a second, nodding back to him. "Thank you, Giovanni. That means a lot."

After the others shook my hand and gave me their condolences, each one's demeanor seemed to shift as they passed Dante. Giovanni clasped his hands in front of him in a gesture of respect. "I know he was like a father to you. I'm very sorry for your loss. I'm confident that you'll be able to fill his shoes, and I look forward to working for you, Don Castellano." He tilted his head slightly, almost like he was bowing. Each man in turn did the same.

Dante took conscious effort not to glance my way while this was happening, even though he saw me gaping at him. He exuded power and authority, giving them subtle nods of acknowledgment as they paid their respects. They spoke like everything had been decided already.

Maybe it had, and I was too determined to stay in denial.

This isn't the real him.

I reminded myself of that over and over again as we left my uncle to rest.

Chapter Two

Dante

I expected the funeral to be difficult, but nothing could have prepared me for the sight of Livia breaking down during her eulogy. When she fell to her knees in front of the casket, it took everything in me not to break down right along with her. Losing Michael destroyed me, but there was still one ray of light left behind for me. I felt a twinge of fear in my gut when I thought about losing her, too. *Never happening. I won't let it.*

A few people from the crowd looked shocked when I rose from the pew to go to her; I didn't give a shit. None of them understood the pain of being left alone in the world, without a shred of family left to lean on. I did, and now Livia did, too. I wouldn't wish that pain on most people, but especially not her. In her short life, she had suffered more loss than anyone should ever have to endure. By some miracle, this resilient woman was still standing. Just barely. As much as I hurt, I still wished I could take all of her sorrow from her.

All I had was Liv, and the lingering memories of Michael that popped up at the most inopportune times. As they lowered him in the ground, I thought about all the times he was there for me when my own father wasn't. Whenever he and his crew would come into Castellano's Italian Bistro, Michael would always shove a wad of cash into my hand and request a song. If he noticed I was stressed, he would pull me aside and put on his fatherly act, telling me to stay out of trouble. It was almost as if he knew the road I would be going down before even I did. Eventually, after my parents' deaths, he deemed it safer under his wing than being left to my own devices.

Even though I'd proven my worth to him over the years, maybe he could never see past my terrible decision-making enough to trust me with Livia's heart. *Too late now.*

During the burial, I felt her eyes burning into my skin as Giovanni and the others started talking business right in front of her. I wanted to kill them, but I couldn't avoid this conversation for much longer. Livia knew me better than any living soul, and she loved me. Nothing but my title was going to change, and even though I had no faith that anyone would hear it, I prayed that she could find a way to look past this. I could think of nothing else as we headed back to Michael's house for the funeral reception.

Her silence told me she was agonizing about the same thing. I glanced at her and couldn't help but notice the sizable distance between us. With me on one end of the backseat, and her on the other, she was about as far as she could possibly get from me without being outside of the car. I couldn't stand to have her that far away from me, and before I could stop myself, I reached out to her and took her hand in mine. "Baby, don't shut me out," I pleaded. "What's on your mind?"

Livia shook her head lightly, still staring straight out the window. "Nothing."

"I don't believe you."

With a sudden huff, she straightened her back and turned on me with a frustrated glare. "Is it so crazy that I'm upset right now?"

"No, it's not. But this day has been hard enough for you, and I don't want anything making it worse. Talk to me." Obviously, she was heartbroken after losing her uncle, but her furrowed brows told me she was thinking about something else entirely, and I knew damn well what it was. Maybe it wasn't the time to talk about it, but every second we avoided it, I felt her drifting further away from me. "And don't lie to me."

My stern tone put fire in her eyes. "Fine, you want to talk about it now? Let's talk about it. What's going to happen with *the family*?" Her question came out as a shout, and then her nervous eyes darted forward to the driver.

At least we were finally addressing it. After closing the divider between us and the driver, I reached for her again. "I'm not sure yet."

"They called you Don Castellano. I know I'm sheltered, but is that how it works? They expect you to take over now?"

A few uncomfortable moments of silence passed while I tried to think of a response that wouldn't send her running. "When Michael went to prison, he wanted to make sure someone was available to look after you in case something happened. He only trusted me to do that." It was the moment of truth. Now that she was asking me directly, I couldn't lie. "Augustine was never supposed to be the acting boss."

Livia's face went ashen. "What are you saying?"

"I'm his *consigliere*. The second-in-command."

At the time, I'd been relieved because I wasn't sure

I wanted the responsibility of being the boss, but now I saw I should have taken it. It was going to end this way no matter what, and all I'd done was delay the inevitable.

She jolted back, ripping her hand from mine. "I thought you were just my uncle's…bodyguard, or whatever! You knew it would come to this if he died. How could you not tell me?"

I'd prepared myself for her anger, but not for the look of pure terror in her eyes. "I didn't think it would happen! And what difference would it make? You knew I was part of this life before. I'll just have to take a bigger hand in it now."

She backed away again, staring me down in the way only she could. "But you expressed an interest in leaving it behind someday. The don doesn't get to retire! It's either death or prison, don't you see that? Weren't you there at the funeral?"

Livia started to lose it, scrunching herself up against the car door to get away from me, as if I disgusted her. Wounded, I dropped my hands, stopping all attempts to touch her. "I won't let that happen."

The sudden silence was deafening, and I clenched my fists on top of my knees, almost feeling the thickness of the air in my grasp. It was all I could do not to punch the car window out, or yank Livia onto my lap and hold on to her as tightly as I could. Anything to keep her with me.

When she spoke again, I jolted out of my self-loathing spiral. Desperation tinged her soft voice, and I felt my anger melting away. "We just buried my uncle, and the idea of losing you scares me so much, I don't think I can cope. Please…I don't want to talk about this anymore."

"Come here," I ordered, waving her toward me. After a few moments of deliberation with herself, she finally slid over and swung her legs over mine, and I hauled her onto my lap. The fear gripping my chest told me to hold on as tightly as I could, so I did. I crushed her to my body, pouring my need into her.

When she turned her face toward me, I kissed her hard on her mouth and held her in my intense stare. "You are never going to lose me. I only wanted to give you time to process everything. It was never my intention to hide it from you. Please believe that."

"I know." She nodded and let her head fall onto my shoulder. "I wish we were back at the house upstate. Everything was so perfect there. Just you, me, and Nero. My uncle was alive, and none of this had happened yet. We should have just stayed there."

To quell the unease I felt, I peppered kisses on top of her soft chestnut waves. "You have no idea how much I wish we had. But, my beautiful *principessa*—" I tilted her head back to look at me again. "—we can't turn back time. We have to deal with what we have. And what we have is each other. You are everything to me, and I will make it my life's mission to make you happy. Just please bear with me for now, okay?"

Short of begging her not to give up on me, I didn't know what else to say. How would I cope with the loss of the only meaningful father figure I'd ever had, followed by the only meaningful love I'd ever had? I buried my face in her hair to regain my equilibrium just as we pulled into the rounded driveway of Michael's house. "We're here."

We turned to look out the window at the brick mansion before us. It was Georgian in style on the outside, and contemporary on the inside. I remembered when Michael had bought that house, because it was right around the time he pulled me off the streets to work for him. My throat tightened at the memory. I remembered him complaining about how stuffy it was on the inside. He had spared no expense having the interior completely redone. Even though it was quite the contrast to the exterior of the house, I had to admit it was beautiful.

It felt like years since I stepped into this house, but in reality, it had only been two months. While he'd been in prison, his Manhattan mansion had basically remained the Rossi family HQ, even though the "acting boss" rarely showed his face, preferring the company of his strippers. I'd gotten used to being here without him, making sure nothing fell apart, and I was the only one he trusted to go through his important files in his office.

But it felt different this time, knowing I'd never see Michael in his study again, sitting behind his desk with his customary glass of whiskey and a cigar. *I could go for a smoke right now*. I had to force myself to let the image go. Whatever I was feeling, it had to be magnified ten times for Livia, and she needed me to be there for her. I couldn't fall apart now.

With the difficult conversation shelved, we exited the car, and I ushered her into the house. It must have been strange for her to see it again, having not stepped foot inside this place for years. We were the first to arrive, and that was a deliberate move on my part. I wanted to give her a minute to explore and gain her bearings before she had to deal with the onslaught of people.

Her tense shoulders betrayed her state of mind. "It

hasn't changed at all."

She seemed almost in a haze and didn't take notice of me as she wandered up the stairs. Giving her a minute to look around, I noticed Giovanni and the rest of Michael's men pulling up to the house. I didn't trust anyone not to try something today. Anyone still loyal to Augustine wouldn't see anything as sacred—not even a funeral. With my authoritative expression firmly in place, I approached.

"Gio, I want you and the guys to space out around the outside of the property, and a few inside as well. Keep your eyes peeled for anything strange, and make sure no one is armed but you." When he signaled his assent, I met his eyes with a warning glare. I wasn't going to let anything make this day even harder for Liv, or myself, for that matter. "If anything goes wrong, I'm personally holding you responsible."

Completely unfazed by my threat, he nodded eagerly. "Understood, boss. Do you want someone to keep an eye on Livia as well?"

"No, I'll be with her. If you see anything off, then come find me immediately."

He only meant to be helpful, but I couldn't help getting defensive when anyone even so much as hinted I couldn't protect Livia myself. The unpleasant memory of that night came roaring back, and I forced it back down quickly. Toning down the irritation as much as possible, I muttered, "I just want to get through one day without any fucking catastrophes."

"Of course. I understand. We'll make sure everything goes smoothly. I'll personally handle the door, okay?" he suggested with a genuinely sympathetic smile.

I had always liked Gio. He was the kind of guy to bust someone's kneecaps if they disrespected a woman in front of him. Otherwise, he was friendly and gregarious. I trusted him more than most of Michael's guys. Not to say I didn't trust them, but I still had yet to sniff out all of Augustine's sympathizers, so I found myself being very careful about what I told any of them. Guilty until proven innocent.

Gio had been distraught when he learned Livia was missing, so I trusted he had no knowledge of it. He acted like a grandfather with her, even though he was barely fifty years old. He'd known her for most of her life, and I was sure he still saw her as that little girl playing with her paints. After the mass, I watched as he offered her a piece of candy out of his pocket and had to hold in the inappropriate laughter that threatened to come out.

Once he had his assignment, people began to arrive, and I realized Livia had been inside the house alone for at least half an hour. I turned around and went back inside to find her. Several people stopped me as I made my way upstairs where I assumed she would be, and I became slightly more frantic with each person who wanted to chat about meaningless shit. The last guy, I threw aside by the collar of his shirt with only two words, "Go away."

I'd have been a liar if I said I didn't have the same fears she did. Every minute she was out of my sight sent me into a panic that wasn't entirely normal. Nothing about our situation was normal. In our brief relationship, it felt like we'd been through an entire lifetime together. All I was sure of was that I was obsessed with her, and it only grew stronger every day. I refused to go back to my old life—living for no purpose other than fulfilling my obligations, separated by meaningless distractions in between.

Whatever I had to do to keep her, I would do it.

I took the stairs two at a time, and once I was on the landing, I realized I didn't actually know which room was hers. This house had six bedrooms, most of which were usually vacant these days. Back when Livia lived here, there were at least three of Michael's men staying in those bedrooms at all times. Honestly, it was almost eerie how quiet it was—it felt empty even though there were twenty or so people here already. Michael's presence was so robust, I imagined it would feel empty with even a hundred people here, if he wasn't one of them.

My men made sure nobody ventured up to the second floor. There were two bathrooms downstairs for guests to use, one being right off to the left of the living room, and another to the right of the study. It was a small way for me to ensure Livia had a safe place to run off to if she needed to be alone. I hoped my presence would have been all she needed, but maybe that was too much to hope for.

Two bedrooms were to the left of the landing, and the other three were to the right, the master bedroom being downstairs. It didn't take me long to find her when I spotted the only room where the door wasn't completely shut. Not wanting to startle her, I lifted my fist to knock on the door, but before I made contact, I heard her sniffling and quickly abandoned my manners. Livia sat on the bed with a fluffy purple blanket wrapped around her shoulders.

"There you are."

With no clue what to say to ease her obvious

distress, I settled myself down beside her and kissed the top of her head. She leaned into me instantly, which made me feel better about bursting in on her private moment. I was glad she still wanted me near her after our argument in the car, but the relief faded away once I heard her shaky voice.

"Have you seen my mom's work before?"

Not what I expected her to say, but okay. At least she was thinking about something other than Michael or my new position, and that was a relief. "Yeah, one of her paintings is hung in the study. She gifted you with her talent."

"Yeah, right. I could never be as good as her. I haven't seen these paintings in years, and suddenly I feel like I learned nothing in art school. My paintings don't compare to this." She gestured toward the wall above her bed. On top of her headboard hung a large abstract painting of the ocean, with thick layers of different shades of blue paint, and white ocean spray along the edges of each wave. "You know, I didn't go to the beach once in California? I haven't lived at all."

"So I'll take you to Jones beach." I didn't like where this was going. "What brought this on? Your paintings are beautiful. You have your own style, and every artist is different. I don't play the violin like the pros, but does that make me any less talented? More than once, my music moved you to tears."

She nodded hesitantly. "True. I'm just being silly… It's weird to be back here, and all the memories are coming back to me at once. I can hear the voices of all those people downstairs, and yet this house has never felt emptier."

Her words struck a chord in me, mirroring my

previous thoughts. I silently agreed and held her close to me for a few more minutes. Mostly, I was getting a little uncomfortable with the direction the conversation was headed before she changed the subject. Any other time, and I would have loved to spend a while reminiscing with her, but now I was only feeling the dread in the pit of my stomach growing with every passing moment.

Livia always seemed so wise beyond her years; it was easy for me to forget how young she was. I had lived a very busy life before her, yet she was just beginning hers. A voice inside me told me I should have let her go, but I told myself I knew better and that I could make her happy. The insecurity began to gnaw at me, followed by guilt. Maybe Michael had been right to warn me away from her, but it was too late now. I needed her, and I wasn't letting her go.

Technically, we were engaged, even though I had yet to put a ring on her finger. With Michael's funeral taking precedence, we had barely spoken about it since, and I couldn't fault her for it. She was the last of the Rossi line; a wedding was probably the last thing on her mind right now. Clearing my throat, I brushed her hair from her face and nuzzled her cheek. "Should we make the rounds downstairs before we send everyone home?"

Livia rose from the bed. "Yes, let's get it over with. I just want to go home and cuddle with you and Nero."

Hearing her refer to my apartment, which paled in comparison to the garish mansion, as *home* lightened my sour mood. Even though she lived here longer than she'd lived anywhere else, she was at home with me. That would have to be enough to convince me I deserved her and that she wasn't going anywhere.

Chapter Three

Livia

Dante's paranoia about a new adversary coming out of the woodwork was understandable, but it was difficult to see him so wound up. With an obviously armed guard everywhere I looked, and Dante staying glued to my side, it told me he was worried. Why had he been so determined to make nice with all the mobsters downstairs if he thought one of them might betray us?

If anyone dared, I'd be angry enough to do some damage myself. The thought would shock Dante, surely. He thought I was such a sweet girl, and I usually was, but everyone has their limit.

The wake and funeral had gone smoothly, but now I ached to go back home and bury my sorrows. I couldn't stand for one more person who didn't know me or my uncle to give me platitudes and hollow sympathies. All of their claims that things would get better made me feel worse; I couldn't imagine a time when the loss of my entire family wouldn't hurt.

I turned to Dante, watching his shoulders and face relax the farther we got away from my uncle's house. He looked completely exhausted, and I couldn't blame him. Holding down the fort today must have taken a toll on him, and I was sure our earlier argument didn't help matters. I wanted so badly to assuage his fears that were bubbling under the surface, but I couldn't do it. How could I promise him something I wasn't sure of?

Beyond the fact that Dante owned my heart, I didn't know anything. We'd let our powerful connection draw us together without thinking about the ramifications our relationship would have on our lives. I'd been swept up in his captivating presence until I couldn't resist the deepening feelings blooming inside me.

He didn't have to tell me he was worried about our future. I could see it all over his face and was certain he could see it on mine. Neither of us wanted to be the one to rock the boat and cause more pain. Our relationship was the one thing that kept us afloat. After we got home, we didn't say a word as we undressed and fell into an exhausted heap on the bed.

****

The softness of Dante's kisses peppering my neck woke me from a fretful sleep. My body's response to his arousal was involuntary; I scooted closer to absorb his soothing warmth, which prompted him to snake his arms around me, answering my wordless request for closeness. After a few moments of his gentle caresses, I gained enough awareness to open my eyes and check the clock on the nightstand. Four in the morning?

I wiggled against him, wondering if he was even fully conscious. "Having horny dreams, *caro*?"

He moaned lightly against my neck and nuzzled it. "Only yourself to blame—you're irresistible."

His hand slipped under the hem of my T-shirt, and my breath caught in my throat when he flattened his roughened palm over my belly, slowly rising up to cup my breast. His fingers brushed against my nipple with feather-light touches, sending a jolt straight between my legs. The juxtaposition of soft touches from his worn hands stimulated every nerve ending in my body. A quiet whimper escaped when he took my nipple between his fingers and rolled it. The twinge of need throbbed at my core.

A sharp pain interrupted my sudden onset of pleasure as he sank his teeth into the side of my neck. Dante chuckled when he heard my gasp of surprise, then he gently licked and sucked the spot, soothing it. It would definitely leave a mark, and I was sure he'd intended to do so. His breaths came out shallow and quick as he traced his tongue along the shell of my ear. "I need you, Liv. Now."

I reached behind me to stroke his bulge through his boxers, and I could already feel the moistness of his arousal through the fabric. Before I could reach inside, he stopped me, rising up from the bed and shoving them hastily down his thighs.

"You're eager tonight."

"On your knees. Hold on to the headboard," he ordered quietly, ignoring my observation. The ache in my lower belly magnified when my eyes fell to his shaft, which was harder than I'd ever seen it. I watched it throb as I followed suit, tearing off my shirt and throwing it to the floor.

I gripped the edge of the headboard and scooted up closer so I was kneeling on the bed, and a second later I felt Dante's broad chest heaving against my back. Holding my hip to keep me steady, he positioned himself behind me.

When he hesitated for a moment, I turned to investigate; the predatory look on his face both shocked and turned me on. In my attempt to urge him on, I pushed my hips against him, and he shuddered. As he slid inside, he breathed, "I'm going to make everything right for you, baby. I promise."

His passionate declaration kept repeating in my head, but my mind quickly went blank when he thrust deep again. He worked hard to keep me distracted from it, as if he hadn't meant to say it out loud. After a few smooth pumps, he sped his movements, and my voice was suddenly nowhere to be found.

With his face buried in my hair, his hot breath came out in quick puffs against my ear. He panted his words out between increasingly sharp thrusts. "Tell me you're mine. That this body belongs to me."

I felt his hand drifting up between my breasts until he cupped my throat. The gentle, yet possessive hold sent me into another level of ecstasy; my knuckles whitened as I held onto the headboard for dear life. "I'm all yours…only yours."

"Damn straight. This is where you belong… Oh, God, it feels fucking perfect."

His thrusts became more desperate. His grunts and growls in my ear felt almost primal, accompanying every swivel of his hips. I would have fallen forward if it weren't for my iron grip on the headboard and his arms around me, holding me close. When he tightened his hand around my throat slightly, I felt the familiar fluttering of my inner walls.

Listening to his deep voice in my ear, telling me how good it felt, and how beautiful I was, made my heart pound. My climax came over me in a powerful wave, which had my legs wobbling under me and my voice hoarse. "Oh God, Dante, I'm coming!"

Banding his arms across my midsection, he held me

up as I shook furiously. He panted against the back of my neck, his shallow breaths cooling my skin as he came. "*Baby, yes*. Take it all."

Completely replete, I fell limply against his chest. "Wow…"

"I've got you. Come here." He gently shifted us back down to the bed and lay on his back with me beside him, head resting on his chest. For a few minutes, I traced the wings of the owl tattoo on his pecs with my index finger. Neither of us seemed willing to move again, and after a few minutes, we fell into a peaceful slumber. I could still feel the pulsing between my legs as I drifted off.

****

When I awoke again, I felt like I was still high from the explosive sex from only a few hours ago. It wasn't just making love this time—it was something primal, possessive. His passionate declaration before he entered me stuck in my mind. It was as if my uncle's death had opened a dam, and he couldn't slam the door shut. The raw emotion he displayed showed he was terrified of losing me. I wasn't ready to open that can of worms.

Why couldn't the world just leave us alone in our bubble? Hadn't we been through enough?

My eyes snapped open when I slid my hand toward his side of the bed, only to find it empty and cold. I quickly sat up and looked around the room. The closet door was open, and he exited the bathroom a second later, accompanied by the steam drifting out from the shower. He smiled when he spotted me. "Morning, beautiful. Sleep well?"

I had to smile back at his cheekiness, shoving aside the negative thoughts. "Yep, like a baby all night."

He snorted. "You're a brat, Liv."

"That's why you fell in love with me, though. What good would it do for me to change now?" I jumped out of bed and threw my arms around his neck to give him a kiss, then rushed past him to use the bathroom and brush my teeth. When I looked into the mirror, I let out a shriek, dropping the toothbrush from my mouth when it fell open in shock. "Oh my God!"

Dante sauntered back into the bathroom with a knowing smirk on his face and an unconvincing tone. "What's wrong?"

"You! Look at my neck! I'm going to have to wear a turtleneck if I want to go out." It was no secret that his possessiveness turned me on, but I couldn't let him get away with *everything*. "Why do you have to be such a beast?"

His wolfish grin widened in the mirror's reflection. "May I turn your own words back on you, my love? What good would it do for me to change now?"

Our eyes met in the mirror, and I shook my head at him, even as the corners of my lips turned up in amusement. It was moments like these when everything else fell away. My pain, my loneliness, and every insecurity were gone when he beamed at me like I was the only thing in his world. Those eyes melted me every time I basked in their glow.

He gave me a peck on my forehead before he went back to the bedroom and started getting dressed. I was about to ask him what he was getting dressed for when I heard a sharp rap on the door. Dante hadn't heard the knock, and I rushed to answer it while throwing on my clothes.

The man on the doorstep looked somewhat familiar,

but I couldn't quite place him. He looked to be a little older than Dante, maybe in his forties, with sandy brown hair swept to the side. Cocking my head, I asked, "Yes?"

Even though he seemed surprised to see me answering Dante's door, he quickly went into professional mode. "Livia, good to see you again. I'm Carlo Basile. I used to be Michael's driver…" He trailed off, shoving his hands in the pockets of his slacks. "I'm sorry for your loss."

I really wished people would stop reminding me. Every time I managed to forget about my grief for a moment, something would remind me that my uncle was gone, and he was never coming back. Not wanting to be rude, I nodded slowly. "Thank you, Carlo. I remember you. Can I help you with something?"

As if worried about revealing too much, he answered curtly, "I'm here to pick up Dante."

I felt the hairs on the back of my neck stand up, and then Dante's warmth against my back. When I faced him, he had his expressionless mask on, and a sleek black suit, paired with a crimson-red tie. Though he looked mouth-wateringly handsome, the formal attire meant one thing. The anxiety returned with a vengeance.

He shot Carlo a steely look. "I'll be out in a minute. Wait for me downstairs." When the door shut behind him, the icy stare thawed, replaced by nervousness as he waited for me to explode.

I didn't want to jump to any conclusions just yet. "You didn't tell me you had to work today. What's happening?"

Dante sighed and took my hand. "I was going to fill you in later when I had all the information…I have a meeting with the five families."

"What is the meeting about?" I regretted the question immediately when Dante's bottom lip disappeared between his teeth.

"I think you know." He straightened his tie. "I have to do this."

My worst fears were realized at that moment. I knew I had to face it eventually, but why did it have to be now? Just when I was feeling so good about us, the rug was ripped from underneath my feet. "Why can't someone else do it? You let Augustine take charge before. Isn't there anyone else who can take my uncle's place?"

He glared at me, as if wondering how I could be so naïve. "Are you serious? Look at the things he's done! What he did to *you*. I want to honor Michael, and the way to do that is to take his place myself. It'll be better this way."

I couldn't hold it inside anymore; the words came out in a hoarse cry. "How will it be better if you go to prison? Or if you don't come home one day, then I'm left to wonder if you're working late, stuck in a traffic jam, or at the bottom of the river? What if we have children? How can this possibly work?"

He let out a groan of exasperation. "We will figure it out together. We can talk about this as soon as I get back, but I have to leave now."

Now he was eager to get away from me? When he turned to leave, I stepped in front of him to prevent him from walking away. He wanted so badly to hash this out, and now I did too. There was no avoiding it anymore. "You can't come into my life and make me need you, then leave me with nothing!"

Dante didn't try to loosen my grip on his biceps when I clung to him. Staring deeply into my eyes, he rasped, "I promised you that would never happen. You and I are going to have a long life together and we're going to be happy. You just have to look past this one piece of me. I know it's selfish, but don't act like you're alone in this. I didn't want to need you this much either, but it happened. We were always going to happen, Livia."

How could he be so foolish? He must have acquired selective amnesia, because I couldn't understand how he thought we would just sail through life unscathed. His parents were gone, my parents were gone, and now my uncle too. And here he was, offering up his head on the chopping block, as if in penance for a death he blamed himself for. He didn't understand how I saw it as him choosing the Mafia over me. Choosing death over me. I'd hoped he was growing past his self-destructive tendencies. *If he hates himself this much...*

The despondency hit me hard, and the words fell from my lips in a whisper. "I didn't sign on to be a don's wife."

"*What did you say?*"

When I ignored him and stalked into the bedroom, I instantly heard his heavy footfall trailing behind me. My feet carried me to the closet almost without my knowledge, and I threw open the doors. My fight-or-flight instincts kicked in, and the only word repeating in my mind was *run*.

"Don't walk away from me."

I spun around and stared daggers at him as he studied me, shoulders tensed. "You're the one walking away. I'm not going to watch someone else I love be ripped away from me. Not again."

My heart ached when I saw the pain he failed to fully

cover, the flash of fear and anger behind his eyes. "You knew what I was from the minute we started this." He stalked closer, reaching up to cup my face in his hands as he grated out his words. "You willfully pushed me to let you in. You made me feel things I've never felt before, and you pursued me even when I tried to distance myself. You agreed to marry me! Remember that? What's changed besides my fucking title?"

The words that spilled out of my mouth surprised me but frustration at the situation sent me over the edge. "If I hadn't come back with you, none of this would have happened! Maybe I wouldn't get to see my uncle, but at least he would still be alive, and you wouldn't be forced to follow him to the goddamned grave!"

Dante dropped his hands to his sides. "You blame me for Michael's death…"

How could he suggest that? Back when I was still afraid Dante would kidnap me and drag me back to New York in a cage, I'd planned to run away. If I'd done that, I could have prevented all of this. If I hadn't needed rescuing when I was grabbed off the street, Uncle Michael would still be alive.

Damning myself for my poor decisions, I tore my clothes down from the hangers haphazardly, all while ignoring Dante's heavy breathing. The pain in his voice was almost too much to bear, so I didn't dare turn around when I finally answered him. "I would never blame you for what happened. It's my own fault for coming back here. That's why I'm taking myself out of the equation now, before it gets any more painful."

I felt his hands on my shoulders, and he spun me around to face him again. "You can't do this," he stammered in disbelief, making no more attempts to hide his frantic state from me. "You don't get to give up on us—I haven't. I'm in *love* with you. Do you have any idea what that means for me? I didn't even know I was capable of it before you. You make me feel like a man, and not a monster. The only other person who made me feel human was Michael."

Too afraid of what I'd see if I looked up, I averted my gaze. "I love you too...which is why it will hurt too much to stay."

A strangled noise escaped from deep in his throat. "I fucking knew you would do this. I knew you'd run..." He paced in front of me, running his fingers through his impeccably slicked-back hair, mussing it up. "This can't have all been for nothing."

The tears fell, even as I tried desperately to blink them away. "I'm sorry. I...can't watch you go down this road. I'll break."

"You've broken me already, Livia Rossi." His words came out hoarse and broken before he stalked away from me, slamming the door so brutally I was sure it came off its hinges.

The bang sent Nero into a barking frenzy from his perch on the couch, and after packing my things, I paused to say goodbye to him. His knowing eyes looked so similar to Dante's, and it only made the tears spring forth again. "I'm sorry, Nero. Take care of him."

Chapter Four

Dante

Once Carlo saw the look on my face as I jumped into the passenger's seat, he must have known better than to ask what was wrong. It took everything in me not to rip the car door off its hinges, but I felt a little satisfaction when I slammed it shut with a bang. He jumped slightly. Good. Right then, I wanted *someone* to be afraid of me.

The idea of scaring Livia into staying with me was tempting, but deep down, I didn't want that. She deserved to be able to choose her happiness for the first time in her life. As much as I wanted that happiness to be with me, I didn't have the right to take her choice away from her.

As I stared out the window, I cursed myself for two things. One, for not taking her hand and running for the fucking hills. And two, for being surprised at her response. What made me think I could take this woman from her peaceful life in California and bring her back to her worst nightmare, expecting her to acclimate with no issues?

At least in my world, no one could hurt me where it really mattered.

"Ready, boss?" Carlo uttered in a wary voice.

My only response was a scowl and a tight nod. He was likely worried that he had done something wrong by talking to Livia. With Michael gone, my men didn't know what the protocol was anymore. I could have told him I wasn't her warden anymore, but I wasn't feeling empathetic enough to put his mind at ease.

I had my own reasons for not wanting them around her. I didn't want to take the chance that a traitor might get too close to her—or worse, seduce her away from me. Judging by the way she had just ripped out my heart, that concern was unfounded. She wanted nothing to do with men like me. And she could pretend it was about safety all she wanted, but I knew the truth. Livia saw the monster side of me, and once it sank in, she decided she couldn't love me like this.

Until I fell for her, I couldn't fully appreciate Michael's unrelenting willingness to risk anything for her. His dying wish had been to ensure his niece was always protected, and I planned to do just that, no matter how much it hurt to see her. It was the one promise I couldn't break.

I spent the rest of the drive compartmentalizing everything that had happened in the last half hour into a neat little box in the back of my mind. By the time we arrived at the restaurant, I had my self-assured mask firmly on.

I hadn't stepped foot in Castellano's since the place was sold. Those last few weeks working there after my parents' deaths had been hell. I was shit faced through every shift, and the manager was relieved when I stopped showing up for work. Customers complained about my terrible performance, and once I left, Augustine made it easier for me to slip further into that self-loathing spiral I'd become so comfortable in.

The dining area looked similar to the way it had

when my parents owned it, with some updated décor and furniture. It had been old-school Italian back in the day, but now it was slightly more high-end. Unfortunately, they kept the tacky, bright red paint, though. And there was no live band anymore, just music piping through the smart speakers mounted on the walls. The owners were connected as well and willingly shut the place down for the day so we would have a place to meet on my territory.

My territory. It gave me an immense rush of adrenaline. I told myself this was something I had to do, but a secret part of me reveled in the authority my new position would grant me. It was a feeling I wasn't entirely comfortable with, but I vowed not to let the power go to my head, or I would be no better than my predecessor. The relief I felt four years ago when Michael let Lombardi take the reins instead of me made me laugh. If only I had known I couldn't escape my fate.

As I led the way for my crew into the restaurant, the entire room went dead quiet. Immediately, I spotted Lorenzo Leone, who was called Enzo by friends and family. But we weren't friends—I only called him that to annoy him. Judging by his general look of boredom, he must not have known that Michael and I had roughed up his little brother, Luca.

A nod of acknowledgment was the most he'd get from me this day. He had a reputation for serious drug use, which was reason enough to keep my distance from him.

Sitting beside him was Anthony Conti, and he gave me a slightly more friendly greeting. With a sympathetic smile on his overly tanned face, he said, "Don Castellano. We were sorry to hear about Michael…and less sorry to hear about Augustine."

Several of the other men let out chuckles of agreement. Augustine Lombardi was not a popular man with most of our...I couldn't quite call them allies, but they weren't enemies either. They all saw how arrogant he had become once I made the mistake of handing him the crown. My bitterness made me wonder if it would have been better if I'd taken the role and stayed in Manhattan back then, but I couldn't picture not knowing Liv the way I did now. Even the sick feeling in my stomach whenever the image of her face popped into my mind was preferable to the emptiness that was there before.

"Thank you, Don Conti. Let's get started."

Pushing Livia out of my thoughts, I pulled out a chair at the long mahogany table and settled in, straightening my tie as I took in the heads of the other four families. "As you all know, I was Michael's *consigliere*, and I'm prepared to take his place as soon as possible. I'd like to go over any prior agreements and partnerships Augustine held with any of you so we can renegotiate. I have a few caveats that I'm not willing to budge on, and some others that are up for discussion."

Enzo raised a brow, then glanced around the table before he let out a humorless laugh. "You've got demands already? *Madonn'*. This is what happens when they let the kiddies sit at the adult table."

"My *caveats* are quite reasonable and will help all of us in the long run," I corrected him with a hint of menace to my tone before I addressed the rest of them. "The so-called 'war on drugs' is going strong right now, and I think all of us would rather not go on the way we have been. We're losing good men to prison, and less are willing to stay loyal when heftier prison sentences are being handed down. If you're behind bars, you're not earning."

Rocco Esposito spoke up from his seat across from me, raking his fingers through his graying mane, streaked with what remained of his original brown color. "I agree with Don Castellano. Back in my day, we didn't mess with that shit. We have construction contracts, the unions, and even some dealings with cryptocurrency. I don't pretend to understand it, but the younger men on my crew deal with that. As I understand, it's quite lucrative and damn near untraceable."

Sergio Bianchi usually stayed quiet in most of the meetings where I'd been present, but he agreed as well. "Not to mention, I would prefer not to have drugs around my guys. I've lost a few to overdoses in the past. It's a fucking waste of life, in my opinion. We don't want to go to war with the cartels, and that's the way we were headed with Augustine at the helm of your ship."

With that settled, I moved on to the most important part, attempting to keep my tone even. "Also, I'm sure everyone here has been made aware of what transpired the day of Michael Rossi's death. I want it known that harassing loved ones will not be tolerated. You have a problem, you come to the source to discuss it. We all have blood on our hands, but we're not fucking animals."

"Terrible thing, what Lombardi did…in front of his niece, too," Sergio commented with a shake of his head. "Shameful."

With what sounded like genuine concern, Anthony leaned toward me. "How is Livia doing?"

I tried to avoid mentioning her directly, not wanting these men thinking about her any more than necessary. Right before I snapped Augustine's neck with my boot,

I threatened his men, and anyone who even thought about touching her. I'd essentially showcased my number one weakness for anyone to exploit.

With a straight face, I willed confidence into my voice. "She's in mourning, but she's coping, as far as I'm aware."

"As far as you're aware?" Anthony smirked. "I thought you two were an item."

My eyebrows shot up immediately. I liked the guy, but he was too damn nosy, and I didn't have time to gossip about my love life with a bunch of business associates. The fact it was a topic of conversation put me on edge. "You misunderstood. She's the niece of my mentor. She's my responsibility now."

It wasn't a lie, but it stung. Acting as if Livia meant nothing more than a chore was for her safety, and something I should have done earlier.

"Oh, so she's available then?" Enzo asked. He didn't smile often, and his smarmy grin twisted up his thin lips, giving him the look of a cartoon lecher.

The look in his eyes when her name came up made my blood boil. "Off-limits, Enzo. Besides, you're much too old for her. I doubt you could keep up," I snarled.

His fists clenched but he kept his face straight. "Well, apparently the girl has a thing for older men."

It was meant to be a whisper, but it had been loud enough that I heard every word. I didn't even want to think about what insinuations he was trying to make as I felt my blood pressure rise to an unhealthy level. I opened my mouth to let expletives fly, but another voice interrupted me.

As if sensing that I was a breath away from launching myself across the table at him, Rocco Esposito grated, "Let's not start a brawl during the meeting. We leave the families alone. Agreed?" He looked to be losing patience with this conversation. "Let's not have some Helen of Troy bullshit. We have work to do."

Since these kinds of near altercations weren't uncommon at these meetings, we moved on quickly. Augustine's club was now mine, and I planned on keeping it a neutral territory. Not because I trusted any of these men, but because I wanted to keep an eye on them.

Ever since Livia's confession that night in Chicago, I wanted to burn the place to the ground. Since it made us good money, I wasn't actually going to do that. I was, however, going to remove the stripper poles from the VIP room and completely renovate it. At least then I wouldn't want to throw up every time I went inside. Just thinking about it made my skin heat with fury.

Once they all left, I rounded up my own men to reassess their positions. I named Giovanni Gallo my *consigliere*, or underboss. It had been a simple decision. He loved and respected Michael, so I chose to trust him with the position of my right hand. I rearranged my crews, pairing suspicious characters with those who would watch them and inform me of any strange behavior. I wasn't about to take any chances of being betrayed again.

When I wasn't able to be around to keep an eye on Livia, Carlo Basile would watch her. I would have been *stunad* to take everyone at their word that they would leave her alone. They all knew it was bullshit when I informed them she was nothing but the former boss's niece. She meant much more to me than that, and she had for a long time.

Back when Michael first went to prison, I wasn't thrilled about being on babysitter duty. But the more I watched her, the more I believed the praise Michael constantly showered her with. She was special, but I couldn't let myself acknowledge it. It was easier to watch her from afar and keep my distance.

It didn't matter whether we were together or miles apart. Livia was mine to care for. Even if I wasn't bound by my promise, I could never erase the mark she'd left on me. The pain I felt was excruciating, but at least I felt something. Her safety was my number one priority, and I wasn't going to tolerate any resistance on her part. She didn't want me anymore? Fine, but she would be safe if it fucking killed me. This time I wasn't going to give her the chance to protest, because I just wasn't going to tell her.

The all-too-familiar cloud of loneliness set in as Carlo drove me back to my apartment. I'd almost forgotten what it felt like, and the anger bubbled up inside me. Anger at Livia for making me feel, only to run away like she promised she wouldn't. Anger at Augustine for reminding her why she hated life in Manhattan. But most of all, anger at myself for even daring to hope for happiness. I dreaded the despondence that would hit me when I faced my empty apartment, alone with Nero again.

It wasn't until that moment that I thought about my poor dog. Nero was going to be heartbroken. On top of grieving Michael and losing Livia, I'd have to comfort that lovesick dog if she never returned. *Great*.

Staring out the window, I watched other cars pass by to block her out of my mind. Even though the meeting had been productive for the most part, I felt my decent mood slip away as I got closer to home. Carlo was quiet for the entire drive, but I was sure he noticed. I was tense, and everyone damn well knew it. They were afraid to push any buttons that would cause my temper to detonate.

Taking the stairs was mostly an excuse to prolong the inevitable pain I would feel as soon as I entered my lifeless home. But the longer I didn't have proof, the longer I could stay in denial. I agonized over the memory of us joking together as she taught me how to make meatballs in my tiny kitchen. They were sub-par, but it was fun to let loose with her—I didn't care what we were doing.

Another memory flashed across my mind. The last time I made love to her, I'd felt desperate, almost frantic. At that moment, I knew I was telling her goodbye. I had known it from the beginning. She was too good for me— too innocent. I dreaded the day she'd realize she deserved better, and then she would run like hell. *This goddamned woman has gutted me.*

Nero's whining was audible when I got to my floor. The door was hanging onto one hinge for dear life, and he attempted to jam his nose through the crack when he sniffed me out. He barked with alarm when I walked inside; he must have realized I was alone. "I know. I chased her off. I'm sorry, okay?"

Saying it out loud made me wince, but when I thought I heard a noise coming from the bedroom, I felt a tiny bloom of hope inside my chest. I rushed into the bedroom, finding the closet thrown open as it had been when I left. Peeking around the door, I saw that half of the contents were gone. All her clothes.

Something caught my eye on the bed, and my heart

instantly sank into my stomach. My gaze fell to a note sitting on her pillow, with just my name written on the front. My hands trembled a little as I unfolded the piece of paper.

Dante,

I love you, but I can't live in fear. We'll end up resenting each other, and that's the last thing I want. You'll find someone who can be the kind of partner you need, and maybe someday we'll be able to have a friendship again. I just need some time. I'm sorry about everything. Please believe that.

Liv

I read the note three times before I slumped down onto the bed and reread it, almost hoping the contents of the note would change if I checked it again. *A dear John letter? Really?* She wanted to forget that anything had ever happened between us and move on. Could she do that so easily? I knew I couldn't. The idea of touching anyone who wasn't her turned me off so much, I swore my balls shriveled. I was a goddamned slave to her. Didn't she know that?

Nero jumped on the bed and started licking my face. "Stop it. I'm fine."

He gave me a look as if to say, "Yeah, sure, buddy."

I couldn't hold it in anymore. A sob crawled up my throat as I chucked my fist through the headboard. The same headboard that, only this morning, Livia clung to while I fucked her from behind. Her sweet cries of ecstasy were burned into my brain, and it was pure torture.

She had only been here for a week, and yet there wasn't anywhere I could look that didn't remind me of her. I had been with her, or inside her, on most of the surfaces in this place, and I didn't want the reminder. When my gaze fell on her side of the bed—now empty— I made my decision.

I'm getting rid of this apartment.

Chapter Five

Livia

After paying a cab driver an inordinate amount of money to drive me around the city, I finally resigned myself and gave him my uncle's address. No more than twenty-four hours ago, I'd fled this house to escape my uncle's memory—yet here I was again.

My life was in a constant state of flux. I'd planned to graduate from college, then see where life in California might lead me. Then Dante happened. He swept me back into my old life, and I trusted him. Now that he was gone, I didn't know what my future would hold anymore. It wasn't as if I'd planned out a life where I was single again, in Manhattan, living alone. This was the last place I expected to find myself when I left California.

Multiple times during the drive around the city, the cabbie asked if I was okay as I sobbed like a child in the back seat. I couldn't even get words out to answer him. Eventually, he stopped asking. When he dropped me off with my pathetic few bags, I stood on the rounded driveway, staring up at the mansion for several minutes, unable to force myself into taking a step in any direction.

Anxiety twisted up my stomach. What I'd just done couldn't be taken back. I wasn't sure if Dante had come home yet, but it wasn't going to be a pretty sight when he did. I was well aware of his volatile temper, as the front door hanging on just one hinge testified. I had tried my best to close it so that Nero wouldn't run out and get lost.

I hope he won't drink. If I said I wasn't worried about what he would do after I left, I would have been lying. I'd known for a long time that he tended toward self-destruction, especially when his turmoil came from a source he couldn't subdue—I was one of them. Maybe he would have been happier with someone more submissive. Someone who wouldn't question him as much as I did.

Being in a different place for what felt like the millionth time this month, I was emotional. This place wasn't home anymore. There was nothing that didn't stir painful memories, reminding me of the gnawing ache of loss. It hit me then how completely alone I was. Fear that I had made the wrong decision plagued me. I loved Dante. Could I really not get past the idea of him being the boss? The fact I let things get this far only proved how determined I was to bury my head in the sand. Dante's ultimate question hung over my head as I stared up at what used to be my bedroom window. *What's changed besides my fucking title?*

From the moment he kissed me, I saw nothing else but who he was with me. No reason could have stopped me from letting myself be consumed by the passion that bloomed between us, like something about our union unlocked a secret only we shared.

"Livia?"

The sudden sound startled me, but when I recognized the voice, I turned around. "Carlo? What are you doing here?"

"Dante figured you'd come here." He shifted his weight from one foot to the other, anxious for my reaction to his statement. "Let me help you with these."

It annoyed me that the second I left, Dante immediately sent one of his men after me, but I couldn't blame Carlo for being too afraid to say no. I didn't envy him having to deal with Dante after our argument, so I chose not to make his job more difficult. "Thank you."

Carlo smiled. "Of course. Anything you need."

I led the way to the front door, but once I reached it, I halted. Unsure if Dante would have told him anything, I couldn't resist the urge to ask, "How is he doing?"

His thick, furrowed brows answered my question. As he stared at my tear-stained cheeks, confused, he gradually put the pieces together. "Oh, so it's true, then." As if it had only been a rumor on the street, but never confirmed. "Shit. I'm sorry, it's not my business."

It really wasn't, but I couldn't help my curiosity. By now, I thought everyone had known we were together. After all, he'd practically screamed it from the rooftops the night my uncle died. "You didn't know?"

He cleared his throat, dropping my bags at the bottom of the stairs. "He doesn't talk about personal things, at least not with me. All he said was to watch after you, but he was more…irritable than usual."

He was obviously downplaying things for my sake. *Irritable* was not in his vocabulary. Rage, definitely. "Well, I guess it really doesn't matter what he said or didn't say. We're not together anymore," I responded in a low voice. "So, I'll be staying here."

I didn't hide the fact that I wasn't happy about it. It was too close for comfort just a week after my uncle's death, but it was the best alternative to staying with

Dante. If I had to watch him die too, there was no way I'd be able to survive it.

When I ventured farther into the house, I avoided the places that my uncle used to frequent. I didn't even care if it made me look weak—I asked Carlo to make sure his office and bedroom doors were closed. I didn't even want to be tempted to go inside or see a flash of his knickknacks through the crack of a half-open door. Carlo gave me a sad smile as if to say he understood without me having to explain, then he rushed off to do as I asked.

While standing in the foyer waiting for him to come back, I saw someone from the corner of my eye in the dining room. Turning back, I found a familiar man sitting at the table on his computer, but his name eluded me. I had to get used to having armed guards wandering around again. It used to be nothing strange to me years ago, but my short involvement with Dante changed everything.

Carlo poked his head around the corner from the foyer and I gestured for him to follow me. When he reached me, I lowered my voice and asked, "I want to talk to you and ask…"

Catching my drift, he grinned. "His name is Stefano Marchesi."

"Thanks."

We entered the dining room, and as Carlo stepped in front of me to make eye contact with the dark-haired man hovering over his laptop, they exchanged a nervous glance. Did they think they were in trouble or something? Stefano stood, towering over both Carlo and me. Then he smiled warmly and asked, "What do you need?"

As I tilted my head back to look at him, I didn't

know how to start, or whether they would even listen to me. I was just the former boss's niece, but this was my life. I didn't want things to revert to the way they were before—being followed by silent gargoyles every day. "I'm aware that you two are going to be guarding me, but I'm an adult now, and I don't want to be treated like I can't handle myself." When I paused to take a breath, both men waited patiently for me to finish. "And I want the mute act to stop. If something is going on that involves me, I want to know about it. Dante is not my proxy."

Stefano chuckled to himself, his piercing blue eyes sparkling. They were in stark contrast to his inky black hair, and it had been shocking the first few times I'd met him. I found him a little intimidating, even when he was smiling. "He said you could be a bossy thing. I haven't had the opportunity to see it yet. If it makes you feel any better, we're instructed to do anything you ask, anyway."

I rolled my eyes. I didn't believe for a second that they would do something I asked if it went against Dante's wishes. Things wouldn't be so different after all. I still had bodyguards, and the only thing that was going to change was who they'd be reporting to. I wouldn't be able to sneeze without Dante knowing about it.

I thought it better to get everything on the table. "If you say so. You should know I'm going to start looking for a job. I can't sit around here all day and do nothing."

The moment the words left my lips, Carlo cocked his head. "Why is that so surprising?"

"No…it's just…you're the beneficiary of Michael's estate. It's pretty sizable. You wouldn't need to work," he reasoned.

"I need experience in the art world if I want to make

it as an artist. Besides, I'd like the satisfaction of making my own money for once. This isn't negotiable."

Stefano cut him off with a slap on his back just when he was about to respond. "We'll just make sure you get to and from work. Just let us know your schedules and appointments."

That felt too easy.

"Thank you. I'm going upstairs now."

With no desire to see reminders of who I used to be scattered around my room, I didn't bother to turn the lights on before wrapping myself up in my fuzzy blanket and dozing off.

A dreamless nap left me inexplicably more tired than I'd been before I fell asleep. When I looked at the clock, I jolted awake; it was midnight. After my initial shock at seeing the time, naturally, the next thing I thought about was Dante. I wondered what he was doing right then. Was he asleep with Nero? Was he as miserable as I was, awake after midnight, feeling like I had the worst hangover? I couldn't even squeeze any more tears out—I was empty.

Unable to decide what to do now that I was awake and wired in the middle of the night, I decided to rehydrate so I could cry Dante out of my system. Walking through the foyer, I heard voices coming from the living room, and I quietly inched closer. As I pressed myself against the wall separating me from the living room, I heard Carlo talking to Stefano.

"—the way he looked when he came downstairs. When I went up, everything was fine. Ten minutes later, he comes down looking like he wants to kill me. He's going to be just as bad as Michael with her. I'm afraid to do the wrong thing."

Oh, God. He really was driving them crazy. I didn't want to hear any more, but I was frozen in place. If they were this afraid of Dante, then eavesdropping would be the only way I would ever get any information. I couldn't help but wonder what the hell his reputation was with these men. Was he really that ruthless to scare a man at least ten years his senior?

Stefano scoffed at him. "You're worried about nothing. You've been keeping an eye out for her since she was practically a kid. He's just heartbroken and doesn't know where to direct his anger. Shit always falls downhill."

"I can't picture it. I've never seen him act this way over a woman." With a light chortle, Carlo went on, "I mean, come on. You know how he used to be."

"Yeah. I've personally seen him walk into a club and leave with a woman after five minutes. Imagine my surprise when he came back with Livia, a different man—I thought he'd gotten into some of those fancy California drugs."

Dante's "dating history" wasn't something we often talked about, and I couldn't fathom him using women like napkins, sleeping with them and then tossing them away. It only made me question why he chose me over them. Before I got carried away with my thoughts, I realized I'd stopped listening to their conversation. They'd moved on to something else, and I struggled to make sense of it.

When Carlo lowered his voice, I took a step back to ensure they hadn't made me in my not-so-discreet spot in the hallway. "When Enzo made that remark about Livia, I thought he was going to kill him right there."

My hand shot up to my mouth to hold in my gasp.

Why were they talking about me at their meeting? They were going to continue to lie to me, and I was tired of it.

I quietly slipped back to my room, and before I was aware of what I was doing, I had Dante's contact info pulled up on my phone. At that moment, I didn't care if he was sleeping. I dialed him and waited, hoping the adrenaline wouldn't wear off before he picked up.

Almost two full rings in, he answered. He didn't say anything for a moment, and I had to check to make sure the call hadn't disconnected. Another few seconds passed without either of us saying anything, before he finally whispered in disbelief, "Livia?"

I'd been so angry a minute ago, knowing he was keeping things from me, but now I was taken aback. The pain in his voice was evident with just one word. I suddenly didn't know what to say.

"Are you okay?"

I forced myself to slow my breathing before I could answer without my voice breaking. "I'm fine… How are you?"

I was positive he didn't buy my feigned attempt at acting fine. "I miss you so much, Liv."

This line of discussion was one I was desperate to avoid. I really didn't want to lose it over the phone with him, letting him know how much pain I was in. It would only make him feel worse. "I need to ask you something."

"Anything. What is it?"

"I overheard Carlo and Stefano talking just now. They said you talked about me in your meeting, and I wanted to know if I should be worried."

He responded quickly. "No. You're safe. I'm just taking precautions."

Those words sounded all too familiar, but my annoyance melted away after hearing his pained voice. It had been a mistake to call him, because my resolve was cracking already. *Get off the phone.* "Okay. Well, then I guess I'll let you go. I probably woke you up."

The unfamiliar awkwardness between us seemed to anger him. There was a long pause before I heard his heavy breathing and his clipped reply. "That's it?"

"You've successfully fulfilled your promise to keep me safe, and now you can let me go with a clean conscience. Don't worry about me." It came out harsher than I meant it to, but I couldn't shove the words back in my mouth. I clutched the phone tightly in my hand while I waited for the inevitable explosion.

Dante let out a strangled mixture between a gasp and a scoff. "*Clean conscience?* I haven't had that since I was seventeen. You got your last word in. Now it's my turn, and you're going to hear it." He didn't wait for me to respond, his frantic breathing betraying his state of mind. He was furious. "I read your note a hundred times, and if your goal was to hurt me—congratulations. You think you can just walk away and forget how perfect we are together? Maybe you can turn it off that easily, but I can't pretend I don't know everything there is to know about your beautiful mind and body. *I won't.*"

He thought I was trying to hurt him? That couldn't have been further from the truth. I was trying to save us the heartache, but he still refused to see it. "It doesn't matter how happy we are together when people will use that knowledge to hurt us. This can't last forever. Everything good always ends…" My voice broke on a hoarse whisper.

"Not this. Not us. You just have to fight with me."

"Maybe I'm not the determined *principessa* you thought I was."

His voice calmed, and his next words came out in a soothing whisper. "You are. It's one of the reasons I fell so hard for you. You just can't see it right now."

A few moments passed, and I heard the shaking in his breaths. What could I say to convince him we could never work? We'd been kidding ourselves all this time.

Finally, he spoke again. "You were scared yesterday, and I understand that. I should have told you sooner, but I chose to let myself think the longer you didn't ask, the longer I could avoid the fight..." He let out a loud, frustrated sigh into the phone. "Just come home. We'll figure this out together."

Tears streaming down my face, I shook my head violently. "I can't. You have to let me go..."

"That's never going to happen."

Chapter Six

Dante

The idea of forcing myself to go to the bedroom and face the emptiness there was enough to make me camp in the living room. When Livia called, I'd been lying on the couch, attempting to read myself to exhaustion. It was strange to me how quickly I had become accustomed to sleeping with her beside me, and now, without her, sleep eluded me. I felt useless, tossing and turning on the couch, wondering what to do with myself now that she was gone. What had I done before her?

That's right. I would throw myself into work during the day, and strange women at night, until I was so exhausted, I didn't have time to think about how hopeless my existence was. Fucking another woman was out of the question, when just the idea of going on the prowl again turned my stomach. I found I even resented my work, even though there was always something that needed to be done. Knowing this was the reason Livia was gone, I had little desire to go back out and deal with the hundreds of tasks ahead of me.

I always knew she would irrevocably change me, leaving me unable to return to my old self after she was gone. It was the reason I kept my distance all those years ago. If I hadn't gotten weak and let her get under my skin, I could have prevented all of this before it was too late. As broken as I felt, I still knew that Livia was the best thing to ever happen to me. I'd never have given up the memories we shared; I only wished I'd known she was a gift I couldn't keep.

I spent another hour tossing and turning on the couch before I gave up and wandered into the bedroom, passing by my violin case with a frown. Even my music was imbued with memories of her; I wanted to stop being reminded.

Needing to do something with my hands, I went into my barren kitchen to find my power drill and fixed the front door. It seemed like nobody could sleep tonight, because the drill wasn't even the loudest racket in the building, being drowned out by my neighbor's blasting music. Once that was done, I stalked back into my bedroom with purpose, shoving the violin case in the back of the closet.

It was a completely unreasonable time to call my *consigliere* with a new assignment, but I didn't give a shit. A part of me wanted to make everyone as miserable as I was, and any distraction would do. "Gio, I want you to hire contractors to start work at the club tomorrow morning."

He still sounded like he was half-asleep, but he quickly perked up, hearing my stern voice barking orders at him at one in the morning. "Yes, boss. Do you know what you want changed?"

"Everything. I want to turn it into an old-school speakeasy. Classy. It'll be a welcome change," I remarked, not missing any opportunity to show my displeasure at anything having to do with Lombardi. "And I want to rename it."

"Sure thing. I'll get started on that bright and early."

"Okay, good. Then, have Stefano come at seven to take me to the club. I want to make sure these contractors don't fuck anything up. Anything else to report?" He hesitated slightly, and my skin prickled with awareness. "What is it?"

"Stefano told me Livia gave Carlo and him a little talking to earlier. She informed them she's getting a job, and also wants full disclosure on everything." Gio sighed into the phone. "I don't think that's a good idea, all due respect."

Great. She's going to have my men chasing her all around the city. "No, I agree. I'll let them know what they can tell her. I don't want her stressed out for no reason. Make sure Carlo knows to keep his mouth shut unless I give him the okay."

"Yes, of course."

"Okay. Get some sleep. We have a busy day ahead of us."

I slipped the phone back into my pocket and got into my car. I didn't know where I was going until I pulled up in front of the convenience store and found myself on autopilot, going straight to the front counter to buy a carton of cigarettes and a lighter. I'd quit months ago, but I was on edge. As I left, I tore open a pack with voracious urgency. I pulled out a cigarette and held it under my nose, inhaling deeply—I couldn't go back to *all* of my old habits, but this one would have to do for now. The first one made me feel sick, but it didn't stop me from chain-smoking the entire drive back to my apartment. When I snuffed out my third cigarette on the sidewalk outside my place, I let out a heavy sigh and went inside.

Nero was at the door as usual, and he gave me a

suspicious sniff as if to let me know I had disappointed him. "Give me a break, okay?"

I sank back onto the couch and opened one of the books I'd abandoned before I left for California, about the volcanic eruption in Pompeii. Not the most calming bedtime story, I had to admit, but I figured at least I had it better than them.

****

The next week, construction at the club was well underway. Normally, a full renovation would have taken much longer, but I made sure the contractors felt the pressure my guys were putting on them. I needed a project to get my mind off the fact that I hadn't talked to Livia in a week. Somehow, I felt like I was secretly absolving her of her trauma by erasing every trace of sleaziness from the place.

She hadn't called again since that first night we spent apart, and my every update since then came via Carlo. I was glad she wasn't giving him as much trouble as she had me, most likely because she knew he reported to me. I could see through her stubbornness. She wouldn't seek me out, but she wanted me to know she was okay. That was probably less for her sake and more for mine. It gave me a little shred of hope that she still cared about me.

But the negative thoughts inevitably sank in again. I hadn't done a good job of hiding just how bad my temper could get, and I thought she was more worried about me getting fed up with her and coming to scold her into behaving for my guys. The idea that she would cooperate just to avoid seeing me stung.

Castellano, you miserable prick.

Well, she hadn't seen *me*. It was surprisingly easy to

fall back into the habit of stalking her. Carlo must have thought I was over the top since he was already keeping an eye on her, but he did nothing to discourage me from it. He'd only shrugged and said, "If it was my wife, I'd be watching her like a hawk too."

I trailed a couple of cars behind them later that afternoon as he drove her to several interviews at art galleries and museums around Manhattan. Every time she exited the car, I braced myself for the impact of her presence. When I laid eyes on her, it felt like I had been punched in the stomach. Seeing her beauty and knowing I couldn't possess it killed me. I dreaded the day I caught her blushing at another man, because that would probably be the day that I let jealousy, of all things, drive me to murder.

She had her long waves pinned up in a bun that was messy and classy at the same time, donning black slacks and a deep purple blouse. A furious gust of wind blew past her, and I swore I could smell her perfume from where I sat in my car. Unable to help my body's reaction to just the mere proximity of her, I immediately felt myself stiffen.

She gave a smile and a wave to Carlo as she rushed into one of the more high-end museums in Manhattan. I ignored my raging hard-on, adjusting myself so that my cock wasn't being choked by the fly of my pants. I wasn't happy about the idea of her working at some dump where she would be hit on constantly, but it impressed me that she managed to get an interview at a place like this. For the first time in days, I found myself smiling. *That's my girl.*

In a way, I was envious of her. She was making a genuine attempt to make a life for herself outside of the criminal world, which was something I hadn't managed to do in thirty-five years. I could have taken over my parents' restaurant, gone back to school, or joined an orchestra. It was useless to think of those things now. I had made my bed, and now I had to lie in it. I just hoped she would succeed in making a better future for herself. *A better future would be one without me in it.*

Acknowledging that, I couldn't help myself from sticking around anyway, even if it destroyed me to see a smile on her face that wasn't one that I put there.

She looked nervous when she went inside, but when I caught sight of her breezing out the glass double doors with a bright flush on her cheeks and a wide grin, I pumped my fist in victory for her. Carlo stepped out of the car to open the door for her. They were too far ahead for me to hear what they were saying as she chattered excitedly at him, but the pride on Carlo's face was clear.

Once they drove off, I turned around and headed back to the club to oversee the construction. When I got there, I found Gio arguing with another of my guys about that damn VIP room, but they both immediately stopped talking when I walked in. It gave me some satisfaction that I could silence a room with just my presence. At least it gave me some outward control.

"What's the problem?"

Gio scowled at the lanky guy next to him. "Tony thinks we should do bottle service, since we're doing away with the strippers."

I turned to face him, and he shriveled slightly under my pissed-off stare. Willing some bravery into his voice, he forced himself to speak his piece. "Maybe it's not historically accurate, but we're going to lose business if we don't give the customers some ass. What's the problem? Even the old-schoolers love a good striptease."

"I don't give a shit what anyone else wants. If we lose business, I'll burn the place down myself. I'm going to have it the way I want it." I held him in my gaze, daring him to argue with me. A rush of satisfaction filled my veins when he flinched. "Are you even old enough to drink?"

"I'm twenty-six."

Quietly seething, I went on. "Not that I need to explain myself to you, but the one thing that club-goers covet more than tits is exclusivity. There will be a password and a waiting list, and people will flock to get in and see what the big deal is about."

Gio stepped in, if only to avoid me killing the boy in front of the contractors milling around the place. "Okay, now that's settled. What do you want to do with the VIP room?"

"It'll still be a VIP room. I want poker tables back there where the guests can do some light gambling. The office back there will be for the sharks and bookies." I turned to glare at Tony again. "Don't *ever* question my decisions."

"I'm sorry, Don Castellano. I was just trying to show initiative. I wasn't trying to disrespect you, I swear," he sputtered, taking a step back from me.

Ignoring him, I addressed Gio again. "Get him out of my sight until he knows better."

"Yes, boss."

I could have been here earlier to make sure things were going as I wanted, but I let myself get distracted. I wasn't a bodyguard anymore, and I had to come to grips with the fact that I was unabashedly stalking my ex. It wasn't a good look for a don to be all twisted up over a woman, so I felt like I needed to turn up the intimidation to a hundred to make sure my men knew I was to be respected. But when I found myself alone, the mask fell away.

Not wanting to look at myself in the mirror just yet, I found myself driving to Livia's house before I was aware of what I was doing. Carlo informed me she was at home, and I couldn't stop myself from getting one more fix of her before I went home to spend the night alone with Nero. She would recognize my car, so I parked a few blocks away and kept my distance. At first, everything was quiet, and I didn't see anyone outside aside from Carlo keeping watch at the front door. I wasn't worried about him seeing me, since he was used to me checking in on her by now.

There was movement from the corner of my eye, and I spotted Livia at the side of the house on the pergola. She had changed out of her blouse and slacks from earlier and was now in her customary look of jeans and a paint-splattered T-shirt. A canvas sat on the easel in front of her.

I wanted her to be happy, but I couldn't ignore the pang of jealousy I felt, knowing that she was back to painting with a smile on her face, as if she wasn't heartbroken at all. The jealousy soon faded into pure fascination, reminding me of what I felt the first time I saw her hard at work in California. As beautiful as she looked in her sleek outfit earlier, this was the way I fell in love with her. Not a stitch of makeup, messy hair, and completely focused on creating. I couldn't get a glimpse of the canvas without her seeing me, and I wasn't willing to risk that. If she wanted to see me, she would have reached out by now.

As she got to the painting, I watched on in awe. I never thought I'd see the day I would stalk someone for my own pleasure—and it made me feel pathetic.

Castellano, you are such a pussy.

Chapter Seven

Livia

In celebration of my new job at the museum, I decided to take up Carlo on his offer to bring his wife over to dinner. Ever since my conversation with him and Stefano, he'd been tossing around the idea of introducing us, insisting we'd get along since we were close in age. I thought it rude to ask Carlo how old he was, but I was sure he was older than Dante. I laughed to myself. What *mafioso* didn't love a young woman on his arm? The idea felt strange to me at first, but maybe this was what I needed to make a life for myself in Manhattan—to actually mingle with the people here.

Marcella Basile was twenty-six years old and had been married to Carlo for three years. They didn't have children yet, but apparently, it was in the plans. Carlo had admitted he noticed my loneliness and figured setting me up on a friend date with his wife might ease that. It bothered me that even he could see my desolation, but I was grateful to have someone in a similar situation to talk to.

For the past week, all I'd done was run to interviews or paint, and I was starting to miss interacting with people. Now that I had a job, I told myself I needed to start building a life for myself again. Anything to keep Dante from my mind, especially when I felt like every time I turned around, I could almost sense him near me.

When the doorbell chimed, I ran to answer it, ripping off my apron and straightening my hair. I was aghast when I greeted Carlo and the beautiful woman beside him. "You must be Marcella! It's so good to finally meet you. Carlo told me a lot about you."

My attempt to cover my excitement didn't work; luckily, she must have felt the same way. Her raven black hair shone under the sunlight, matching her dark eyes as she beamed at me on the doorstep. "Me too! Carlito has been annoyed with me all day because I've been too excited to meet you."

I noticed a hint of an accent. Carlo had mentioned she was from Colombia. She was here on a student visa when he met her, and he immediately fell for her. After wooing her, he married her to make sure she could never be taken away from him. I thought it was pretty romantic, even though I couldn't picture Carlo being so impulsive.

My first effortless laugh in what felt like forever fell out of my mouth as I gestured them inside. "Carlito? I like that." With a smug grin on my face, I spun around and caught him nudge his wife in a subtle hint that she embarrassed him. "I hope you like pesto. Everything is ready in the kitchen. Do you drink wine?"

Marcella followed me into the kitchen. "Yes, please. All of that sounds amazing."

After everyone had drinks and food, we chatted casually. Carlo mostly sat there and watched his wife rattle off at me, seemingly in awe of her. I knew how that felt, and I started to wonder if anyone would ever look at *me* like that again.

Carlo interrupted my thought process when his phone rang. "Sorry, ladies. I have to take this."

"Workaholic. Dante must be driving you up a wall!" Marcella mused, then realized her mistake and she shot me an embarrassed look, as if hearing his name would send me off the deep end.

"I'm sure we can manage. Go ahead." I watched Carlo retreat into the living room before I turned to Marcella, eager to change the subject from Dante. "So, Carlo tells me you're from Colombia."

"Yes. It's a beautiful country."

"Why did you leave?"

Her gaze fell to her empty plate. "Mostly to get away from the cartels. My brother, Emilio, got mixed up with them."

"Oh no…was he addicted to drugs?"

From what Dante had told me about his experience with his parents and even his own addiction, I knew it could ruin lives. He'd admitted to this day, he still had cravings for alcohol, but he resisted them every day.

She nodded somberly. "We knew we had to hide family heirlooms from him because he would steal anything not nailed down, but he was mostly harmless. Until he got desperate and stole from the cartel leader."

I couldn't hold in my gasp. "That's not good… What happened to him?"

Her chest rose with her deep inhale, and she met my curious gaze. "It's a long story. I had to make a deal with the leader on his behalf." Her eyes darkened for a moment, but she didn't elaborate. "The important thing is that we managed to escape with our family intact, and I'm so fortunate for that. It usually doesn't end that way for most people when they get involved with the criminal underworld."

I'd been sitting across from her at the table, mouth

agape as I listened to her story.

"We had to pool our resources," she continued. "Sell anything we could within a few hours, packed a bag each, and we left everything else behind. It was…hard to leave my childhood home." She sipped her wine, letting her shoulders relax now that she'd offloaded her burden.

There was more to her story, I was sure, but I didn't press her for details. "Where's your family now?"

"They fled to Brazil—they're still there now. My mother, father, my brother, and my two sisters. Once I met Carlo, he offered to help bring them here, but they think America is just as corrupt. We flew to Brazil to see them after we got married. They're happy there, and I've found my happiness here. It's not ideal to be so far, but it's the hand fate dealt me."

"I'm sorry." What I really wanted to ask was how she could reconcile it in her mind—running away from one type of gangster just to end up in another one's arms. "I think in a way, I can understand your brother. My uncle used to keep me sheltered from what he did, but when I got too curious, I got burned…"

I trailed off, realizing I was about to expose myself without even thinking about it. It struck me as strange that just a few hours after meeting Marcella, I was already so comfortable with her.

She must have sensed my hesitation, reaching out to touch my arm. "You can tell me, Livia. We're basically in the same position here."

Maybe I could stand to open up to more people, but I didn't think I had it in me to go into detail. She'd told me her story, and it was only fair to disclose in return. Steadying my voice, I forced myself to talk. "I had an…altercation with someone from one of the rival families four years ago. After that happened, I ran away to California for school. I've only been back in the city for a few weeks, and it's honestly been difficult trying to get my bearings again." I left out the parts that involved Dante, not willing to open that can of worms yet.

She didn't question me more about my situation with the nameless man, and I was sure she sensed it was still painful to think about. She flashed me a bright smile. "Don't worry. I can tell already that we have a lot in common, and I'll be happy to help you get settled again."

"Thank you. I'm glad Carlo suggested this. I needed to start leaving my bubble once in a while."

"He told me some of what went on with you these past few months," she confessed. Her dark gaze met mine, but it was filled with nothing but sympathy. "It must have been hell having to run for your life like that. And then losing your uncle and your boyfriend. I'm so sorry. Do you want to talk about it?"

Considering her question, I picked at the remnants of my food. I knew walking away from Dante would be hard, but I hoped he wasn't going to disappear from my life completely. It seemed like once I connected with someone, it was only a matter of time before they couldn't stand to look at me anymore, or they were taken from me.

I once told Uncle Michael everything. Knowing I couldn't pick up the phone for his advice rattled me more than I wanted to admit. The loneliness hit me like a bucket of ice water. Unable to keep it inside, I let it spill. "I miss my uncle so much, and now that I'm back at home, I expect to see him around every corner. If losing him and my parents hurt that much…I *know* I can't take losing Dante too. It's dangerous for both of us, and now everyone knows I'm a huge weak spot for him. I would rather hurt myself by walking away than to have someone ripped from my arms again."

Marcella nodded with understanding. "Do you want to know what I think?"

With a wave of my hand, I said, "Go for it, because I don't even know what to think anymore."

"I don't know Dante very well, but I can tell he loves you very much. Carlo's phone rings off the hook, asking for updates about you. He's acting like a tyrant, and I think it's because he's suffering without you."

That was news to me; the radio silence all week convinced me he'd given up. It was no secret that I loved him, but if he died because he was being a hero, there was no way I'd survive it. I thought about how he let himself get shot to protect me, and the memory made me shudder. "I'm suffering too, but I don't know how to cope with this. I'm not even worried about my safety because I have an army to protect me. I worry about him more. He has no regard for himself, and that scares me."

"I get where you're coming from. I was wary when Carlo first told me about his…affiliation. My first instinct was to run and run far, but something held me back. To this day, I don't regret that decision."

I almost wanted someone to give permission to give in to what Dante and I both wanted. "What should I do?"

Marcella poured us each our third glass of wine and held hers up for a toast. "You've spent years being told everything is too dangerous, forcing you to live in fear. It's your life, and now your choices are solely up to you. Take advantage of it. Whatever you do, be sure that it's what *you* want, because only you know what feels right."

"It feels right between us, doesn't it?"

Dante's words from that night in Chicago echoed in my head like a bell. Every second I spent away from him did nothing to ease the ache he left behind. Bits of my resolve chipped away every time I thought of him at home alone, in pain and missing me. "Marcella…thank you. It's been a long time since I had a friend to give me a good ass-kicking when I needed it. You've definitely given me a lot to think about."

She leaned in close across the table. "I'm always down for a good ass-kicking. And new friends. *Salud*!"

I clinked my glass against hers. "*Salud*."

Before Marcella and Carlo left, they informed me that Augustine's club would have its grand reopening next week, and suggested I should come check it out. Neither of them knew it had been the source of my trauma, but they most likely chalked up my hesitation to the idea of seeing Dante again. Fortunately, he wasn't telling everyone my business, but how could I explain that Augustine's was the last place in the world I wanted to go? "I don't know about that. I'm not really into that party scene anymore."

"Just think about it. We can get dolled up! We'll ignore the men and just dance together," she said with a giggle, nudging Carlo's arm. He silently nodded and bent down to kiss the top of her head.

The way he beamed at her made my heart ache. "I'll think about it, but I might be working that day I might be too tired." Going through my mental card file of excuses, Marcella shot down every single one. "I have paintings to finish too."

With an exasperated sigh, she said, "*Cariño,* you have to let loose sometime. How about this? I'll come over on Saturday and if you're feeling up to it, you can decide then. If not, I'll just hang with you and we'll watch terrible movies. Sound good?"

It was rare that someone was pushing me to have fun, and I had to admit it was endearing. We exchanged phone numbers and Marcella promised to call me the next day. I hadn't realized how much I needed friendly company until they left and the house fell quiet. Scolding myself for missing Eric in that moment, I groaned to myself and stomped upstairs.

Several bodyguards wandered around the house, as usual, but the ones on shift at night were less friendly than Carlo. I couldn't complain too much about that—he needed to go home to his wife sometimes. These men probably had a million things they'd rather be doing, yet they were stuck babysitting me, which made me feel guilty. It only struck me then just how blind I had been all these years because I let my uncle pull the wool over my eyes.

Interacting with the people in my uncle's world, I quickly realized they weren't the boogeymen he made them out to be. They were regular people with the same problems and lives as anyone else. In my childhood, they were as mundane as the furniture in the house to me, because they were always too afraid to speak to me. I even jokingly called them "Uncle Michael's band of gargoyles." Now things were different, and I could finally make my own judgments about *the family*.

Maybe Marcella was right. I needed to stop living in fear and start figuring out what I wanted from my life. Whether it be in this world or not, I had to make a firm choice. No one was left to influence me. I wanted so badly to let go of the regret I felt when I considered that maybe running away had been pointless.

I decided then that I needed to face my demons. I'd go to the club on Saturday with Marcella and make fresh memories to erase the ones that threatened to plague me forever.

A shiver ran through me. Dante would be there. After a week of no contact at all, I suddenly had no idea how I'd talk to him. Marcella's ass-kicking had me feeling brave at the moment, but I gave myself the week to overthink and possibly chicken out. Somehow, even more than the awful memories of my last visit to that club, the thought that came to the forefront was Dante.

It was always him.

Chapter Eight

Dante

With the opening night of Augustine's—now called Forte—looming, I couldn't ignore the nervous fluttering in my stomach. Not that I cared much if the club did well. Honestly, I would probably have made more from the insurance money than I would from opening night, after the cost of the hurried renovations. I was infinitely more concerned about Livia.

Surprisingly, her reaction to seeing me was my second biggest concern. My first worry was that she would come to the club and then become overwhelmed with memories of her last experience here and immediately flee. It was impossible to completely erase her trauma, but damned if I wasn't going to try. Liv had broken my heart, but I couldn't conjure any malice toward her, no matter how much I may have wanted to. If it meant slaying demons who were already dead, I'd do it for her.

Carlo told me she had been hesitant about my invitation. She didn't know the invite was from me, of course. That was where Marcella came in. I knew Carlo's wife would love her, and that she'd jump at the chance of making a new friend. It was a partially selfish move, but I'd mostly done it so she could have someone she could relate to.

Sure, it helped that Marcella wasn't a man who was secretly in love with Liv. She was rooting for us to patch things up, and that gave her reason enough to make sure Livia didn't balk at the invitation. Everything was working out as I planned, and the only thing left to do was wait and see if she showed up.

If we could just be in the same room again, I could make her remember what she felt when we were together.

Just like the first time I carried her in my arms, away from the Irishman and that ridiculous party, while trying not to notice how soft her skin was. Even as she scowled at me, I could see the heat behind her eyes that threatened to thaw me from the inside out. I didn't let myself see it then, but that moment irrevocably changed me. Our bodies, and our souls knew something we didn't. I just needed to refresh her mind, because I refused to give up. I didn't suffer for so long just to get a taste of heaven, only to have it ripped unceremoniously away from me again.

Two weeks of no contact did nothing to ease the emptiness I felt. In fact, it only made it worse. It was hell on Earth, and I was sure I was making my guys miserable. Not that anyone had the balls to complain to me about it. I had always been good at hiding my emotions, except for anger. It was the only safe emotion to show, and the hardest one to rein in. Showing weakness was the worst thing a man like me could do, yet I couldn't seem to hold it in. To cover up my heartbreak, I had to be more ruthless than ever.

You're going to turn into a man she can't love.

My own hang-ups were part of the reason I could justify it to myself. As the boss, I could prevent young men from being exploited and pushed into addiction-ridden lives, and make sure we always had the means to live comfortably—which was something I'd always craved since childhood. It was the downfall of my family, and I refused to let it happen again. Now that I'd found something precious I wanted to hold onto, it wasn't the time to take risks. Before Livia, maybe I would have turned it down, but not now. This was all for her, even if she didn't want to see it.

As I walked inside, the dartboard drew my attention immediately. I tapped one of the construction workers on the shoulder, causing him to jump when he turned and nearly clocked me. "Get rid of that dartboard. This isn't a dive bar anymore."

He gave me an annoyed expression and drawled, "We've been using that during breaks. We'll take it down when we're finished."

Does he know who he's talking to?

My gaze trailed down from the shaggy brown hair buried under his hard hat to his beat-up work boots. He was about a foot shorter than me, and he seemed to shrink as I took a step closer to him. The corner of my lip tugged upward when I registered the fear in his eyes. "No more breaks. You have three hours to finish up."

I didn't need to elaborate—he understood the threatening undertone perfectly. "Yes, sir."

"Get rid of that board. Now."

It wasn't until I looked down at my phone to check the time that I noticed the date. I shielded the screen from the sun outside the club and checked again, just to be sure. *Shit*. It was no wonder I was even more wound up today than usual. Everyone expected a nasty mood from me lately, but today was on another level. I almost wanted to kill that contractor for taking a break. *Calm down, asshole.*

Driving often helped me clear my head, and today I had more on my mind than just the club, my job, or even Livia. Thinking about my future with her, or my lack of one, had triggered something in me. When given a choice between fight or flight, I always fought. If someone punched me, I would hit back. If I had a vice, I'd deprive myself just to prove I could. But when it came to love, I was a coward. For the past two weeks, I'd done nothing but feel sorry for myself, and where had that gotten me?

I pulled into the cemetery, almost surprised to find myself there. As I got out of the car, I made my way to the only grave other than Michael's I ever visited—my mother's. During my rage following my mother's death, I had my father cremated and sent his remains to my grandparents, who were both gone now. I had no clue where his ashes were now. All I knew was that they had no place anywhere near my mother. Even now, I didn't regret that decision.

The scent of the freshly cut grass wafted up into my nostrils. I'd come here to visit Mom often enough that the smell of the grass would always be associated with her, and I found it comforting. I inhaled deeply and felt the knot in my stomach loosen.

My throat tightened when I found her headstone, and I hitched my pant legs up as I crouched in front of it. "Sorry I didn't bring flowers this time, Mom. I've had a lot on my mind." For the next few minutes, I picked out weeds from the base of the stone where the groundskeeper had missed while I talked to her in a low voice. "A lot has changed since I've been here. I'm the head of the family now. I know you probably won't be proud of me, and I don't expect you to be…"

Her name was carved into the marble, and I brushed my fingers across the letters. *Elisa Castellano. Beloved wife and mother.* It was the only way I could feel close to her anymore. She had always been a gentle woman, and it ended in her demise at my own father's hand. If I could prevent anyone from meeting the same fate, I would.

Even though she couldn't hear me, I still felt the need to explain myself to her. "I might have turned it down, but…there's a woman. I have to protect her, even if it means becoming my own worst enemy. But I'm trying to hold on to myself. I won't let myself forget what you raised me to be."

At that moment, I realized I wasn't only trying to avoid becoming Augustine Lombardi; I was trying to avoid becoming my father. Being the boss was just the ultimate test. The thought rattled me.

Pushing the dark cloud aside, I tried to imagine what it would have been like to introduce Livia to my mom, watching them laugh together and gush over the wedding that was no longer happening. "You'd like her, you know. She's fiercely loyal, and she loves with everything she has. She's stubborn, and so damned talented."

A gust of wind toppled the bouquet of roses sitting on the next grave over, and I reached over to prop the vase up again. One of the blossoms had fallen off; I closed my eyes while I lifted it to my nose. My mother loved roses, specifically yellow roses. They were the only flowers I ever brought to the cemetery.

I could almost feel the warmth of her hand on my arm, telling me that everything would work out as it should. I barely remembered her voice anymore, and that only depressed me more.

"I lost her, but I'm going to get her back and fix everything. I'm going to show you I can be the man my father couldn't be." My earlier irritation dulled into an aching yearning, but somehow getting my thoughts out made me feel a little better. I kissed my fingertips and then touched them to the headstone before standing up again. "Thank you for listening to me. Mom, I really miss you. I love you."

I had only said those words to two women in my life, and I never planned on saying them to another for as long as I lived. I lost one, and I would do anything I could to avoid losing the other. Rather than scare the contractors anymore, I planned to go home and call Gio later for an update on the club.

At this point, I was even getting tired of my shitty mood. It was too bad I couldn't get away from myself, nor could I do any of the things that used to make me forget.

Well...the one thing I could have done that was actually constructive only brought up more painful memories of Livia. But I was kidding myself, because she could only be brought up if she ever left in the first place. She was always at the forefront of my mind, and it was pointless to pretend she wasn't. When I arrived back home, I strode with purpose into the bedroom, only stopping to pat Nero quickly. He'd been quiet for the past week, but I didn't know what to do for him. Being stuck with just me again must have been disappointing. *I feel you, buddy. Sucks for me too.*

I opened the closet and slid my things across the rack to reach the back corner where my violin case lay. Hidden away as if it would help me stop picturing the reverent look on Livia's face every time I played for her. I slipped my fingers inside the leather handle of the case and pulled it out, then put it down on the bed. Even though I saw how stupid it was, I still turned around and pushed my clothes back to one side of the closet, keeping half of the rack empty.

Once I had it positioned, I sucked in a shaky breath. *If I can't stop thinking about her anyway, I might as well bask in it.* It was torture to play her favorite piece all the way through to the end, but it didn't stop me from repeating it several more times, almost as a punishment. My only solace was imagining she was there with me, humming along as she drew in her sketchbook.

Nero sat at my feet, wagging his tail. It was clear he was enjoying himself. "Did you miss this?" Even with the ache in my chest, I chuckled at his enthusiasm and put the violin away to give him some attention. I fell asleep next to Nero. It was rare that I could fall asleep so easily, but my loyal canine must have known I needed his comfort.

****

Photos of jazz musicians and old-fashioned wanted posters lined the walls, hanging above smooth red leather couches, with matching barstools surrounding the bar. The bartender, who was already hard at work, was dressed in period-appropriate attire, complete with a collared shirt, vest, slacks, and newsboy cap. When I approached the bar, he smiled widely and placed a glass on the counter. "Don Castellano, this place looks amazing! Sparkling water?"

"It does. I'm actually impressed." I wished I could have had something harder to ease my nerves, but I ignored the urge. "And yes, thank you."

We would open the doors in an hour, and I spent most of that time walking around the premises, looking for any indication that someone had screwed something up. I'd have taken any excuse to distract myself from wondering if Carlo's wife succeeded in convincing Livia to come tonight. I hadn't forced the woman to ask her, but I'd strongly suggested that I would be very pleased if I had the chance to talk to her, which was usually all it took to get people to do what I wanted. Realizing that everyone was getting sick of dealing with my exaggerated mood swings, I was sure if they had to drag Livia here to calm me down, they would.

I felt a little guilty for Marcella; I had asked a lot from Carlo lately, leaving him exhausted and overworked. The problem was that, aside from prep for the opening, I was still dealing with the traitors left behind in Augustine's wake. I wanted to make sure every single one was eliminated before I could entrust Livia's safety into anyone else's hands. And now that I was more comfortable with the men under me, I could afford to give Carlo a break.

I stepped outside to have a smoke while the line formed in front of the club. Keeping my expression straight as I scanned the faces in the crowd for her, I turned to the bouncer. "If you see Livia Rossi, don't let her wait in line, just send her right in."

"Yes, boss."

I threw the cigarette on the ground and stamped it out before going back inside. When I spotted Gio at the bar, he beamed at me. "Damn, look at you, man. Every woman here is going to be drooling all over you."

"They better not. I paid good money for this suit." I cracked a smile as I smoothed down the lapel of my sleek black suit and adjusted the linen pocket square. "How are things in the back?"

Gio grinned and downed his drink. "Everything is ready. Stefano has a list of approved visitors, and the blackjack dealers just arrived. I might even gamble a little myself. What about you? Feeling lucky?"

"Not particularly. I played a little poker back in the day, but not anymore." I didn't necessarily disapprove of gambling, but any addictive activity was a slippery slope for me, and I usually abstained just to avoid the temptation. "I don't believe in luck. It doesn't matter if I'm expecting good things, or minding my own business, not expecting anything at all. Shit always goes wrong."

"You say that now, but I think things will be looking up soon, boss. I know it's been a rough transition, but this is still leagues above what things were like before. Trust me." Gio nudged me with a knowing look before he walked away.

When I followed the direction of his gaze, I saw her. Livia had her back to me as she talked to Marcella, anxiously darting her head, surveying the room. I couldn't help but wonder if she was looking for me because she was eager, or if she was getting ready to run away. My heart slammed in my chest as I willed her to turn around.

She looked like a Roman goddess. Her hair was half pinned up, the rest left to cascade down her back. It only struck me then that her dress had little material, because I could see her smooth skin where her hair ended, and her lower back began. The silver dress hit mid-thigh, and when she turned around, I noted it was almost as plunging in the front as it was in the back. She wore a long string of pearls that nestled between her breasts, drawing the eyes directly to her cleavage. I had never seen her wear anything like this before, and I couldn't help but stare hopelessly at her.

Jesus Christ. If she was trying to give me a heart attack, it was working. She glided farther into the room, and it seemed like every red-blooded man in the club was giving her the same attention I was. My skin prickled, and it didn't help when Marcella found my gaze from across the room and smirked, then mouthed, "You're welcome."

Suddenly suffering from a severe case of dry mouth, I choked down the rest of my water and approached.

Chapter Nine

Livia

Familiar tingles danced over my skin and rendered me senseless—Dante was here. How could I act normal when merely sensing him from across a room sent me into a flurry of panic?

The second I mustered the courage to seek him out and saw him standing at the bar, I spun around to face Marcella. "I don't think I can do this."

With a playful eye roll, she grinned at me. "Is it about the dress? I think you look amazing! You have an entire department store in your closet."

"It's not about the dress, although now that you mention it, I do feel very…naked."

For the millionth time since we left the house, I adjusted the nonexistent neckline of the silver dress I'd bought during my brief partying phase but never wore. I didn't know what I was thinking when I bought it.

By the time Marcella showed up, I was still on the fence about going to the opening. Of course, once I saw her in her flapper-style getup, I felt too guilty to tell her I'd changed my mind. She definitely knew what she was doing when she tore apart my closet to look for a dress for me to wear. I was prepared to put on the standby little black dress, but Marcella quickly nixed that plan. She told me I needed to exude confidence; I felt anything but confident right then. I was shaking in my insensible heels.

The tingles intensified, and I felt my back straighten. That feeling had been ever-present for the last two weeks, but I'd been ignoring it. I didn't need to turn around to know Dante was still there, actively watching me. Marcella's chin slowly rose as she cast a beaming look over my shoulder. Instinctively, I turned to see what she was looking at, causing me to whip around and crash into his chest.

"Oh!" My skin vibrated the moment I felt his hands land on my hips to hold me steady, and the familiar warmth seeped through the thin fabric of my dress. After being apart for so long, the sensory overload was too much to take. My cheeks flushed. "Dante...hi."

Various emotions crossed his face. There was concern and sadness, but most of all, hunger. If I felt exposed when I first walked in, I felt it tenfold now. His gaze trailed from my head to my toes, almost burning me from the intensity of it, then his hands tightened slightly on my hips. It was a subtle, but obviously possessive move. *Oh no.*

"Livia...you look gorgeous." The low rasp in his throat revealed he was just as affected as I. For several long moments, he stared at me before he spoke. "How are you?"

I retreated. Not because I didn't like the way his hands felt on me, but because the contact brought all our explosive passions to the surface. I needed to distance myself if I wanted to retain any measure of control. After taking a few steps back, I straightened my dress. "Why don't you ask your team of spies?"

Ah, snarky Livia, my best defense mechanism.

I assumed he would come back with an equally cutting remark, but he kept his face straight and his eyes firmly on me. "Can we have a minute alone?"

I shot a pleading glance at Marcella for an excuse not to go with him, but she only nudged me forward. By now, I was positive Dante had asked her to bring me here, and I wasn't sure who I was more annoyed with. It was clear she wasn't going to save me from this.

"I'll be back," I whispered to my deceitful friend, who quickly shooed me off and linked arms with Carlo, a huge grin on her face.

Dante took my hand and led me away. As we passed the bar, we coaxed curious looks from everyone around us. I couldn't see his face, but I imagined he was parting the sea of people with his infamous death stare. His fingers tightened around mine when we stopped in front of an office door, then he brought a key from his pocket and unlocked it.

I went still when he opened the door, showing me the minimal space inside. The office had only a desk with a computer and papers stacked on it and a few chairs. I assumed he wanted privacy just to talk, but I didn't like the idea of being alone with him in a tiny room—I didn't trust myself.

When he tugged on my hand and I didn't move, he exhaled heavily. "Don't make me beg."

The gravelly tone of his voice told me he was distressed. I didn't want to cause a scene in front of all these people, who were still watching us as he silently pleaded with me on the threshold of his office. I responded with a subtle nod and followed him into the room.

Unable to decide whether sitting or standing was

safer, I stayed frozen in place until he shut the door behind us. My chest tightened as I felt the air in the room charge with electricity. Once the boisterousness of the activity outside was blocked out, the office shrank even further.

My voice came out shaky. "What do you want to talk about?"

Dante strode closer, only stopping a foot away from me, and I closed my eyes to steel myself for his touch. I couldn't stand to see the moment his mask slipped, and it would the second we made contact. His palms cupped my cheeks softly, instantly warming me. With my eyes tightly squeezed shut, I tried to fight my body's reaction to him.

"I want to know how you really are, not just what you're telling yourself. Are you happy to have gotten away from me?" He paused, giving me barely a second to answer before he continued, "Goddamn it, look at me, Livia."

His harsh tone, dripping with desperation made my eyes fly open. "I'm…" I stammered. Why was he asking me this? If I told him I was happy—which I certainly wasn't—it would hurt him. But if I told him I wasn't, what good would it do? Nothing had changed.

Marcella talked about living in fear, but I would be damned either way. If I stayed, I'd be constantly wondering about when Dante would be taken from me. And if I didn't, I would be living in fear that I'd never find a love like this again.

I expected Dante to grow frustrated with me, but when I looked into his eyes, all I could see was fear, and it shook me to my core. "Are you as miserable as I am?"

I couldn't hold it in anymore, frustrated tears fill my

eyes. "I'm trying to hold myself together, but everything I'm doing is to distract myself from thoughts of you…"

He turned his face away, as if the words pained him. "What can I do to fix this? I need you, *tesoro*. I can't think of anything else."

"There isn't anything you can do. I understand why you feel the need to do this, and I won't ask you to choose me. But I can't…I can't watch." I took a step back, and Dante let his hands fall to his sides in defeat. "I miss you, but nothing has changed."

Suddenly, he didn't look like the formidable bodyguard-Mafia boss he used as a mask. Nor did he look like the gentle, sweet lover I fell in love with all those weeks ago. He was broken. "Just promise me one thing."

"What?"

"It's hard enough to think about you all the time without worrying about where you are or who you're with. I promised I would always look after you, so don't give my guys a hard time." He ran his fingers through his hair before he dropped the bomb that made it impossible for me to deny him. "If you won't do it for me, then do it for Michael."

Even though I'd been the one to move away, I felt naked without his hands on me. I'd have promised him almost anything in this moment if it meant I could leave before I did something I'd regret later. "I promise."

"Thank you."

We continued to stand there, staring at each other for several minutes. Even though this conversation had accomplished nothing, neither of us wanted to walk away after affirming that our relationship could never work. The second I left, it would be real. Unable to fight the urge to comfort him somehow, I took his hand in mine and squeezed it. "This isn't easy for me, either. You have no idea how hard I'm fighting with myself."

"Because you know as well as I do that we're meant for each other. You're it for me. Anyone else would pale in comparison, and it would be a waste to try." He brought my hand up to his lips to kiss it before letting it go. When I stood there in stunned silence, he went on. "It would be easy for you to find someone better...but the idea of another man touching you, making love to you, it kills me."

"I think you're the more sought-after one, here. You're the boss now. Every woman here would drop to her knees for you."

His reply came in a near whisper. "Except the one I want."

It was all too much. Tears pooled in my eyes, and I turned before he saw. If he touched me in an attempt to comfort me, the thread I was hanging by would snap. "I don't want to hurt you. I need to leave before—"

He interrupted me. "Before what? You won't even look at me because you're afraid you're going to see the love in my eyes, and you won't be able to ignore it. Isn't that right? You can lie to yourself all you damn well want, but you can't lie to me."

I headed for the door, but when my hand touched the knob, I stopped. "Things have changed so much these past few months. I'm having a hard time processing all of it, and I'm scared. Just give me some time."

Dante inhaled deeply as he came closer to me, the heat of his body warming the space between us. "You can have all the time you need, but I know you'll come to the same conclusion I have. Nothing is worth throwing away what we have together." He didn't speak again, and for several minutes we stood there, basking in our closeness.

He walked me back out of the club to give me the chance to say goodbye to Marcella. Her triumphant grin when we said goodnight made it clear she thought we were leaving together, and I quickly dispelled her of that myth. I didn't want to ruin her night out, but after only twenty minutes inside the club, I was too overwhelmed to stay any longer. I hadn't even had a drink yet. Not that I planned on it, anyway. Even with the change in décor, the memories of being drugged in this club were still too fresh.

It wasn't just the décor that was different. Dante had changed the name too, but I had been too distracted to say anything about it until he was depositing me in Stefano's car to take me home. Once inside, I wound down the window. "I like what you did with the place. And the name too."

Dante leaned down to look at me through the open window, his face the picture of victory. "I hoped you would. Good night, Liv." He knocked on the hood to signal Stefano to go, and I watched him shrink as the car sped off, the neon sign of the club glowing above his head.

It read Forte. *Strong* in Italian, but it had a double meaning. In musical terms, it meant to play loudly. He meant to remind me how strong I was, and that he wasn't giving up on me yet. I'd gotten his message loud and clear, but I didn't know what to do with it.

****

An hour later, while lying in bed, I reached for my phone to check it for the first time all day, and nearly dropped it onto my face when I saw the unopened text. Unable to resist the curiosity that shot through me when I read the name of the sender, I opened it without a second thought. Eric Walsh.

—*I know it's been a while, but I'd really like a chance to clear the air. I'm in the city. Can we meet?*—

The text had arrived just as I was leaving the house to go to the club with Marcella, and I remembered hearing my phone ping. I'd assumed it was nothing important, but now I realized I had been walking around all night with a bomb in my pocket.

What the hell was I going to do with this? I hadn't heard from Eric since he left me crying in his apartment after we argued. That day had been the beginning of a chaotic few weeks, and I never had time to really think about his behavior. Did he know I knew what he did? Or did he think I was just mad at him for the way he abandoned me? I couldn't say I wasn't dying to hear what he had to say for himself.

The challenge was finding a way to meet with him without Dante knowing. Carlo or someone else would inform him the second I left the house, and I had *just* promised him not to dodge his men. I was still so angry with Eric, I didn't think I would have it in me to stop Dante from killing him, and the thought sent a chill down my spine. Before I could think about it anymore, I typed out my response.

—*I'm working tomorrow, but we can meet for lunch. Noon outside of my job? I'll text you the address.*—

He answered right away, which surprised me.

—*Thank you. I'll be there.*—

Well, there wasn't any going back now. Carlo didn't

usually stick around while I was at work, so maybe I'd be able to sneak out and see him quickly before I sent him packing. Just because I was willing to hear his excuses, that didn't mean I planned on forgiving him.

****

I tried to distract myself with the wonders of the gallery all morning. It hadn't been very long, but I was sure I would never get sick of talking about the wonderful pieces in residence at the museum. My official title was Museum Educator. I led guided tours, talking about the different styles of paintings and the artists who created them. I'd finished two tours already, and at eleven forty-five, I ducked into the restroom to fix myself up before meeting up with Eric outside.

The desolate look on my face appeared the minute all distractions were gone. I was nervous about seeing him again, and, frankly, I was afraid too. I couldn't live with myself if I didn't call him out, but I secretly hoped that he planned to cop to it himself. Brushing my hair out of my eyes, I braced myself and left the building.

Eric waited just outside the double doors, looking apprehensive and anxious. He took a step forward as if he were about to reach in for a hug but stopped himself. "It's so good to see you again…"

I nodded, feeling much too uncomfortable to feign excitement. The tension between us was so obvious, I was sure the effects could have been felt all the way back in Glendale. "Where do you want to go?"

Flexing his hands at his sides, he made a feeble attempt to cover his discomfort with a smile. "You're the native here. You tell me what's good."

I chose a café around the corner, just in case things went south and I needed to escape. The awkward energy lessened while we waited in line for our food, but once we sat down, neither of us seemed eager to begin "clearing the air." Eric ate half of his BLT in one bite, and I wondered if he was as eager to run away as I was.

His swallow looked painful, but after the lump finally went down, he met my gaze. "How have you been?"

Even though it was a perfectly innocent question, I glared at him. Was he seriously going to act like nothing happened? "If you cared, you wouldn't have waited almost two months to check in. Why don't you just get to the point? Why are you here?"

He looked taken aback by my sudden hostility. "I'm showing a few photos in a gallery nearby. I was embarrassed about the way I acted the last time we saw each other, but I still care...I wouldn't have let this go on forever."

My arms folded across my chest. "Is that all you have to say to me?"

"...What do you mean?"

I pushed back my chair and stood up to leave. "I can't believe I thought for a second that you came to apologize. You really think I don't know what you did?"

All the blood drained from his face then, and his mouth opened to say something then closed again. "Damn it...please, hear me out. I was hoping you'd never have to know. Believe me, Livia, when I say that it kills me every day."

Hesitantly, I sat down again. "I'm listening."

His chest heaved with his heavy breathing as he tried to calm himself down. "A few months ago, a man came to me after class and threw me into his car. He told me he knew where my mom worked and where she lived.

He told me him and his men would kill her if I didn't go along with the plan. I had no choice…" Eric glanced up at me nervously. "Yes, I was upset that you didn't feel the same way about me, but I couldn't face you every day knowing what I did. That thug assured me it was just an intimidation tactic, and that he wasn't going to hurt you. I know that probably doesn't mean anything to you."

"You're right. It doesn't. You have no idea what I've been through this past month. I've been shot at, Eric. That harmless man you talked to? The man who sent him after me kidnapped me the day I stepped foot back in Manhattan."

He gasped. "Oh, shit…I'm so sorry…"

"I'm not even finished. My uncle got out of prison, only for…" I almost choked the next words out. "It was a trap, so they could murder my uncle, and probably pass me around like some kind of expensive bottle of champagne in celebration! So no, his promises that I wouldn't be hurt means *nothing* to me. Maybe I'm in one piece physically, but I'm broken inside."

"Liv…" Eric reached for my hand, but I recoiled from his touch. "Please believe me when I tell you how sorry I am. I have to live with myself knowing I took part in this. I won't ever forgive myself, and I don't expect you to, either."

I ignored his apology and blurted, "How did you even get in to take that photo?"

He dropped his eyes to the table in shame. "When Dante threatened to throw me out of the window that day at your apartment…I pickpocketed him."

That meant when he came over and confessed his feelings for me, he had already been planning to betray me. He'd acted clueless when I told him about my family, when he knew all along who I was. The bile rose in my throat. Desperately willing myself to stop shaking, I asked, "And how did you manage to get past Nero?"

Eric let out the heaviest of sighs. "I shoved bacon under the door…"

"I can't believe you."

"I had to either betray you or let them kill my mom. How could I make that gamble? I didn't grow up around armed thugs like you did. I didn't know what to do!" He blinked back tears, trying to explain himself as his cheeks reddened further. "I figured if I were the one to go inside, then I could be sure you weren't hurt. I made sure nothing was…exposed."

Sometimes knowing more doesn't help.

It fell silent for several minutes as I took deep breaths to slow my heart rate. "I can see where you're coming from, and for some reason, I don't hold any ill will toward you—though God knows I have every right to. But I can't trust you anymore. It's not just about the photo. It's about the way you shrugged me off, like my friendship meant nothing to you. You knew I was in danger, and you never even checked in to see if I was okay." I paused to hastily wipe a tear away and scolded myself for crying over him again. "You really hurt me."

"I know I did. I'm so, so sorry. Give me a chance to make it better," Eric pleaded, grabbing my hand before I could pull away. "Please, Liv. I love you."

I never thought the next time I heard those words, they would be from Eric, of all people. I searched his eyes for any sign his remorse was genuine, but a flash of black hair above his shoulder had me on alert instantly. *Oh no.* With no time to process Eric's many confessions,

I looked up and met Dante's furious gaze as he stalked toward us.

I shot a fear-filled glance back at Eric, realizing I couldn't in good conscience leave him at Dante's mercy. *Shit, shit, shit!*

"Eric, run!"

Chapter Ten

Dante

After our talk at the club last night, Livia had me convinced she was warming to me again. Or at least that was the way it seemed, based on her body language. She'd been struggling not to give in, and I saw the telltale signs of her arousal—the pale blush creeping up her exposed chest to her face, her rapid breathing, and her parted lips. When I cupped her face in my hands, the thinnest sliver of her coffee-colored irises begged me to kiss her, but I stopped myself; she didn't want me like this. Maybe that's all it was to her—the lingering attraction, but she didn't love me anymore.

Barely twenty-four hours after our talk, she was out having lunch with some other man. I felt like a fool. If I'd been murderous watching all the men in my club ogling her last night, I didn't even have the word to describe how I felt now. I pulled into a parking garage near the museum and rounded the corner, looking for the café where Carlo had seen them.

After running up and down the block like some deranged lunatic, I felt the familiar prickle on my skin that signaled her presence. I whipped around. Sure enough, there she was.

From the slightest glimpse of her face, it was clear she wasn't happy. Admittedly, I got a thrill from knowing she wasn't enjoying whatever this was…until a hand rested on top of hers. The person blocking them from my view shifted, and a growl left my lips when I realized who that hand belonged to.

Oh, you've got some real balls.

I recognized Eric Walsh's bushy, flaming curls anywhere. My legs began carrying me toward them before I had time to think about it, and it wasn't long until Livia sensed me coming. She always sensed me coming. I would have preferred for her to look at me with love and passion, but instead she flashed me a terrified gaze as I approached, and she shouted, "Eric, run!"

Let him. I love a good chase.

The coward leaped up from his seat, sending the chair flying back into that of the person behind him. They gave him a filthy look he was oblivious to as he turned around to find me stalking toward him. A sick sense of satisfaction washed over me when his eyes widened in terror, and then he took off running down Fifty-Third.

"Dante, no!" Livia sidestepped Eric as he sprinted past her and held her arms out to stop me from my pursuit. "Please. You promised you'd leave him alone."

I slowed my steps, making sure to keep an eye over her shoulder to see which direction the little shit had run off to. "That was when you assured me he would stay away from you. Get out of the way."

"No!"

Her defensive stance and defiant glare would have turned me on if I weren't so pissed off. I tried to pass her, but she grabbed on to my biceps. She couldn't overpower me if she tried, but I refused to push her out of the way. "Why the hell are you seeing him? Out of everyone in all of New York, why did it have to be him? He had his hands on you…"

Why would she entertain his excuses after what he'd done? She was vulnerable, and he would take advantage of her again. Why couldn't she understand I was only trying to save her more grief?

She furrowed her brows. "What are you talking about? This wasn't a date!"

"Good. I'll be right back then."

When I moved to step around her, I felt a blunt object slam into my jaw. The surprise force sent me back a few steps, until I realized what had happened.

Livia shook out her fist, hissing in pain. It wasn't the hardest punch I'd taken, but the shock of her sudden violence took me aback. I grasped my jaw in one hand and clicked it a few times as I stared at her in astonishment. "Did you just fucking deck me?"

She looked almost as shocked as I was, but she quickly straightened her face again and glared at me. "Yes, I did. Might've broken my damn hand too," she murmured, dropping her hand to her side. "You're acting crazy, and you're not listening to me. Eric was only here to apologize. I have no intention of dating him or anything else. I just wanted to give him a chance to explain. Besides, you promised me you would let it go."

I lost sight of the Irishman's bobbing red head when he darted around a corner, and I sighed audibly. *She made me lose him.* "If you think I'm going to sit back and watch while he tries to screw you over again, then you're dead wrong, my beautiful girl."

"I'm not yours anymore…" she pointed out with a frown. Before I could argue, she went on, "If you're willing to break your promise to me, then why bother keeping the one that forces you to keep tabs on me? Doesn't it hurt you to watch me live my life without you? Why would you want that?" She hurled the words at me, dripping with indignation. "This isn't any of your business."

"That's where you're wrong, Liv."

"About which part?"

I took one step closer to her, watching her pupils dilate the instant she detected my warmth on her skin. "All of it. You are my business, *principessa*. And you will always be mine."

Her mouth fell open in shock, but she couldn't find her words. It was hard to tell if she wanted to argue with me some more, or if she was too busy arguing with herself in her head. All I knew was I couldn't take it anymore.

Before I could rein myself in, I had her in my arms and smashed my mouth into hers. Liv gave a surprised gasp, which gave me the opportunity to slip my tongue inside. The tension in her shoulders loosened as she melted into my arms, taking every bit of passion I had to give her. I fisted my hand in her hair, angling her head as I devoured her lips with desperation, silently pleading with her. Her hands landed on my chest, and when she whimpered into my mouth, I lost my breath.

Covering her hand with mine, I moved it to rest over my heart and pressed down firmly; it pounded like it wanted to escape every time I laid a damn finger on her, and I wanted her to feel it. Not taking my lips away from her soft skin, I trailed them across her jaw, down her neck, and up to her ear. She sagged in my arms when I traced her collarbone with my tongue, signaling her surrender. I didn't give a shit that we were standing outside of a busy café with people gawking at us.

"Stop fighting us, Livia. I love you."

She didn't answer me, gazing up at me with tears in her eyes. I could see the deliberation going on in her head for a split second before she lunged at me. She wrapped her arms around my neck and stood up on the tips of her toes to kiss me again, her tongue dancing with mine.

God, yes.

Livia's explosion of passion felt like someone set a fire in my stomach, and I felt the heat spreading through my entire body. She nibbled on my lower lip, teasing it with her teeth. "Take me somewhere."

"Right now?" Her demand had me taken aback, and I chuckled to myself. "How do you go from 'stay away from me' to 'fuck me' from one day to the next?"

She shrugged nervously. "I can't control myself around you. I need you…"

Without another word, I swept her up into my arms and carried her to my car. Before she could change her mind, I opened the door and practically tossed her inside. "Take off your panties. Show me how soaked you are."

Livia hiked up her skirt to slide her panties down, and I reached out and snatched them from her, stashing them in my pocket like a trophy.

My cock practically throbbed in anticipation of being inside of her again, and I hurriedly undid my fly. "I haven't gotten off since the last time we were together. I'm fucking aching for you, beautiful."

Livia blushed shyly at me. "Neither have I."

I couldn't hide how pleased that made me as I pushed her to lie down across the back seat, sliding my hands up her thighs to pull them apart, and rested myself between them. I flicked a few glances out of the window before I roughly yanked up her blouse to expose her lacy black bra. Pulling the cups down, I bared her beautiful tits, the nipples hardened already. I shot her a fiery gaze before I bent my head down to take one in my mouth, then the other. She writhed under me, running her deft fingers through my hair and tugging.

An animalistic groan came from my chest when I cupped her between her legs and felt how wet she was. I parted her swollen lips, gently tracing my finger up and down from her greedy opening to her clit. "God, I missed you so much."

"Ohh...I need you inside me. Now."

Livia's sudden eagerness surprised me when she had been so determined not to let this happen. I didn't let myself ruminate about the reasons why as I reared back and slammed myself deep inside her, giving her what she was begging for.

She let out a loud shout, "Oh my God!"

Her mouth fell open to let out little pants of pleasure, her brown eyes glazed with ecstasy. Livia grabbed at my shoulders while I steadily drove into her, root to tip, over and over. How could she not see how perfect we were when we melded together like this? To me, this was about me staking my claim. I wanted to make her come so hard that she would become as addicted to me as I was to her, and the thought of leaving me again would be unthinkable.

Instead, she only made me more addicted to her every second I spent near her. She craned her neck to beckon me for a kiss; I met it with fervor, sucking gently on her tongue. She wrapped her legs around my hips and used her heels to push me in deeper. Accepting her demand, I grabbed both of her thighs and yanked her forward until the base of my shaft was flush with her lips. My vision blurred from the sensitivity—every time she tensed, I could feel it like a vise.

As she quivered, she let out a strangled moan. "Please, please, *please…*"

Her head thrashed back and forth against the seat, and when she began spasming around me, I held her chin in my grasp so she couldn't look away. She couldn't ignore our connection while I was buried inside her, pleasing her, and staring down at her with devotion. "Nothing compares to this. I love your body, the sounds you make, and the way you look at me…Tell me how it feels."

"Oh, *God…*it's so good. Please don't stop, I'm close!"

One more jolt of my hips set off her orgasm. She buried her face in my neck, her breathless moans echoing in the car. I tipped her head back, swallowing every single one of her pleasured cries. I couldn't hold on anymore. My grip tightened on her thighs and I let out an ear-splitting roar as I emptied myself into her.

When we were finally spent, I collapsed on top of her for a few minutes, still feeling her clenching around me. She lay limp beneath me; I was pretty confident I'd fucked her to exhaustion. Once I finally gained enough strength in my arms to lift myself, I slipped out of her, then met her hesitant gaze.

Suddenly worried I'd been too rough with her, I reached for her, but she recoiled from my touch. *What the hell?* "What's wrong, baby? Did I hurt you?"

"No, I'm fine." Livia quickly sat up and straightened herself out, not even looking at me. She yanked her skirt back down and reached for her purse to check her phone.

"Shit! I have to go back to work now. I'll be late."

She fled from the car so fast, while I hadn't even put my dick away yet. I didn't understand how she was even able to stand after what we'd just done, much less think about going on with her day like it was nothing. Even *my* legs were a little shaky when I zipped up my fly and got out of the car to chase after her. "Liv, wait! We need to talk about this."

She shook her head, avoiding my confused stare. "No, we don't. I had a moment of weakness. It was bound to happen when you keep showing up and tempting me."

I couldn't believe what I was hearing. She was really going to leave me feeling like a girl who got dumped on prom night. *What the fuck?* "I'm not going to lie—I'm feeling a little used right now."

"I just thought this would be a good way for us to get each other out of our systems…it doesn't change anything. But I need to go before I get fired."

She started to walk away, but I reached forward and grabbed her wrist. *Get each other out of our systems?* "You can't be serious. That was more than just sex."

Scoffing, she blurted, "What more do you need? This can't work between us."

"Maybe this meant nothing to you, but it meant something to me." I ran my fingers through my hair, feeling the desperation clawing at my chest. "You know what else means something to me that you don't seem to give a shit about? Our engagement. You made a promise to me, too." I tightened my grip on her wrist when I saw the flicker of emotion in her eyes. *Finally, something!*

Livia wrenched her arm from me and took several steps back. "Of course, it means something to me. How can you say that? I just don't want to be a widow!"

I didn't get a chance to respond—she'd already turned tail and ran. Sighing deeply, I shoved my hands into my pockets and felt the lacy fabric of her panties against my fingertips.

If she was willing to have meaningless sex with me, how soon would it be before she would do it with someone else? Knowing that her little photographer chased her to New York only concerned me more. The thought of it had me feeling more possessive than ever. Would she run after him and let him get between us?

All I wanted was to march into the museum, drag her back home and stop playing these games. It took everything in me to get back in my car and go home, kicking the shit out of a couple garbage cans on the way.

Exerting sexual dominance over Livia didn't have the outcome I'd expected. If I was going to get her back, it would have to be in a way that I had never really tried with a woman before. Romance. If only I knew how I could do that, when I didn't know how she fell in love with me in the first place. It couldn't have been as simple as a little violin music. California was littered with *dudes* who played guitar on the beach, and she hadn't given any of them the time of day.

I realized my problem wasn't her. It was my disbelief that someone as pure as her could ever love a monster like me. If I couldn't find any redeemable qualities in myself, how could I expect her to?

Chapter Eleven

Livia

It was a miracle my weak knees carried me back to the museum. I immediately rushed to the restroom to collect myself. Once I was sure I was alone, I leaned over the sink, chest heaving. My rude awakening came when I glanced at my reflection in the mirror, only to see a desperate, stupid, weak girl staring back at me.

What was I thinking, giving in to him like that? I'd only wanted to erase the memories of him making sweet love to me and making me fall for him. In the heat of the moment, I pretended Dante was just a man who meant nothing to me. It was nothing but a delusion.

He used to struggle with showing vulnerability, but he wasn't that man anymore. Everything about his demeanor showcased exactly how he felt. Even as he was screwing me like a wild animal, I felt his reverence with every graze of his hands and the way he looked at me when he was inside me.

The soul-deep connection was still there, even stronger than before. I knew without a shadow of a doubt that I still loved him. He'd told me he still loved me, yet I couldn't make myself return the words.

The only option was to let him think I was getting over him. Instead of fighting to possibly gain something more, I was fighting to lose something.

I shot a quick text to Eric, assuring him he shouldn't fear for his life. My phone pinged with a text seconds later, and I opened it right away, assuming it was him.

—This conversation is not over.—

I let the phone drop into my bag with the text unanswered and rushed back into work five minutes late, trudging through the rest of my day in a haze.

When my shift ended, the fact that I still hadn't heard from Eric disturbed me. I hoped Dante wasn't hunting him down right now. My phone went off just as I got in the front door, and I scrambled for my phone to check it, then announced my disappointment to an empty living room when I saw it was Dante again. "Shit."

—We need to talk. I don't like the way we left things earlier. Please, let me see you.—

I wanted so badly to let him convince me we could be together again, but it felt like that would just be an excuse for me to slip back into denial. Why did he think our weak moment changed anything? Dante thought my concerns were silly, and that pissed me off like nothing else. His parents, my parents, and my uncle were gone. The track record was staring right at us, and still he refused to see it.

—I don't think that's a good idea.—

The later it got, the more frustrated I was that I still hadn't heard from Eric. I tossed and turned in bed for another hour, but I couldn't stop the questions from swirling in my head, keeping me too wound up to fall asleep. Giving up on sleep for now, I found my phone to call Eric.

He picked up instantly, and without preamble, he drawled, "Yes, I'm still alive."

I let out a quiet sigh of relief. "I'm sorry about

Dante. He's only trying to protect me."

With a scoff of disbelief, he said, "I get that, but I honestly can't remember the last time I could finish a conversation with you without him busting in on us. What's his deal? Is he in love with you?"

I had never really admitted my feelings for Dante to Eric. I was so used to telling him everything, but all I could think about was how he betrayed me. And yet, it still spilled out of my mouth before I could stop myself. "When things started getting dangerous, something changed between us. Dante opened up to me and even risked his life to protect me—I couldn't ignore how he made me feel anymore." Taking a deep breath, I kept the tears at bay. "We tried to make it work, but after my uncle was killed, everything fell apart."

Eric was silent for a few moments. "Wow… Yeah, I kind of figured. The way he acted with you before you left, and the way he looked at you today… What are you going to do?"

"It's complicated. He's put himself in a position that's dangerous, and after everyone I've lost…I couldn't deal with the idea of losing him too. We had a huge argument, and I broke up with him."

"That's heavy. For what it's worth, I am sorry this is happening to you…" Despite his soft tone, his next words were abrasive to my fragile heart. "But if you ask me, I think it's for the best. He's going to hurt you somehow—I just know it."

I felt my hackles rise a little. "He would *never* hurt me. Why do you even care? You said we were never really friends, anyway."

"I didn't mean it. I've been going crazy these past few months wondering if you were okay. The only reason I didn't contact you was because I was sure you'd figured out what I did and wanted nothing to do with me." He let out a sigh of frustration. "I was a coward."

I didn't disagree. "Yes, you were. I wish you hadn't waited so long... I really missed you."

Eric's quick intake of breath sounded through the phone. Perhaps he hadn't expected me to admit I still cared about him. "When the gallery wanted my photos, I was terrified to face you, but I couldn't stay away any longer. God...I'm so sorry about your uncle."

I twisted my bed sheet up in my fist. I really didn't want to think about Michael Rossi right then, not when I was wallowing in the many losses that kept being dangled in front of my eyes. My parents, Dante, Eric, and my uncle. I had Marcella to talk to, but she didn't even try to hide the fact that she was rooting for Dante a hundred percent—I couldn't trust her not to be biased.

Maybe someday I could have a friendship with Eric again and have someone who knew me apart from this world. Would it be so wrong to let this go so I could hold on to one small part of my life from Glendale?

"Thanks..." I squeezed my handful of blankets one more time before I let go. "I'm still mad at you, but if you prove you're trustworthy...then maybe we can get past this."

He let out a breath of relief. "I hope so, Liv."

"I'll talk to you soon."

The day was barely over, and I felt like I had been awake for a week. In one twelve-hour period, I had two confrontations with my ex-lover and one with an ex-best friend. One issue was semi-resolved, and all that remained was my relationship with Dante—whatever that relationship might have been. I couldn't make sense of his behavior at all. He was overtly sexual one minute, and the next he was melting my heart with sweet declarations. And then, as if I weren't already confused enough, he kept reappearing to remind me how good it would feel to just stop fighting.

I sat frozen with my phone in my hand; my heart wouldn't allow me to turn my back on him. Resigning myself, I replied again.

—Maybe we can meet up. Just to talk.—

Jesus Christ, what are you doing, Liv? Losing him once was difficult enough; why couldn't I stop myself from gravitating to him again?

My phone alerted me to his response—a smiley face.

Hopefully, he would make me feel better about our situation, but fear stuck in the back of my mind, like a bomb waiting to go off. Augustine Lombardi was gone, but for all we knew, he could have left behind an army of allies waiting for an opportunity to strike.

I tried to force the thought aside and think about us. Dante made me happy. He was supportive, loving, and he believed in me. He always treated me like a valued equal, even with his dominant personality being what it was. What he said that night at the club was true. Being together felt right.

****

Dante didn't tell me where we were going—he only told me when to be ready. He reiterated that he only wanted to talk, which meant there would be no sex. He'd always been full of raw sexual energy, but he was holding himself back now. I was positive he felt guilty for our dalliance in his car; I did too, given his wounded expression when I ran away from him. He was serious about this being an honest reconciliation, instead of letting our chemistry overshadow everything, like it had in the past.

Keeping that in mind, I settled on a long, flowy skirt and a fitted sweater for our date. I was thankful for the cold weather, because if we had to resist each other, I didn't need the temptation I felt when he touched me. Part of me wanted some sort of armor—not just from his touch, but from the tactile sensation his intense gaze elicited in me.

When I answered the door, Dante stood before me in his usual work boots, paired with black jeans, a navy button-up shirt, and a leather jacket. I thought he was just as delectable in casual wear as he was in a three-piece suit. He cleared his throat. "You look stunning, Liv…"

No matter how many times he complimented me, I always felt a responding blush creep up to my cheeks. Where did this sudden shyness come from? Just a few days ago, I begged him to have sex with me, practically right there on the street—now I was acting like a girl on her first date. Well, it *was* my first proper date.

In an attempt to act casual, I responded, "Thank you. So, where are we going?"

His entire face lit up. "I want to show you my favorite place in New York."

He refused to give me any hints about the destination and kept the conversation light. It made me wonder if he was afraid he'd scare me off before we even got there. He didn't touch me either, which felt odd. It was nearly impossible to be in an enclosed space without Dante's big hands all over me.

When we pulled up in front of an old-fashioned jazz bar, I cocked my head. The hanging sign read Grooves.

He seemed to read my mind, and shook his head. "We're here for the music."

The place was styled as a forties-era jazz bar inside. Low purple lighting, live music, and round tables surrounding a stage near the back. "This is amazing."

"I knew you'd love it. This place gave me some wonderful memories." He led me to a table right in front of the stage, nodding to the sax player hard at work who returned a slight nod in acknowledgement.

"Oh, yeah?" I coaxed him gently. What I did know of Dante's past was all negative, and I was curious to learn more.

"My dad used to bring me here when I was a kid. At first, we came for the music, but then he started drinking, and soon, I was the only one listening. But I didn't care, because while he was at the bar ignoring me, I was pressing my chin up against the stage, watching the musicians with stars in my eyes. Coming here is what made me want to learn the violin."

Dante leaned back in his seat and sighed. Knowing his father had only done it as a way to keep his son entertained while he got wasted was sad, but at least something good had come out of it. "Even after everything happened with my family," he said, "I never stopped coming back."

We fell silent for a few minutes while we listened to the music. During a brief lull, Dante rose from his seat and leaned in close to whisper to the piano player. I couldn't hear what was said, but the long-haired musician glanced my way, then nodded. Without a word, Dante rejoined me at the table while the players on stage coordinated for their next set.

I resisted the urge to ask. "I can see why you love it

here. It's so warm and comfortable."

"It is." His dark brows furrowed slightly as he seemed to deliberate about saying more. Dante extended his hand out to me, waiting for me to make the next move. I obeyed immediately, and he flashed me a grateful look as he affectionately stroked the back of my hand with his thumb. "That's how I realized I was in love with you. You made me feel the way I feel when I'm here. Calm and content one minute, then overcome with powerful emotion the next. But beyond that, just pure bliss."

I broke the gaze and turned away. "Dante…you make me happy too."

He squeezed my hand tightly, pleadingly. "Then why are we torturing ourselves? I'll do whatever I need to do to prove I'll come home to you every day. I'll assign more armed guards. I'll buy a tank. I don't need all that shit, but I'll do it for your peace of mind."

His words were spoken so low, no one could overhear us, but I didn't miss a single word. Losing me had brought this dominant man to his knees, and seeing the raw emotion on his face only chipped at my resolve more. The band resumed their playing, and the familiar song Dante had played for me months ago filled the room.

"This has all been so intense, so fast. It scares me how much I need you already."

His eyes warmed. "It scares me too, but living without you terrifies me more than any danger out there. I know you need time to adjust to all of this. All I'm asking for is a chance to show you that I can keep us safe and make you happy." A few moments of silence passed before he asked, "Do you trust me, *tesoro*?"

The answer was obvious, but the uncertainty in his eyes killed me. I already knew what I wanted.

I'm done being afraid.

Chapter Twelve

Dante

Tension hung in the air. If Liv said no, nothing else mattered. A relationship couldn't exist without trust, and if I'd lost hers, I didn't know what I would do. The swell of the music almost drowned out her response; I strained to make sure I heard her.

"With my life."

In reality, this was uncharted territory for both of us. She'd never dated anyone before me, and the duration of my relationships with women were inconsequential. Before Liv, the only time women slept over was when we fucked each other into oblivion, and afterward I felt too guilty to send them home. In that very moment, I decided there was something to be said about romancing a woman.

Back when Livia struggled not to admit what we both knew was happening between us, she must have known she was fighting a losing battle. The factor that tipped things over the edge was me. I hadn't tried to impress her with my music, yet I unknowingly showed her a piece of myself that resonated with her.

I needed to show her I was still the same man she fell for. The plan was working. This date was exactly what we needed.

As she listened to the music, the serene smile on her

face completely enthralled me. While she let herself get lost in the melody, I let myself get lost in her. I could hardly believe I had her again, but over the years I'd learned better than to receive a gift and ask why.

"You're staring, Mr. Tough Guy."

Even in the low lighting, I could see the color rising to her cheeks. I would never get tired of seeing her blush whenever I appreciated her beauty. It felt only natural to me now. "Do you have a problem with that, *principessa*?"

Her sly grin was quite the change from her previous reaction to my little pet name for her. "What were you thinking about just now?"

"I'm thinking about how happy I am that you came tonight."

"I'm glad you convinced me to come. This is the last place I expected you to take me, and yet somehow, it's exactly *you*."

I brought her hand up to my lips to kiss it. "You're really going to be surprised when you see where I'm taking you for dinner."

Her face brightened immediately. "Can I have a hint?"

I covered my nervousness about what was coming next with a bright smile. "We're having Italian. That's all you're getting out of me, beautiful."

When we pulled up in front of my apartment building, she immediately did a double take—more like a quadruple take, finally settling on my poker face with a questioning look. "Are you having a chef come out to your place, or am I cooking?"

"*I'm* cooking. Go easy on me, okay?"

She stared at me for several long, agonizing

seconds. "You keep throwing me curveballs."

It was my way of demonstrating to her that, even though I was who I was, I was willing to adapt to her needs. I refused to let Livia save me, and Nero was beside himself from the moment he got a whiff of her floral perfume, so I left them to it while I struggled alone in the kitchen. The nerves were getting to me, and the last thing I wanted was for her to watch me flailing while I attempted to replicate her lasagna.

There was no way it would be as good as hers. I could still close my eyes and imagine the explosion of flavor every time I tasted her cooking. The tomato sauce was well-seasoned and rich—homemade, of course. And the sausage had the perfect amount of spice—just like the woman who made it. It had been one of those moments that seemed innocuous at the time but turned out to be one of the defining moments that led to me falling for her. Even as she was pulling the wool over my eyes, she was charming me with her cooking. Livia was like a tempest, catching me completely off guard until I was helpless against her affections. I wanted to do the same for her now, in my own way.

My endeavor wasn't off to the best start when I almost broke the glass baking dish I'd bought precisely for this date. The damn thing tumbled out of my hands onto the counter when I grabbed it from the cabinet above the stove. Luckily, it didn't shatter, but the clanging of cans and a dull thud must have alerted her.

"Are you sure you don't need help?"

My grumpiness came to the surface; I masked it with a teasing threat. "I'm a grown man, Liv—I can handle it. If your ass leaves that couch, I'll have Carlo come over here and stand guard."

"You're lucky I like him. His wife is super sweet, too…" Her voice trailed off before she shouted across the apartment, "She's a good wing woman, I hear."

I was unable to see her while fist deep in a casserole dish, but I knew damn well she was wearing that knowing smirk on her beautiful face. Maybe I could have been sneakier about using Marcella to get closer to her again, but they got along well, so I figured there had been no harm done. "You never let me get away with anything, do you?"

"No. It would be off-brand for me, don't you think?"

When she laughed to herself, I felt a pang in my chest. It was everything I'd been longing for these past few weeks—to have her joyous nature filling my apartment again. Trying to gain my composure, I put the lasagna in the oven before I screwed up anything else and joined Livia on the couch. Nero protested when I squeezed in beside her, then finally settled in on her other side, his head possessively placed in her lap.

"Just so you know, Stefano is downstairs keeping watch tonight. He and a few others take shifts."

The smile on her face faded. I hated killing the mood by bringing our issue to the forefront, but I couldn't spend the entire date trying to charm her into taking me back only to have it backfire when the truth came out. Livia needed me to address the issues she had with my new position, or all of this would be for nothing.

After a minute, she nodded. "Okay. That's good. Is he armed?"

I gave her an incredulous look. "Of course he is. They all are. I rarely even drive myself, except when I've been…following you." Out of the corner of my eye, I peeked at her to gauge her reaction to my confession.

She wasn't surprised. "I figured that."

"Did you now?"

"Something happens when you're near me. I can feel it in my body somehow. It's strange. Nothing else has ever made me feel that way before." She averted her gaze and gnawed on her lip. "Do you feel it?"

I let my arm close in around her, pressing her against my side. "The first time I carried you in my arms, I felt it, and it's tethered us together ever since. And I am so goddamned grateful for it, because I'm a better man with you, Livia."

She tilted her face back to look at me, her chin trembling with emotion. "I really want to be okay with this because I miss you so much…I feel like a piece of me is missing when we're not together."

Her eyes glazed over when I placed an innocent peck on her cheek, filling me with satisfaction. "Don't worry. I'm going to do everything I can to reassure you that we're safe. We'll start over and do it right this time." I'd thought I was doing the right thing to ease some of her fears, but something was still plaguing her. She twisted the fabric of her skirt in her fingers over and over as she stared ahead in silence. I cupped her cheek and angled her to face me. "What is it?"

Her brown eyes glistened as she spoke. "About what happened the other day after we had sex… I never should have run off like that. I thought it would be easier if I pretended I was over you, but I could never be. I'm sorry…"

As her shoulders shook, I grabbed her tightly, holding her close to me. "Shh…I know, *tesoro*. Thank you for saying it, though. Honestly, you were forgiven the moment you accepted the date."

"Thank you."

The oven timer beeped to let me know the lasagna was finished, and I braced myself for whatever monstrosity was about to come out of the oven. After I set it down on my rickety kitchen table, I was actually impressed; it didn't even look half-bad. Livia sat across from me, taking a generous whiff of the food. "It smells great! I can't wait."

After failing to not be offended by her surprised tone, I cut us portions of lasagna. Maybe I had cooked it too long, because sawing into it with the knife took a lot more effort than I expected. Livia kept her mouth shut and waited until we were both served, then carved into it and took a tentative bite.

While chewing, we stared at each other as we waited for the other's reaction. Once Livia finally swallowed, her mouth stretched into a wide smile, making her best attempt not to laugh at me. "It tastes good…but um…"

The fork clinked loudly against the plate where I let it fall. "I didn't boil the noodles long enough. I thought they'd cook the rest of the way in the oven. *Damn it.*"

She grinned at me, trying to hold back her amusement at my childish frustration. "Your parents owned a restaurant. How is it that you never picked up any tricks?"

"I spent more time in the dining room playing music than in the kitchen. Romance isn't my strong suit, Liv."

With a knowing smile, she rose from her chair and joined me at the other side of the table. "All this time, I've been coping with the idea of being single for the rest of my life, because I knew nobody would ever compare after you. You don't even know how romantic you are without trying. Every time you look at me and smile the way you do, I can see that you love me. When you talk to me about painful things, or about nothing at all, I'm blown away by you." Her arms wrapped around me as I sank like a cranky baby into my seat. "I want *you*, Dante. Just you."

Goosebumps traveled down my arms, listening to her soft voice, and feeling her warm body against mine. "Thank you. It means a lot to hear that from you. Just…please don't tell anyone about my crunchy lasagna."

She laid a soft kiss on my temple and whispered sweetly in my ear, "You got it, *boss*."

I had to admit she was a good sport, because I was sure she strained her jaw from forcing herself to eat her entire portion of lasagna. This was *not* the way I usually enjoyed making her sore.

Even though Stefano was there, I chose to drive her home myself as an excuse to spend another twenty minutes with her. As much as I wanted to keep her at my place and indulge in her all night to make up for lost time, it would have been foolish. Not to say I wasn't hard as a steel pipe the entire night—I most certainly was. Our physical connection was too powerful, and I didn't want it to give me a false sense of security with Livia. With the fragile state of our relationship, I had to go about this the right way if I wanted to get her back for good.

This meant bringing up our broken engagement again would be a bad idea, although I was tempted to at least ask her to move back in. *Patience.*

As I pulled into the rounded driveway, it felt weird to think of this giant mansion as being anything but Michael's home, and even stranger to imagine her staying here alone. Well, basically alone. Out of the men

I had guarding the house at all times, Carlo was the only one she was really friendly with, and now she was becoming friends with his wife, Marcella, as well. Even though it had just been a means to an end at first, the added benefit was knowing she had a friend she could talk to and trust. Especially when it came to things that involved our lifestyle.

Stefano was civil to her, but he wasn't shy about letting me know he disapproved of her involvement in any of this. He was almost as traditional as old-timers like Anthony Conti, who was nearly twice his age. He believed women had no place in the Mafia, except as a liability. Chivalry to a fault. In a way, it reminded me of myself not too long ago. *He'll learn his lesson when a stubborn beauty comes along and turns him on his head.*

Luckily, it seemed we had more cheerleaders than nay-sayers, but all that mattered to me was the opinion of my own stubborn beauty. I walked her up to the front step like a proper gentleman. Carlo waited at the door and flashed an enthusiastic grin the moment he clocked us. "Hey, you two. Have a good time?"

"Very good. Can you give us a minute, man?" I hinted, jerking my head toward the door.

"Of course, boss. I'll be inside."

Before we had that awkward *standing at the doorstep* moment, I yanked her close and hugged her tight. "Did you enjoy yourself, beautiful?"

"I loved every second, *caro.*"

My chest constricted almost painfully. I still remembered the last time she called me that, and I wondered if I would ever hear it again. Thinking about the day she left me gave me a shudder, and I squeezed tighter. I *never* wanted to feel that way again. "I'm going to kiss you now."

She nodded wordlessly, letting my hands slip into her soft waves to bring her face to mine. Her warm, panting breaths tickled my lips, and I stared down at her, helpless in my grasp like a fallen angel. Heaving a breath of pure relief, I closed my eyes and brushed my lips softly against hers, so softly that I felt an immediate tingle from the contact.

She let out a quiet whimper. "It's just like the first time you kissed me."

I smiled against her lips, then broke the contact to nuzzle her hair, inhaling deeply. It had been too long since I got my fix of her intoxicating scent. Leaning in, I whispered into her ear, "It feels right, doesn't it?"

Chapter Thirteen

Livia

Dante left me with lips tingling at the front door. He breezed back to his car, giving me a casual wave and wink as he got in. *Cocky.*

Even with his failed attempt at making my famous lasagna, he had plenty of reasons to be confident. He opened up more about his past, brought me to a place that was special to him, and tried to woo me with a home-cooked dinner. It was the most thoughtful thing a man had ever done for me, not that I had much to compare it to. I appreciated all the effort he'd made to get me back, and I had to admit it was working.

It wasn't just him showing me his romantic side that was winning me over. Maybe he didn't understand my apprehension at first because he was so confident about his immunity to threats, but he was taking my fears seriously now. Part of me wanted to dig my heels in, insisting that he give it all up, but deep down, there was a side of me that was proud of what he was doing. Dante had informed me in detail the reasons he felt it would be better for everyone if he remained the head of the family—he truly wanted to protect people. And while I didn't have any delusions that his or my uncle's hands were free of blood, they still held to their own moral code.

My uncle had been the boss, and I never maligned him for it—not really. They were both people I loved and respected with everything I had. Being the don didn't make them like Augustine. Dante was stronger than that, and if he had me, I hoped he would hold on to his humanity even tighter.

It was strange to see this powerful man yielding to me, to give up his upper hand for me. *Being so damn respectful*. Dante had looked so hot in his semi-casual wear, and that leather jacket that screamed danger. All night he held me in his worshipful gaze, polarized by his intimidatingly sexy look. I'd caught him staring many times with a grin on his face, like he didn't have a care in the world. I did that to him.

****

On the dining room table, I set out a bottle of rosé and two wine glasses, then prepared a quick snack—a charcuterie board with cheese, nuts, and different kinds of crackers. I wanted to nurture this new friendship with Marcella since I'd never had a close friendship with another woman in the past. I'd been avoiding her since the night at Forte, and I wanted to make up for it. If I were being honest with myself, I was sure part of the reason she went along with Dante's plan was to get him off her husband's back. Could I blame her?

When she arrived, she seemed pleased about the snacks and wine, but she was more eager to hear what I'd been up to these past few days. After giving me a kiss on the cheek and joining me in the kitchen, she wasted no time before grilling me. "So?"

I sipped my wine, watching her over the rim of the glass as I tried to hide my smug grin. "Yes?"

Marcella scoffed at me and popped some almonds

into her mouth. "Oh, come on. Everyone at the club could see the sexual tension between you and Dante when he was dragging you away. Did he ravage you in his office or not?"

I felt the blood rush to my face instantly. "No, no. We talked. He asked me to give him another chance."

She shook her head in disbelief. "I can't picture that man *asking* anyone for anything. What happened?"

After I filled her in on the events leading up to now, including the meeting with Eric and the car sex that came after, I confessed, "We went on a date yesterday."

"You have been busy!" she joked. "Carlito told me he saw you two coming home together, and Dante was actually smiling. I've got to get a picture next time that happens."

It seemed my first impression of Dante was the same as everyone else's. A cold, stoic man. I couldn't picture it anymore, not since that night he carried me home from the art show; he'd looked at me with tenderness in his eyes, and my entire perception of him shifted. The man everyone else knew was just a small sliver of the whole.

"I keep forgetting how small this world can be." As I gushed to her about our first official date, I held back the hilarity of him trying to cook for me, as per my promise. She swooned when I told her about our kiss at the front door. "No one else has ever made me feel so loved before."

Marcella sipped her wine, looking a little guilty. "That's why I've been rooting for you guys since the moment we met."

"Oh, I'm aware. Dante told me you were scheming with him to get us back together," I said in a chiding tone. "So much for not knowing him very well."

She shifted in her seat. "Part of it was for selfish reasons—an angry don is no good for anyone. But once I met you, I really saw how well-matched you two are. Don't be upset with me... It's just that I see myself in you, and I want you to have the same happy ending I got. You deserve it."

Her affectionate tone convinced me she genuinely cared. "I'm not upset with you. I actually want to thank you for the kick in the ass. It means so much to me to have a friend who has my best interests at heart. I'm just so used to people having ulterior motives for involving themselves with me."

Looking pleased with herself, Marcella picked at the cheese selection and munched.

"How could I not help? The way he talked about you...I was thinking there was no way a woman existed who could turn Dante Castellano into a romantic, but there you were, and suddenly I totally understood it."

"Believe me, I couldn't understand it either. Sometimes I still don't know what he sees in me." I ignored her chastising look and changed the subject. "Tell me, how did you actually meet Carlo? You know so much about my love life, and now I want the scoop on yours."

With a grin, she washed down her mouthful of cheese with some wine. "He used to come to the diner I worked at. Steak and eggs, toast, and coffee—every Monday and Thursday around noon. He'd sit in my section and flirt with me. I always assumed he was just being friendly, because I was still learning English at the time and didn't catch his subtle hints." She chuckled to herself. "One time he suggested a restaurant for lunch, but I didn't understand he was asking me to go with him, and I told him I'd just eaten lunch."

Picturing Carlo desperately flirting with a woman who couldn't understand him made me giggle. "Oh, God. Poor guy probably thought he was getting rejected."

She waved me off, as if to say, *psh, he got over it.* "After a few weeks of that, he finally came out with it, and I think he was quite flustered at this point, so he didn't even ask me—he made me write my number down and told me he'd call me."

I laughed to myself. Dante had been the same way—so sure the outcome would be the one he wanted, he barely considered my hesitation at all. I wasn't complaining, because he was right in the end.

Marcella gulped down some more wine. "That was basically the end of it. He wasn't like the men from home and somehow, I felt I could trust him. I still can't explain it. We fell for each other so fast, and we were married two months later."

I shoveled nuts into my mouth like popcorn, listening to her story and seeing the flush of happiness on her cheeks. She really loved Carlo, and they were still content after years of marriage. *This could be me and Dante someday.* "That's such a sweet story. They should make it a movie or something."

"No way. Your story with Dante is much more interesting. You've got intrigue, mystery, running across the country from death threats. Not to mention hot car sex," she said with a wink.

I blushed furiously, choking down the contents of my glass to cover my embarrassment. "Don't make me regret telling you about that, you perv."

"*Cariño*, who else are you going to tell but your best

girlfriend? Neither of has many of those, so we might as well dish to each other. I'll tell you about mine and Carlo's first time if that evens the playing field."

I clapped my hands excitedly. "I may never be able to look your husband in the face again, but I need to hear this!"

After Marcella left—many embarrassing stories later—I dragged my tipsy self upstairs to get ready for bed. In my inebriated state, I was incapable of keeping Dante out of my mind. I wanted more than anything else to have him here with me, holding me, and stroking my hair as he always did when we slept. We were trying to take things slow and seeing him every day would just be a temptation neither of us needed. I picked up my phone and noticed a text from him, sent an hour ago.

—I hope you're having fun with Marcella. I miss you, beautiful girl.—

Instead of texting him back, I decided to call, and was relieved when he picked up immediately. "I didn't tell her about your lasagna, so your reputation is unscathed." I giggled into the phone, hiccupping.

"That's very good to know. I can't have my men disrespecting me because I can't cook for shit. Gio makes a mean manicotti." His voice sounded raspier than usual, like he'd been asleep when I called.

I snapped my fingers. "Damn, I should have snatched him up first."

When I heard his low growl through the phone, I instantly regretted my joke. *That woke him up.* "Don't joke like that, Liv. It's hard enough not to kill every man who looks your way."

"Crazy man. I was only kidding. Besides, I like it better when you play music for me while I'm in the kitchen. Fair deal?" I smiled to myself, imagining a normal life with Dante. Having dinner, hearing him play, cuddling to sleep every night. I realized how much I had taken it for granted when I actually had it, and I vowed not to make that mistake again.

"Fair deal, baby. When can I see you again? I'll stay far away from the kitchen this time."

"I have work the rest of the week, and I've been painting up a storm lately. How about Saturday?"

"Saturday?" He sighed, clearly disappointed. "Fine."

"It's only two more days. Besides, I have something I need to do."

I wasn't intending on telling him that I planned to see Eric again before he went back to California, but I was well aware someone would be watching, and I really didn't want to sign Eric's death warrant this time.

Of course, he became suspicious immediately. "And what is that?"

I expelled a heavy breath. "I need to see Eric again before he goes back—"

"I don't trust him," he said immediately.

"But you trust me. Please. He was my only friend for the past four years. You didn't see the remorse. He just wants to make it better," I explained softly. "I don't want you to worry about people who don't hold any threat to you. You're everything, *caro mio*."

I knew that would soften his burgeoning temper, and he sighed again. "Fine, but I want a play-by-play as soon as it's over. If he does anything to disrespect you, I'm not playing games anymore. He's done."

"Yes, *boss*."

His sulking tone told me he wasn't pleased at all. "I

think we've established by now that you're the one pulling the strings, my beautiful girl."

I couldn't help the smug grin that spread across my face, even though he couldn't see it. "Oh, please!"

"That's what makes it all the more satisfying when you finally yield to me."

My heart skipped a beat at his seductive tone. "Are you trying to torture me?"

"I would much prefer to be making you moan. Goodnight, *principessa*."

I could kill him!

Chapter Fourteen

Dante

Though it felt weird to wake up without Livia in my arms, I still felt lighter than I had in weeks. She seemed tipsy on the phone last night, and when I rolled over to check my phone in the morning, I saw a message, sent well after I had gone back to sleep. It wasn't easy to shock me, but when I opened it and saw the photo, my jaw dropped.

"*Holy fuck.*"

The deep purple sheets cascaded across Liv's naked body like otherworldly ocean waves, just barely covering her nipples. There was a little sliver of her midriff showing where the sheet crossed back over to conceal her pelvis, but it was her face that captured me most. She dragged her lower lip through her teeth, flashing me those beautiful fuck-me eyes. A tendril of her hair partially obscured her face, and I longed to reach into the photo to brush it away—I didn't want anything depriving me of her awe-inspiring face.

Three words accompanied the photo: *Dream of me.*

If she only knew that she invaded my daydreams just as often as my sleeping ones. I'd been awake for less than five minutes, and I was already hard enough to pound through a concrete wall. Whose idea had it been to abstain again? I was pretty sure it was me, and I already wanted to kick my own ass. There was no way I could get through my day like this, knowing that a hard-on inspired by Liv rarely went down on its own.

I padded into the bathroom, turning the faucet as cold as I could stand it before I got in. The icy water pelted me like a thousand tiny needles on my heated skin, and I let it flow down my body, enduring the discomfort until I grew accustomed to it. Unfortunately, my dick was still ready from that photo burning into my brain.

Every time I closed my eyes, I pictured ripping that sheet from her delectable body and covering it with my own. Her soft skin against mine and her limbs wrapped around me as I surged into her over and over. I hated myself for being so weak when it came to her, but I couldn't resist slowly stroking myself from root to tip. Livia really had a direct line to my libido. She was too addictive.

Feeling her come was as satisfying, if not more, than my own orgasms. And the sounds she made were just as erotic as the way she looked—flushed from her cheeks to her voluptuous breasts, her hair wild on the pillow or bunched around my fist, and her body shaking in anticipation of the explosive orgasms she had only with me. With a gravelly groan, I pumped myself faster. I couldn't wait until I could make her mine again.

Since having a taste of the pleasure Livia brought me, nothing could compare—not another woman, and especially not a sad jerk-off in the shower that had merely taken the edge off. Once I had my head on straight again, I went back to immediately save that picture to my phone, and I tapped out my reply.

—*You love to torture me. Gave me a hell of a wake-up call.*—

It struck me as odd that she would send me a picture like that. That wasn't the kind of woman she was, and I had an unpleasant thought that made me insanely jealous. Livia had never slept with a man before me, but that didn't mean she hadn't sent nude photos before. I hoped she hadn't, because if they were anything like me, they would hold on to those photos as prime jerk-off material forever. I wanted her to be only for my eyes.

As she had awakened the beast in me, I had created a sensual goddess in her. She was so reserved with her body after what happened to her. Even though she was drunk, it felt special that she would do that just for me. After I was out of the shower, I sat on my bed staring at that damn photo. Looking into her chocolate eyes soothed me enough to stop acting like a jealous prick.

She'd probably been drinking wine with Marcella and felt a little frisky. I tried not to let it bother me that she drank sometimes when she wasn't with me. She never touched a drop in my presence, and I was sure that was intentional on her part. After the way she shoved her drinking in my face all those months ago, it was obvious she felt too guilty to ever do it again.

My ringing phone interrupted my downward spiral, and I scrambled to answer it. Liv spoke in a rush before I even had the chance to say hello. "I can't believe I actually sent that picture! I was missing you, and being silly…"

Hearing her embarrassed tone mitigated my worries about her sending nude pictures to other men. "You were drunk, but that's neither here nor there. I loved it, baby. Why are you ashamed?"

She hesitated for a minute. "Last night, I kept wishing you were there with me. But we're taking things slow. I'm afraid to jump back in like nothing happened."

This morning had started out so well, and suddenly it all came tumbling down, only partially due to Livia's continued hesitance. The rest was all me, with my negative thinking. I cleared my throat, ready to set her straight. "When you find the *one*, there's little point in dancing around the subject. And don't ever be embarrassed about showing your body to me. You are breathtakingly beautiful, and all mine."

"You're grumpier than you usually are in the morning."

I let out an involuntary chuckle. "That's because I woke up to be teased by an infuriating woman, then I had to settle for a mediocre jerk-off in the shower, just for said infuriating woman to tell *me* to slow down. Of course, I'm grumpy."

Livia knew just how to push my buttons, and she did so when she laughed at me over the phone. "Oh, you poor man. Is your right hand not good enough anymore?"

"No," I said without hesitation. "It was depressing. What I need is to feel you clinging to me, hear your little whimpers, taste your soft skin…I want to watch those eyes smoke out the way they always do when you come hard for me."

She let out a little moan at my words that had me stiffening up again. "*Dante*…I want that, too."

"Maybe I'll hold out on you until you admit what we both know is true." *Funny, Castellano.* If she were in front of me now, soaking with desire for me, nothing would be able to stop me from taking her.

"That's bullshit and you know it. But if that's how you want to play it, we'll see who gives in first."

"Game on, Liv."

It's one I'll happily lose.

****

Before I got on with my day, I took Nero for a walk. I couldn't seem to shake off the unsettling feeling that developed after my conversation with Livia. It bothered me that she was still so hesitant. We'd been engaged to be married, for fuck's sake. We still were, as far as I saw it. Her words meant more to me than a ring on her finger. You could take off a ring, but you couldn't erase the promise that was made.

I looked down at Nero, at the little scar above his eye where Augustine's goon had slashed him. Even he loved Liv inexplicably. I took a moment to commiserate with my buddy. "Your mom is a pain in the ass. She made us fall for her, and then she keeps running away. We're going to have to fix that, aren't we?"

I took his little *woof* as an agreement.

Eventually, I dragged myself to the club to get through several sit-downs with my disgruntled men. As the meeting commenced, my mood crumbled after I was informed someone had picked up where Augustine left off.

"What do we know so far?"

Gio sat across my desk with Stefano and Carlo; he cleared his throat. "We picked up some punk on the street. Couldn't be more than sixteen-years-old with half a kilo of coke on him. We tried to get him to tell us who he got it from, but he wouldn't spill."

All I could picture was myself, seventeen years old again and trolling on the street for junkies to supply. "Was he high?"

Carlo sighed. "Out of his mind. I dumped the coke and called his parents. Gave them some info for a rehab center, but obviously, that's not going to solve the big issue."

"God*damn* it. Find out who's doing it, and fast. Everyone at the restaurant was in agreement about this. What good is a meeting with the five families when everyone leaves and does whatever the hell they want?"

I clenched my fists hard enough to turn my knuckles white. The only thing that could improve my mood was Liv, but I told myself to give her space until our next date. It was barely noon, and I was over this day already.

"Someone is bound to come out of the woodwork when they realize they're missing a dealer and probably over ten grand worth of product. They'll expose themselves," Stefano pointed out, trying to calm me. "We'll deal with it, boss."

As the meeting went on, Carlo seemed to grow increasingly anxious, but kept his mouth tightly sealed. Gio stepped forward like an eager Roman soldier, ready for his assignment, so I turned my attention to him. "You and Stefano, go see if you can find out anything else. And keep an eye out. I don't want to see any repeats of today."

"Of course. I'll call if I find anything." Gio and Stefano quickly left, leaving me alone with the nervous Carlo, and it was beginning to piss me off.

Rounding on him, I snapped, "Okay, what the hell is going on with you? You've been squirming all morning."

His eyes widened slightly, then he squared his shoulders and met my eyes—a hard feat for most men, especially if they knew me well. "I saw a suspicious vehicle this morning."

"*Where?*"

He took a deep breath and let it out. "Livia's place. I got the license plate, but it turned out to be a stolen car. Could be anyone."

"Why the hell didn't you tell me as soon as it happened? Why wait for the end of the meeting to bring this up?" I shouted.

"I was trying to get more info before I said anything, hoping that it would be a coincidence."

"And? Is it?"

"After what happened just now, I don't think so, boss." He stood to pace back and forth in front of my desk. "Someone is doing everything they can to mess with you. They know your triggers and they won't hesitate to use them."

"Go to her. Now. Watch the museum like your life depends on it." I didn't even need to add, *because it does*. "If anyone, and I mean *anyone*, looks suspicious in any way, you call me immediately. Don't take your fucking eyes off of her, Carlo."

He rushed out of my office before I grabbed my glass of seltzer and downed it. I was even angry at the drink for not being what I needed, and I hurled it against the wall, watching it explode into a million tiny shards. Sinking down into the seat Carlo vacated, I stared at the floor for what felt like an hour, studying the shiny specks of glass embedded into the carpet.

The box that had been burning a hole in my pocket all morning fell out onto the floor, and I carefully fished it out of the shards of glass. I wouldn't be seeing Livia for another twenty-four hours, and it comforted me to have something that made me think of her. Until now, anyway.

Thinking of her now only filled me with pure

desperation. I foolishly thought when I dealt with Augustine and his merry band of traitors, everything would eventually smooth over. Whoever was fucking with us hadn't gotten a proper taste of how ruthless I could be when they threatened what was mine. And I had no problem rectifying that.

I opened the box and gazed down at the ring I had bought that very morning. It embodied Livia perfectly with its casual beauty. Gorgeous without trying too hard, almost as if unaware of its own appeal. The platinum band would pop against the olive tone of her skin, and the rose-tinted teardrop diamond reminded me of her sweet lips when they were pink and swollen from my kiss. Maybe it was foolish of me to listen to her protestation and answer it with a proposal, but that was just how desperate she made me. I couldn't help myself with her.

The longer she dragged this on, the more desperate I became. At first, I'd protected her because I cared for Michael, but now I *needed* to protect her because I loved her. Livia had been used as target practice so much at this point, I was surprised she was still in one piece. And it was all happening again because of me—because I was too selfish and obsessed to let her go.

Chapter Fifteen

Livia

I couldn't summon the energy to be excited about my last meeting with Eric. I would have preferred to let Dante take me out and distract me from the many disasters in my life, but I needed to take my life into my own hands without him continually jumping in to save me. He promised to stay away, leaving only Carlo to keep an eye on me. He took no chances when it came to other men paying attention to me, but Eric seemed to get under his skin like nobody else.

I'd been so consumed with my mental turmoil, it was easy to forget that Dante was still battling his own demons. But I was sure he got some satisfaction from knowing Eric would likely look over his shoulder for the rest of his life. Dante didn't care about the reasons Eric allowed himself to be used as a pawn—he was condemned the moment he stepped into my apartment to take that photo at Augustine's demand. In his eyes, he was a rat.

He thought I was too soft-hearted, but with everything I'd been through, how could I hold a grudge against someone, knowing it could easily be the last time I saw them? Dante's losses hardened him, but for me, it only made me see how important it was to hold on to those you loved. It didn't matter whether Eric deserved my forgiveness—I needed to give it for myself.

When we arrived at Central Park, I waved Carlo off and entered at the Fifty-Ninth street entrance to find Eric already waiting by the fountain. For a split second, the wave of happiness I used to feel whenever I would see him washed over me, until his somber face reminded me of the present. Things between us could never go back to the way they were, but despite myself, my anger, and my hurt, I wanted to hold on to the friendship. This was our last chance to smooth things over before Eric went back to California—the place he now saw as home.

My place was in New York, as much as I'd tried to fight the inevitable.

Eric sat at the edge of the fountain, his hair a bright contrast against all the green surrounding us. I took a mental picture and stored it somewhere deep in my subconscious so that I could always remember him this way. An air of awkwardness was present between us that had never been there before, not even the first time we met. Suddenly at a loss, I wrung my hands as I approached him. "Hey, Eric. How have you been?"

"The show went well…I wish you had been there," he said with a hint of sadness as he rose and shuffled uncomfortably in front of me. After what happened last week where Dante chased him off, he didn't dare to attempt a hug.

I pushed away the twang of guilt I felt for skipping out on his show. Over the past four years, many times we'd promised to never miss a show one of us was in, and I'd already gone back on that promise. "I'm sorry I didn't come. There's just been a lot going on."

He watched me fiddling with the buttons on my coat with a suspicious eye. I was always a terrible liar, and he knew that. "You don't have to lie, Liv. I don't deserve to have a friend like you. I know that. I broke us." His guilt gave me no pleasure as I watched him shove his curls out of his face in frustration. "I just hope that you'll forgive me someday."

"I do forgive you…but that doesn't mean I trust you." I glanced up at Eric's hopeful face that always used to comfort me. Our last conversation was unpleasant, but I didn't want any more secrets between us. "There's something that's been bothering me about what happened before I left."

"What is it?"

I stepped back, not sure I wanted him touching me, given the nature of what I had to say. "Back in Glendale, when I came over and we had that fight, and you were so desperate to get away you left me in your apartment…I knew something was wrong then. Had you been in my apartment already?"

Eric stilled, widening the gap between us. "Yes…but I can explain. I figured I would take the picture, and then take you away somewhere to start a new life. When you told me you didn't want to be with me, I didn't know what to do. I felt so guilty, I could barely look you in the eye."

There were no words to describe the pain I felt, knowing Eric had not only betrayed me, but he subsequently pushed me away so he wouldn't have to feel the guilt. I found myself opening and closing my mouth several times, unable to come up with any coherent response to his confession.

"I'm sorry. So sorry," he whispered. When I didn't respond, he retreated farther. "Maybe I should go before Dante shows up to kick my ass."

The tears sprang from my eyes so fast they caught me off-guard. "Don't you dare walk away from me, Eric! Not again."

My emotional outburst stopped him in his tracks. He spun around to face me, his eyes welling up. "Everything I do only seems to make it worse. I don't want you to hate me."

I'd wanted to come across as strong and confident, unaffected by him, but my shaky voice betrayed me. "Is there *anything* else I need to know?"

"There was one thing… It's why I wanted to meet up again without the interruptions." He paused when my brows furrowed, but then he placed his hand on my arm. "Not something I did, just something you should know. The guy who threatened me…the way he explained what he wanted me to do, it seemed like it was more about you than your uncle. It was almost like he was obsessed with you or something. He specifically wanted a photo of you in bed. It felt…off to me."

My breath hitched. "What did he look like?"

"He had straight, slicked-back hair. Dirty blond, it looked to me. Almost black eyes. The guy gave me the creeps, big time. You need to be careful." Eric sat down again, taking in my shell-shocked expression. "Do you know who he is?"

The moment the image appeared in my head, I shuddered violently. "I know exactly who you're talking about. If you ever see him again, don't talk to him and don't tell him anything. Just run the other way like your life depends on it—because it will. If you ever want me to trust you again, you have to promise me that."

The words came out in a rush before the nausea overtook me. Throwing my purse onto Eric's lap, I ran to the nearest trash can and emptied the contents of my stomach. The alarm was plain on his face when I rushed away from him. He followed me to the trash can and began rubbing soothing circles on my back as I heaved.

"I promise. I'd rather die than hurt you again," he said. "Who is he?"

I couldn't go into this again, especially not with Eric. Having to relive it via the security footage the night my uncle died was bad enough, but this revelation was exponentially worse.

Whoever assured Dante this nameless man had been dealt with was either dishonest or misinformed. For the past month, I'd wandered around New York, stupidly thinking I was safe from him. I was suddenly more grateful than ever that Dante refused to let me out of his sight. I'd never question his protectiveness again.

Unfortunately, it brought an even more disturbing thought to the forefront. Did Dante know him? Did he interact with him on a daily basis?

"Livia?" Eric's face came into focus in front of me while I remained bent over, hugging the trash can. "Talk to me, please."

"Am I ever going to be allowed to live my life in peace?"

"You will. If it helps, I can stay in New York. I can be there for you. I want to," he offered.

It warmed me to know he still cared about me, but I burdened Dante and his men enough as it was, and the idea of painting a huge target on Eric's back terrified me. Months ago, Dante said that I couldn't trust outsiders. Maybe I could come to trust Eric again someday, but he would always be an outsider. I wouldn't let him get involved in my mess. "No. You have a life in California.

I won't ask you to drop everything for me. I have Dante and his crew—I'll be fine."

"Actually, about that—" he started, but his hand halted its movements on my back. "Wait, I thought you guys broke up."

"Don't," I warned, straightening again. "I love him, okay? He makes me happy."

Eric gave me a skeptical look, but seeing my determined face made it clear there was nothing he could say to convince me to stay away from Dante. "I only want what's best for you. You're an adult, and you can make your own choices. I'm just hurt there's no place for me in your life anymore."

"Maybe there will be again someday, but there just isn't room for anything other than what I already have on my plate. I need stability, and my friendship with you is anything but that right now. I'm sorry. Please understand."

"Believe it or not, I do. Take care of yourself. You know where to find me if you need me, okay?"

"I know. Thank you…" We stood in front of each other awkwardly for a few minutes before I reached for him, giving him a tight hug. "Thank you for the best college experience I could have wished for. I'm never going to forget it."

"Me neither. I'm glad that I forced myself to talk to you at that party. You were, and still are, the most interesting person I know." Eric squeezed me tightly for a few more moments before he let go, gave me a sad smile, and walked away.

The information Eric had given me about the nameless man stayed on the tip of my tongue. I couldn't get the words out when I spoke to Dante later that evening. I would have been lying if I said I wasn't afraid of what he would do if he knew that the man who tormented me was still breathing. Did I really want to send him on the warpath again, and start a battle for my honor?

Once I assured Dante that Eric was well on his way back to Glendale, he seemed to relax. Even through the phone lines, I heard profound relief in his voice. Had Dante really been that threatened by puny Eric? For four years, I had spent nearly every day with him and never once looked at him as more than a friend.

****

While getting dressed for my official second date with Dante, I changed three times before I settled on a crimson knee-length dress, trying desperately to ignore my nervousness. After pinning my hair away from my face the way I knew he liked, I breezed outside to find Carlo waiting in the driveway.

"Hey, Carlito," I teased him with a grin.

"Marcella is a pain in my ass," he grumbled, but I saw the corners of his mouth tugging upward into a smile. "You can get in the car, but I've got to wait for the boss to tell me where I'm going."

"He hasn't told you where we're going yet?"

He shrugged and leaned against the car with amusement. "No, he was too worried that I'd tell you or my wife. He can be a paranoid guy sometimes, and he really didn't want to spoil the surprise."

It must have been strange for him to see Dante acting like a lovesick schoolboy. It was interesting to be privy to a part of him no one else got to see. "I was ten minutes late, though. Isn't it weird that he hasn't called?"

Carlo checked his watch. "Maybe he got held up. I

know he had a few things to take care of before he could leave. I'll call him."

"No, I'll do it. He might ignore you if he's in a meeting, but he won't ignore me."

When he didn't pick up on the first ring as he usually did, I wasn't too concerned. As the ringing continued, and the call rolled over to voicemail, my mouth fell open in shock. Feeling sheepish about bragging, I complained to Carlo, "I can't believe this. He didn't pick up!"

Suppressing his smirk, Carlo tried to call and also got no answer. The situation became less funny as another twenty minutes passed, with both of us repeatedly trying to call and getting sent to voicemail. "Something must have come up. I should probably go to him and see what's going on. Stay here."

Alarm bells went off. "If something's wrong, I need to see him. Let me come with you."

"No. You have to stay put. I'm sure everything is fine. I just want to be cautious." He took a tone that a father might take with his daughter, and for some reason, I felt a wave of nostalgia that reminded me of my uncle. "Please, don't argue. Your safety is top priority."

"Fine, but please call me as soon as you find him."

With a reassuring nod and smile, he tore down the driveway. Carlo knew something was up, and like these men always did, downplayed it for my sake.

The moment of paternal concern wore off as I went back inside and paced around the living room, trying to call Dante over and over. This time, I left a voicemail. "Dante, I don't care if something came up with our date, but can you at least have the decency to call me and tell me that? Don't leave me to freak out all night. Call me, please!"

I hung up and immediately redialed. This time, it went straight to voicemail. He turned off his phone? My frustration reached its boiling point, and before I was aware of it, I was heading straight for my uncle's office for the first time in four years.

Chapter Sixteen

Dante

It was probably a monumentally stupid idea to propose again so soon, but Livia made me do things that didn't make sense to me all the time. This beautiful, kind woman loved me beyond all reason, and I needed to make her mine, for good this time. While aimlessly pacing, I lost count of how many times I patted my pocket to make sure the ring was still there.

Last count was fifty-two.

Aside from agonizing over my very impulsive and foolish decision, my mind was consumed with finding the man stalking Livia's house. Michael was gone, leaving behind enemies who saw both Liv and me as extensions of him. As much as I hated it, the twinge of uncertainty made me wonder if I'd made a mistake by bringing her back here.

How much longer would we have to battle the demons of a dead man?

Pushing aside the dark thoughts, I straightened my tie in the mirror and smoothed down the lapels of my best navy suit. I looked damn good, and I wasn't even being cocky. The gel I used to slick my hair to the side gave it some volume, and I hadn't shaved. Livia loved my beard, and I would take any extra incentive I could get. As I wiped the sweat from my brow, I asked myself how sure

I was that she would say yes a second time. *She loves you.* The mantra repeated on a loop in my head over and over as I finished getting ready.

With nothing left to do but sit on the couch, I waited for the moment I would get to see my beautiful girl again. We were getting closer every day, and a romantic night out would shred the last bit of her resolve to keep fighting this.

Nero launched himself from his perch on the couch and ran toward the front door. Not wanting to waste another moment thinking about my potentially lonely future, I rose and followed him as he trotted to the door. "What is it now?"

My peephole revealed nothing. I turned my back and headed back to the living room thinking it was just some kids messing around in the hall, but the doorbell rang moments later. I asked Carlo to check in with me for directions to where I planned to take Livia, but I assumed he'd call rather than show up. *If he tells me she isn't coming, I'm going to lose my shit.*

Upon ripping open the door, ready to lash out at him, I saw nothing but black as a burlap bag was shoved over my head. I heard the footsteps of several other people— heavy work boots creating dull thuds in the hall. Trying to get away from the attacker's hands and the open stairwell, I jerked my body a few feet back into the apartment.

Nero charged past me, barking and snarling, causing several men to shout out in fear. "Get the fucking dog out of here!"

No. "Don't fucking touch him!" The bag on my head made it hard to yell, and I tried to rip it off while they were distracted.

I heard a dull thud and Nero's whimper when he was likely kicked out of the way. Before I could say anything, a violent shove against my back sent me flying into the hallway before they slammed the door shut, locking Nero inside. My arms were yanked behind my back, but I forced myself not to make any outward signs of pain.

A voice cried out, "Fucker bit me!"

Good boy, Nero. The voice sounded familiar, and I wished I could see who the coward was. I just needed my arms free so I could tear him apart myself. Once I recovered from the shock of the first blow, I started to wrench my body back and forth, fighting against the hands holding my arms behind my back, throwing my foot blindly behind me, trying to connect with someone's kneecaps. *If I can just inflict enough pain, I can stop this.*

I didn't bother to shout for help from my neighbors. People in this area knew the score. If you heard something, you knew enough to keep your mouth shut.

My assailant kicked me in the stomach, the sheer force of it causing me to double over with the wind knocked out of me. I tried in vain to reach for my gun, knowing I hadn't put it in my holster, yet, in my desperation, I hoped it would magically materialize in my hand. Another blow hit me in the back of my head, causing me to sag helplessly as the men half-dragged me downstairs.

"I've got him. Let's go."

After they tossed me into a car, and the men filed in behind me, we started to drive away. Every time I sucked in a deep breath, it was immediately followed by a sharp pain, and I couldn't stop the hiss of discomfort that came from my mouth. Unable to move or breathe comfortably, I sank into my seat in defeat.

My head pounded, and it took immense effort to pay attention to what my abductors were saying. The men took no notice of me, carrying on their conversation as if it didn't matter that I could hear everything. Between dull throbs that sounded like thunder in my brain, I caught a few broken sentences that made my blood run cold.

"Where is she?" one of the voices asked.

"…with the driver. Looking real pretty, too."

"Good…" I faded for a while before I heard the same voice again. "Driver's on the move? Keep an eye on her. I don't want anything to interfere…"

The rough rope was bound tightly around my ankles and wrists, abrading my skin, and making movement nearly impossible. I felt my eyelids drooping no matter how hard I tried to keep them open. Even though I couldn't see anything, I desperately didn't want to lose consciousness when I had no idea where I was. Eventually, I lost the fight.

As I faded in and out, I'd felt myself being dragged, then slammed down onto a hard surface. The instant sharp pain in my back brought awareness back. It was pitch black inside the bag, and my shallow, panicked exhales made it hard to breathe or think straight. There was no acting tough anymore. Whoever had taken me was going to kill me. This was it.

I love you, Livia. You'll never know how much. Mom, I don't know where you are, but I'm coming home.

At least four men held me down while they wrenched my arms out across the table and tied me down, the brutal jerking motion sending a sharp pain between my shoulder blades. With barely time to catch my breath, a slightly raspy drawl coming from my left addressed me. "Michael's surrogate son. What a pathetic excuse for a don you are."

I racked my rattled brain for a face to match the voice, but none ever came. Taking advantage of the lucid moment, I desperately tried to pick up any clues about my surroundings I could use to my advantage. I wriggled against my restraints. "Fuck you, coward."

I felt pressure against my face along with a slight odor I recognized immediately, and the cloud of darkness engulfed me. The last things I remembered were the constant drip of sweat rolling down my brow, my drenched suit shirt sticking to my chest, and my desperation for a gulp of fresh air.

When I jolted awake to find myself lying prostrate on the sidewalk outside of my building, I realized I'd been drugged. After gaining my bearings and letting free a slew of expletives, I took a few deep breaths before I tried to peel myself off the sidewalk. I leaned back to get myself up, and a searing pain brought hot tears to my eyes. "*Jesus Christ…*"

As I held up my hands to inspect the damage, I choked on my breath.

Blood drenched the right sleeve of my suit jacket, and I stared at it for a moment, in complete denial of what I was looking at. Or what I *wasn't* looking at.

My hand was gone.

Chapter Seventeen

Livia

The scent of stale cigars punched me in the face the moment I threw open the door to my uncle's office, but my worry about Dante overshadowed my fear of being reminded of my uncle's memory. No one had been inside this office since his death, because I wanted everything untouched until I mustered the nerve to go through his things. Unfortunately, that wasn't why I was here now.

One of my mother's paintings hung over the mantel. It was Uncle Michael's favorite, and one of mine as well. The wide, colorful strokes resembled a lush forest with deep oranges and reds, like fall in New York. When I tore my gaze away, I'd drawn some strength from the memory of her and paced toward the desk with newfound confidence.

Even a hint of his aftershave lingered when I set myself down in his chair as if he'd just been here. Somehow, imagining that he'd only stepped out made me feel better, and I managed to push the grief aside. I still had someone to hold on to. I was here for Dante. *Get yourself together, Liv.*

After rifling through his drawers, I found the keys to Uncle Michael's sports car under his appointment book. Gripping them tightly in my hand, I shoved the papers back into the drawer and rushed to the garage. Carlo had likely alerted Stefano to the order he gave me to stay put, and I wasn't about to risk him trying to stop me. This was the one time I would put my foot down, even if I had to kick *him* in the balls.

Once I got into the car, I pressed the garage door button on the dash. Stefano would soon be alerted to what I had done, but I didn't plan on idling in the driveway long enough for him to do anything about it. It felt odd to be behind the wheel of a car, when the last time had been in a similarly stressful situation involving Dante. And he'd gotten hurt back then.

With no time left to waste, I slammed my foot down on the pedal and sped out of the garage; the tires squealed as I rounded the driveway.

Stefano appeared in the rearview mirror, emerging from the house with his icy stare set on me. Slowly, he shook his head before he brought his phone to his ear. I was sure he was calling Carlo, but I didn't care. I was still hoping to myself that Dante just got held up—but I couldn't hold on to that hope. He was nothing if not reliable when it came to me. He never failed to pick up when I called him, even if it was the middle of the night and I just wanted to hear his voice. The sick feeling in my stomach told me Dante was in trouble.

Deciding to check his apartment first, my native New Yorker came out when I got stuck in a traffic jam three blocks away. "Come on, move it! Can't you drive?"

I slammed my fist on the horn and let it blare. I was ready to get out and run the rest of the way when the cars in front of me finally moved, and I made it to his place in one piece.

His apartment door wasn't even locked. My heart

pounded as I slowly turned the knob and pushed the door open, and my jaw dropped. It looked like a tornado had blown through the living room, with glass all over the floor, books, and papers—but the thing that drew my eyes immediately was Dante's violin. Someone had shattered it beyond recognition, then left it lying on the floor in several chunks of splintered wood and broken strings.

"What the hell…"

For someone to destroy his most precious possession…I couldn't even imagine what he was feeling. I didn't understand, having just spoken to him that morning. What the hell went wrong between then and now?

A high-pitched whine coming from the kitchen interrupted my frenzied thoughts, and when I realized Nero had probably seen everything, I ran to him. *Poor thing.* He sat scrunched in the corner against the cabinets, shaking. Whatever happened must have traumatized him, because I'd never seen this giant beast look like a shivering Chihuahua. I kneeled down in front of him.

"Nero, it's okay. I'm here." I stroked his snout, watching as he visibly relaxed under my touch. "I wish you could tell me what you saw. Where is Dante?"

He answered with another heartbreaking whimper, and I realized I couldn't leave him here. I grabbed his leash and hooked him. "When we find your dad, we'll sort this out."

I did a quick sweep of the rest of the apartment to make sure I hadn't missed anything. The feeling I got whenever he was near was absent, which only scared me more. He was so far removed from me—I worried I would never feel the prickling on my skin again.

Nero jumped into the passenger seat, and I peeled out a little more carefully than I had when I was escaping the mansion earlier. I didn't really know where else to check, or who to ask. The men at my house—namely Stefano—definitely weren't going to be of any help to me, unless that *help* was locking me in the house so I couldn't leave. Why was it okay for Dante to make demands on my behalf, but I couldn't for him? As far as I saw it, if I was going to be the boss's girlfriend, that gave me some rights.

There were usually some of his guys stationed at Forte, formerly known as Augustine's. If he wasn't there, I planned on refusing to leave until someone gave me answers. Someone had to know where he was and why he was dodging my calls. I had fought him for so long that I hadn't considered how I would feel if he turned away from me, and the thought was jarring. Ever since that night in Chicago, he fought for us, and now it was my turn.

I threw the car in park, and with it being a frigid day, I left it running with the heat on for Nero before I got out and strode up to the front of the club. From the outside, everything looked normal for a Saturday night. There were people in line outside, with the usual bouncer at the front. When I skipped straight to the front of the line, I had to ignore a few dirty looks from the people waiting behind me.

The bouncer glowered at me immediately, as if he'd rather do anything than deal with a pissed-off woman, which he could clearly read on my face as I approached. "Livia, you can't be here right now."

Of course, he knew who I was. Dante had probably made everyone even remotely "connected" memorize my face and swear on their lives to keep me safe. I reared back slightly, cocking my eyebrow at him. "The hell I can't! Is Dante here?"

He expelled a deep sigh and folded his arms across his chest. "He's not seeing anyone right now. Go home and I'll make sure he knows you asked for him." His tone was rife with indifference, but the flash of uncertainty in his eyes told me he knew something.

Several people in the line quieted down to listen to the heated exchange. "Whatever is going on, he needs me right now. His apartment is completely trashed, and I have his traumatized dog in the car. Unless you're going to explain to me what the hell is going on, then you can get out of my goddamned way!"

After a minute of deliberation, he leaned in and whispered, "If anyone asks, you snuck past me."

"Thank you."

I pushed my way through the crowds inside, and the tingles danced on my skin the moment I found myself in front of his office door. He was here. I ignored the fear of what state I was about to find him in as I lifted my fist to knock.

Nothing. After rapping three more times, there was still no response. I pressed my ear against the door and heard no movement inside. Pounding on the door this time, I shouted, "Dante, please let me in! I'm worried about you!"

When I was about to look for a chair to bash the door down with, the lock clicked. I hesitantly turned the knob and stepped into almost complete darkness, with just his computer screen illuminating his roughened face. "Why are you here?" he rasped.

"*Why*? Because we had a date, and then you

disappeared on me! What happened to your apartment? Your violin was smashed. Did you get robbed or something?" I let everything out in a rush, desperate for answers, but also relieved to see him sitting in front of me, alive. "I was scared out of my mind…"

He sat like a statue, refusing to look at me. "I've lost everything, Livia. I have nothing left to offer you."

I noticed a slight slur to his words, and a gasp of astonishment left my mouth as the realization came to me. "*Are you drunk?*"

He didn't answer my question. He didn't need to— I could practically smell the fumes coming off of him from where I stood. "I'm done with this. With you."

After everything he'd done to tear down my resistance, *now* he wanted to give up? My voice cracked when I choked out my response. "What? Where is this coming from? I thought you wanted—"

"Things have changed." Dante ignored the bewildered expression on my face, pouring himself another glass of amber liquid and tossing it back.

The same words he uttered in Chicago spilled out of my mouth in desperation. "There's nothing you can tell me that will make me see you any differently! You know all of my secrets, and I know all of yours. Just talk to me, please."

His eyes flew up to meet mine finally, and I almost wished they hadn't. They looked soulless and dark. The Dante I knew wasn't home. Pushing back his chair, he slammed his arm down on the desk with a wince. "Not all of them. Take a good look, little girl, and run away as you should have all those months ago."

With the office shrouded in darkness, I inched closer to look down at the desk as he turned his face away from me. I couldn't hold in my gasp when my eyes followed down the length of his right *arm* to his wrist, which was clumsily wrapped in gauze and still bleeding. When the stench of burned skin, mixed with bourbon hit my nostrils, I held my breath to stave off the wave of nausea.

My head spun. "Oh my God…Who did this to you?"

Dante looked down at the bloodied bandage on his arm. "It doesn't matter. Violence and depravity is what I have to offer you, and you'd be pretty fucked up to want that. I've woken up from the fantasy, and now I'm letting you go."

Broken glass crunched under my shoes as I dug my heels in. "Stop saying that! I'm not leaving you again."

All the breath left my lungs when Dante charged forward out of his chair, coming at me so suddenly I didn't have time to react before he had me pinned to the wall. With his left hand on my throat, he applied just enough pressure to keep me there. His eyes were dead as they bored into me. "Michael was right to warn me away from you, but I fell for your goddamned siren song anyway. No more."

The mention of my uncle caused a pang in my chest; his vicious tone only added to it. "You pursued me first!"

With his fingers still wrapped around my neck, he stroked his thumb against my hammering pulse, as if to cruelly remind me of the night everything changed between us. "That's right, Liv. I did. And I shouldn't have. You need to go home, where you belong."

Angry tears fell from my eyes when his touch evoked the familiar sparks I really didn't want to feel right then. "Where is that? Glendale? That is not my home, Dante."

"Sure, it is. You were happier there, before I came

along like a...what was it? *Giant walking, talking refrigerator*?" As if he needed to twist the knife in further, he leaned in close, his lips practically touching my ear and whispered, "I'm sure Walsh would love to pick up the pieces of your broken heart."

He warned me he was a nasty drunk, and now I'm seeing it firsthand.

Just the mention of Eric normally sent Dante into a jealous tirade—how could he possibly suggest such a thing? He knew damn well my home was here. I'd finally accepted it, and I wasn't going to let him backpedal now. "You know I was only existing there. My home is in Manhattan, with you..."

He chuckled humorlessly, dropping his hand from my throat. "You're not built for this life. Look at you, you're fucking shaking like a leaf in the wind. You're scared of me, aren't you?"

After waiting less than a second for my response, he roared in my face, "*Admit it!*"

I wasn't afraid of the Dante I knew, but I didn't know the man in front of me. After jumping at the sudden loudness, I willed confidence into my voice. "No. I'm scared *for* you. There's a difference."

As he seemed to shrivel under my penetrative gaze, I silently thanked God I'd finally reached him. "Stop looking at me like that. I'm a monster, and I don't need to be constantly reminded of that when I see you. You're too pure. Just go, Livia. Please."

He was doing what I had done weeks earlier, putting the illusion of safety over happiness. The world was dangerous, but Manhattan was the danger we knew, and that gave us an advantage. Now I'd finally seen it his way, he was giving me an out. The trepidation in his glowing eyes betrayed that he was terrified, but I would call his bluff.

Without giving him a chance to retreat again, I wrapped my arms around his torso, being careful to avoid his injury. "Nothing you say will convince me we don't belong together. I need you just as much as you need me. Let me help you, *caro mio*."

"You're going to regret this."

"The only regret I have is ever leaving you in the first place."

"Baby…"

Avoiding the shattered glass on my way to the desk, I didn't wait for him to try to kick me out again as I dialed Carlo from the desk phone. He seemed surprised to hear my voice when he picked up. "I found Dante at the club, but I have Nero in the car. I need you to come and take them back to my house, okay?"

Without a second's hesitation, he responded, "Of course. I'm on the way right now. Is Dante okay?"

"No, he's not." I hesitated for a minute, wondering if I should tell him, but I knew they'd all find out sooner or later. After quickly filling him in, I said, "I'm taking him to the hospital. When he's released, he'll need things. Can you maybe bring some of his clothes to the house? His place is in no shape for him right now."

Carlo must have sensed my frantic tone and attempted to soothe me. "Of course, we'll take care of everything. I'm sending Stefano to meet you at the hospital to keep an eye out, just in case. And if anything else comes up, you just call me, okay?"

Stefano wasn't going to be happy about that after my escape earlier, but could anyone have blamed me? I'd been the one to find Dante, suffering alone, when everyone else wanted me to sit and wait. Luckily, I knew Carlo would understand. "Thank you. I will."

Dante glanced at me expectantly when I hung up, but I didn't give him the chance to argue with me. "Don't make me drag you, because I will. You stopped me from taking you to the hospital once before, and I'm not letting you get away with it again."

Dante staggered slightly on his feet. "You should run before it's too late."

Chapter Eighteen

Dante

The whiskey amplified every dark thought, but as my mind cleared, shame reared its ugly head. Despite my best efforts to scare her away from me, Livia remained undeterred. I'd always promised I'd never hurt her, but in my effort to save her from me, I broke that promise. If Michael were alive, I'd expect to have the barrel of his pistol at the back of my head right now.

We didn't speak for the longest time as I sat there on the bed in the ER exam room, still in my once-fresh suit, holding at least a yard of wadded-up gauze to my wrist. Livia averted her eyes to avoid looking at it as much as she could—I wasn't sure if that was meant to make me feel better, or herself. If she couldn't look at me now that I'd been disfigured, it would break my goddamned heart. In my sober mind, I knew she never would.

Initially the wound stopped bleeding because the *pezzo di merda* had cauterized it. But after I started on the booze, it began to ooze and never really stopped. I began to feel light-headed.

When Liv caught me wobbling as I tried to remain sitting up in the bed, she jumped into action. She pushed me back and propped a couple rolled blankets under my arm to elevate it while we waited for the arrival of the surgeon they'd called in to consult.

"Lie back," she ordered. "You're going to be okay. I'm not leaving your side."

While she fussed over me, all my feelings of regret and guilt came to the surface. "Why are you still here? You deserve better than this."

Her hands stilled while she started in on fluffing the pillows at my back. "Don't put me on a pedestal. I'll decide what I deserve."

I lifted my head to look into those chocolate brown eyes, filled with nothing but love and compassion. How could I have treated her that way? The things I said to her disgusted me, but the heady combination of alcohol and fear had that effect on me.

Sound familiar, Castellano? The bastard apple doesn't fall far from the tree.

The very idea of Livia going back to California to be with the goddamned Irishman made me nauseous. "What I said back there…it was horrible. You have to know I didn't mean any of it. I'm so sorry I hurt you."

Her eyes hardened for a split second, as if she didn't want to be reminded, then softened. "I wouldn't still be here if I thought otherwise."

"I can't fathom why, but I'm glad you are."

Broken and riddled with emotional baggage, I was a mess. And Livia herself admitted my music was what made her first fall in love with me. With my right hand gone, I couldn't play anymore. What bargaining chip did I have to keep her with me? The pain I experienced when she left me the first time was almost unimaginable.

If it happened a second time, I didn't think I could survive it.

****

Through some clever wordplay, I was able to

convince the surgeon to overlook my bullshit explanation of how the *incident* occurred. The lie was slightly more believable when I admitted I was drunk, which I knew they'd find out anyway once my blood tests came back.

After he informed me they would need to take me to the operating room to remove more of my wrist in order to close the wound properly, which would eventually allow me to be fitted with a prosthetic, disappointment washed over me. The image of me as a scraggly pirate with a hook for a hand stuck in my head.

At least this time I was able to sleep through the nightmare. Upon waking up after the surgery, I was more irritable than ever, but Livia didn't let it faze her. She was the first thing I saw when I opened my eyes, and she was the only pleasant sight I was graced with for the rest of my stay.

Each day brought a new medical provider who lent new meaning to the Inquisition. Occupational therapists, young, hip, and grinning like they had the world by a string, showed me how to take care of my basic needs with only one hand. I wanted to punch them so many times I lost count.

The physical therapists were just as bubbly, but for the most part seemed to realize the gravity of the situation and made me do exercises to prepare the stump for the prosthetic. It killed me to prepare for a reality of something I'd hardly accepted myself.

The true fun started when the surgical team oohed and aahed over the ugliest goddamned incision ever made like it was a work of art. Most days I just looked out the window and ordered myself not to cry.

Not my Livia. She arrived each morning before the

breakfast tray arrived to make sure I had everything nearby to feed myself—and didn't leave till after my evening shower. She stood by while I dressed myself with my left hand, even brought new slip-on shoes so I didn't need to fiddle with fucking laces.

The whole time she never once babied me, never once let me whine.

"You don't have to stay here constantly. I'm not going to fade away," I told her, again, after the fifth day.

I felt like a selfish bastard for hoping she would insist on staying, and I was betting on her stubbornness to save me. She put her life on hold just for me. Her job. Her painting. I hated to be a burden on her when things between us were still shaky. We hadn't discussed our relationship, or anything else, for that matter. She hadn't even pressed me for details about what happened that night, even though I was positive she was dying to know—so was I.

"I'm only here to keep you from trying to escape."

The glint in her eyes made me smile for the first time in a while. "I'm getting out of here tomorrow, whether the doctor likes it or not. I'm going crazy here, and I have a job to do."

She responded with a huff and crossed her arms over her chest. "That's why you have a second-in-command. Gio is taking care of things until you feel you can manage."

I found it humorous that Michael had been afraid to let her even talk to me, yet she'd been running interference for me with my *consigliere* all week. "It's *Gio* now?"

"Well, you've been barking at everyone else, so now I'm the middleman. It's not my fault the guys like me more than you."

She wasn't wrong. For the past week, I'd been filled with rage over my situation with no outlet for it; Livia had borne the brunt of it enough the night she found me. My men made up the difference, and understandably, none of them were very pleased with me at the moment.

****

A trio of men transported us to her house, remaining at a respectful distance, while Stefano trailed behind Livia and me as we made our way to what was now her home. At that moment, I would have given anything to know what she was thinking. I steeled myself for the possibility that she was going to leave at the first possible chance—that she was only hanging around until she was sure I was all right on my own.

She'd hardly said a word since we left the hospital, and when I climbed into bed beside her that night, she finally graced me with a smile. "I missed this. Just lying with you."

"Me too, baby."

The moment I started to drift off with her curled up beside me, her soft voice jarred me awake again. "Will you tell me how it happened?"

You knew she would ask, eventually.

After blinking the drowsiness out of my eyes, I turned on my side to face her. "A group of men took me from my apartment. I assumed it was Carlo at the door, so I opened it without thinking." At the moment, I'd been too consumed with the task ahead—proposing to Liv— to worry about checking the peephole first. A huge lapse of judgment on my part.

"They shoved a bag over my head and dragged me downstairs, then took me somewhere else. There was someone there, talking to me. He was goading me, but it's all fuzzy…I'm not sure what was real and what was just a nightmare."

Livia snuggled in closer. "God…I'm so sorry. I realized something was wrong when you weren't answering your cell. I came looking for you right away." She wiped a tear away from her cheek and cuddled up to me. "I'm going to take care of you, okay? Please don't shut me out."

I propped my head on top of hers, letting her bury her face in my neck as I pressed gentle kisses to the crown of her head. "I'm just worried…all the things you keep having to endure just to be with me. What if you decide it's not worth it? What if it changes you? Michael was always so afraid of that, and the last thing I want is to ruin your life or allow you to be hurt."

"I'm already changed. It doesn't have to be a bad thing. Before you, I was just going through the motions of my life. I've tried to fight it, but my place is here. My destiny is with you. I'll take the good with the bad, because you are *worth* it to me. I love you so much."

Her soft, warm lips pressed against my neck as she reached up to run her fingers through my hair. I was too exhausted to even feel aroused by her gentle kisses and her sweet touch, but her words lulled me into a pure state of calm. *She's mine again.*

"Mmm…I love you too, Liv."

****

The moment I opened my eyes the next morning, the first thing I did was check to see if my hand was still there. In my half-asleep state, I almost managed to convince myself that it had all been a terrible nightmare. A tired sigh left my lips when I saw the less bloodied bandage on my arm and three pill bottles on the nightstand beside me, reminding me of the horrifying past week. I was still in a fair amount of pain, but my head felt clearer now that I was free from the sterile white walls of the hospital and had gotten a decent night of sleep with Livia curled up next to me. She'd offered to sleep elsewhere because she was worried about accidentally hitting my wound in her sleep, but I refused. I would have tied her to the bed if I had to. She had made her choice, and she wasn't going anywhere.

I glanced around the room filled with all of Livia's things from her old life. She hadn't changed much since she moved back in. Everything was in shades of pinks and purples, like a little girl's room. It made sense, knowing that she'd never been able to convince Michael she wasn't a child anymore. I swung my feet out of bed and was met with the unpleasant sight of my reflection in her vanity. My hair hung limply in my eyes, which were bloodshot and weary. I felt nothing like the man I'd been the week before.

The warm glow of the sunset shone through the huge floor-to-ceiling windows in the kitchen where I found Livia at the stove, stirring a pot of soup. And of course, Nero wasn't far away, perched happily beside the kitchen island. When he trotted over to me, Livia finally glanced up and noticed me. "What are you doing out of bed? I was going to bring you something to eat once you woke up."

"Is it really getting dark already?" What had been going on all day while I was laid up in bed?

Livia didn't seem concerned about my work at all, as she tried to push me out of the kitchen. "Your body obviously needed the rest. Why don't you go sit and I'll bring you the food?"

"I'm not an invalid. I'm just maimed." Saying the word out loud made me recoil.

She frowned at me with a tinge of frustration she tried to hide. "I want to take care of you. Can't you just let me have the control for a few minutes?"

The minute her hand landed on my back to push me out of the kitchen, I jolted away from her. "You're getting pretty bossy for someone who doesn't want to be a don's wife."

I wished I could take it back the second it came out, but it was too late. There was no one left to punish for my predicament, and I didn't think I could take much more self-destruction.

As she stirred the pot on the stove, her hand halted in its movements. She flicked off the stove before she faced me head on. "And I never will if you keep talking to me like this."

She quickly brushed past me and stalked off. After a few minutes of waiting, I couldn't help the flurry of panic when I wondered if I had just pushed her too far.

The living room was empty, as was Michael's office. Climbing the stairs was more taxing than it should have been as I headed upstairs to find her. Her bedroom door was closed, as were all the others except the one at the very end of the hallway. It was cracked just slightly, and I found myself drawn to the room.

She had turned this small bedroom into an art studio; there were art supplies and easels with canvases on them everywhere. It looked like she'd made some changes after all. I'd only been looking in the wrong place.

I wandered around, taking a thorough look at each one. Her paintings exuded confidence I hadn't seen in her work before. She was developing a style all her own, and it was breathtaking to witness. For a moment I managed to forget about our current situation until my eyes fell on the last painting sitting on its easel, and I froze. I recognized the portrait of me right away.

Though she'd drawn my eyes closed, the reverence on my face was clear. The broad strokes of paint magnified every feature. The dozens of different shades accentuated every shadow perfectly. It felt like years ago that I stood in front of the bay window, playing music for her, while falling even more deeply in love with every second that passed. It was beautiful, and it was agony at the same time. My breathing grew heavier as the fury set in. Everywhere I looked, there was another reminder of what I'd be missing out on for the rest of my life. I could never play the violin again. I could never use both of my own hands to hold the woman I loved. If we had children, how would I play with them? Everything felt hopeless.

The hair on the back of my neck rose when I felt her presence behind me. Without turning around, my shoulders began to shake. I needed to get out of this room before I did something I'd regret. "Get me out of here, Liv. I can't…"

She gasped lightly, surprised to hear the vulnerable tone of my voice. Her warm hands wrapped around my shoulders as she steered me away from the painting. "I'm sorry. I didn't think you would come in here…"

Once she clicked the door shut behind us, I held her close, my forehead resting on hers. "No, I'm sorry. I shouldn't have spoken to you that way. I was coming to apologize, and I saw the door was open."

"I know things are difficult for you right now. I don't want to make it any harder on you than it has to be." She reached up and stroked my bearded cheek. "You're not running me off that easily, but I won't be a punching bag, either."

I frowned, suddenly even more ashamed about my outburst. "I've been taking out my anger on you...I am so sorry, *tesoro*."

"I know. Come, eat."

She led me back down to the kitchen and served me some soup before filling me in on what I'd missed while I slept the day away. "A few days ago, Stefano and Carlo scoured your apartment to see if they could find any clues, but they didn't tell me what they found. Now that you're out of the hospital, they'll come by with Gio."

"Okay. Good."

"And they're also going to be bringing some clothes for you. I just think it's safer for you to be here with me. That way, we can stop having your men move back and forth."

Hope bloomed in my chest. "I thought you didn't want to live together again so soon."

She was silent for a while and I waited, hoping that she wasn't about to tell me this was only temporary. "When I couldn't find you, I truly understood how you felt when I disappeared off the street that night. It was like I couldn't breathe. What you said was true; if we can't stay away from each other, then what's the point in fighting it anymore? I'm here, and I still want you..."

It was a relief to finally hear what I had been wanting for weeks. I set my gaze on hers, not hiding the intensity behind my eyes or my words. "You'd better be damn sure, because if we do this, I'm never letting you go again. You're the love of my life, Livia Rossi."

"I've never been more sure of anything in my life. It

hurts too much to be without you."

As she gazed at me in wonder, I wondered what it was that made her look at me like I had hung the moon for her, but it was a look I would never take for granted again.

Chapter Nineteen

Livia

Fortunately, I'd made an enormous pot of soup. As soon as Dante's men arrived, they flocked to the kitchen like a group of starved teenage boys panhandling for scraps. Carlo sniffed the air with an appreciative grin on his face. "*Madonna mia*, is that minestrone?"

I rolled my eyes and gestured to the stove. "Help yourselves."

I never imagined taking a bigger hand in this world beyond being the clueless partner of the don, but I was beginning to notice his men were changing in the way they perceived me. They respected me, and it was almost as if they viewed me as an extension of him. In the past five days, I had probably exchanged more words with Gio and Carlo than I had with the grumpy Dante.

Once everyone settled in at the table with their food, Dante didn't waste any time grilling them. "So, what do we know?"

"The place was completely destroyed," Stefano pointed out.

"I know that. That was my doing."

My breath hitched in my throat. I assumed whoever had kidnapped him also trashed his apartment, but it was all him. "You wrecked your own place? And the vi—"

He held up his good hand. "I don't want to think

173

about it, Liv. Please."

I clamped my mouth shut, flicking a nervous glance to Gio, who took the opportunity to break the tension. "We found some blood, too, but we assumed it was yours."

"No. Before they dragged me away, Nero bit one of them."

"Good. I wish he'd finished the job," I bit out, earning me a shocked glance from all four men sitting at the table. "What?"

Carlo grinned with pride. "You don't want to piss off this one, boss. You should have seen her when I left that night. Half of me was speeding away to find you, the other half was running away from her."

"Livia is clearly more capable than I give her credit for. I intend to remedy that," Dante said as he pressed a kiss to my temple, making me blush. It was strange for him to be openly affectionate with me in front of his men, but they knew by now what we meant to each other.

I leaned into Dante's side. "So, did you find anything else?"

Stefano picked up a duffle bag which sat at his feet and handed it to Dante, ignoring me. "I brought some casual clothes and a few suits. The garment bags are in the living room. I only found one of your cufflinks though," he said as he dug into one of the pockets to procure a small gold cufflink, and he placed it on the table for Dante to see.

He picked it up and studied it for a moment. "This isn't mine."

The overhead light in the kitchen glinted over the surface of the smooth metal round. The engraving on it caught my eye, and I leaned closer to get a better look.

When the realization hit me, the room spun. As the images flashed through my mind in fast forward, my heart thudded out of control, and I swayed in my seat. "No, no, no…"

Dante went on alert. "What is it? Do you recognize this?"

Everyone's eyes were suddenly glued on me, and my hands shook as I took it from him to examine it closer—like the metal would burn my skin when I touched it. "It's him…the nameless man."

His eyes hardened the instant he grasped what I was saying. "*What?* How is that possible?"

When Stefano saw me struggling to catch my breath, he bolted out of his chair to get me a glass of water. He rushed back to me, and I took a heavy gulp before I answered. "I don't know. These cufflinks…When he put his hands on me, it was all I could see…"

Gio leaned in closer to take the cufflink from me. "Don't fucking tell me…"

Dante slammed his bandaged arm against the table; a roar of agony immediately followed. "Fuck! I always assumed that it was one of his underlings…but I know who did this. Goddamned Lorenzo Leone."

"Whenever there's some bullshit, I know Enzo is involved," Stefano added, shaking his head.

Putting a name to the face of the man who haunted my every memory of New York only made it all seem more real. I'd thought the engraving was only a design, but the cursive letters stared back at me, mocking me for being so blind. LL for Lorenzo Leone, or as everyone else knew him, just Enzo. "I…I have something to confess."

"Tell me."

Bracing myself for his anger, I let it spill out. "The last time I saw Eric Walsh, he told me he wanted to warn me about the man who threatened him. I asked him to describe the guy, and…it's him. He was in California, stalking me."

Dante launched himself out of his chair, then made a motion like he was about to punch the wall but stopped himself. The pure murder in his eyes made me wonder who he was more angry with—me or Enzo. "*Christ*, Liv! If I knew the bastard who hurt you was still alive, I would have tracked him down and torn him apart before I *ever* let you step foot back here. Why would you keep this from me?"

I'd been embarrassed by his semi-public display of affection earlier, but now I was embarrassed to be arguing in front of his men, about this of all things. Trying to ignore the questions in all their eyes, I whispered to Dante alone, "You told me the Leones dealt with it. I didn't want to send you into a blind rage when I wasn't sure if it was the same man, or if he was even alive."

Gio laid a hand on Dante's shoulder in an attempt to calm him down. "Let's not fly off the handle yet. At least now we know who it is."

Dante's statement chilled my blood. "You know this could mean war, right?"

Gio said, "The Leones started this—we're just finishing it. No one is going to mourn Enzo, not even his brother. He's just a power-hungry maggot eager to become the next Augustine."

Once Gio made his point, Stefano turned his laptop to face Dante. I had to peek over his shoulder to see the collection of photos. In one, Enzo was visible standing next to a disheveled child with dark brown hair and piercing blue eyes. He looked miserable. "What's he doing with that boy?"

Stefano finally made eye contact with me. "I wasn't for sure certain he had anything to do with this vendetta against you, but I knew right away he was behind those teenaged drug mules."

Dante said nothing for several minutes as he stared straight ahead. No one spoke, and I could almost see him replaying flashbacks of his memories with Augustine's crew. Was Enzo really doing this just to get under Dante's skin?

His voice came out quiet and calm. *Too* calm. "Luca is a goddamned liar."

"Luca?" I asked, starting to feel lost in this conversation.

"We questioned one of the Leone men when you went missing. Michael and I let him go when he gave us a hint that pointed at Augustine."

The guilty expression on his face meant he'd been keeping things from me too. Maybe I didn't need to know every detail of his crimes, but he'd interrogated someone to find me and never thought to mention it? *Hypocrite.*

"I know this might be uncomfortable, but what happened with you and Lorenzo Leone?" Gio asked gently. "It might help us figure out what his goal is."

Dante flicked his eyes to mine, full of sympathy. He wasn't going to push me to tell them, but I felt I had to. "He…Enzo cornered me at the club, back when it was Augustine's. He held me at gunpoint and forced me to strip for everyone in the VIP room. He threatened me and my uncle if I ever told anyone, so I kept my mouth shut and left New York."

The room fell dead quiet, and when I looked up, there wasn't a shred of judgment on any of the men's faces. I blew out a sigh of relief.

Carlo reached out and took my hand. "I'm so sorry this happened to you. We're not going to let him near you again, I swear it."

Dante sank back in the chair beside me and wrapped his good arm around me. "Does he want to hurt me because I took a piece of his livelihood away? What does Livia have to do with all this?"

"With Michael gone, I don't know why he'd be holding a grudge still. It has to be about you, boss." Gio heaved a sigh and leaned his elbows on the table. "Maybe he wants to take Livia from you."

Stefano's face hardened with determination. "We need to see what he's been up to. I can get into his house and take a look around."

Dante's voice took on its familiar dominant tone that I hadn't heard in what felt like forever. "You do that. And I need some men watching Enzo at all times. Be discreet. Chances are he doesn't know we know yet, and I want to keep it that way until we come up with a plan."

The nameless man wasn't only alive, but right here in my backyard. Knowing Enzo took joy in hurting me only terrified me more. By amputating Dante's hand, he was sending a message to show everyone the Rossi family wasn't untouchable.

Dante took a few minutes to talk to Gio alone before his men left. Feeling exhausted, we settled on the couch in the living room to take in the hectic past hour. A thought came to me. I was pretty sure he wouldn't approve, but I needed to try. "Would you teach me how to shoot?"

His head reared back. "What? Are you serious?"

"Yes. Maybe none of this would have happened if I could have protected myself to begin with." I hung my head down in shame, thinking about how easily this could have been over with if I'd just had a gun four years ago. I wouldn't have needed to run away like the coward I was, and Dante wouldn't have been hurt.

"Please tell me you're not blaming yourself for this." He held up his wrist for me to see, hitting the nail right on the head. I looked away. "If you want me to show you how to protect yourself, I would never say no. But if this is just you acting out of guilt, then you can forget about it, Liv. You have nothing to feel guilty for."

"I don't want to be a burden on you. I know you'd protect me, but you shouldn't have to all the time."

He laughed. "Out of the two of us, right now, I think *I'm* the burden."

"You're not! Even with one hand, I'm sure you could do more damage than I could…"

"Ask my balls how much damage you can do. I hope you didn't want kids, baby," he joked, only making me grow more frustrated.

"You're being an ass."

"No. I plan on pulling out that card when you yell at me to take out the garbage, or whatever normal couples fight about."

"We could never be normal." I wanted to stay annoyed at him, but his amusement was infectious. It was nice to see him smile after everything he'd been through. "Just show me how to use a gun. Please? Wouldn't it be better if I were familiar with it, instead of accidentally shooting myself in the foot or something?"

The grin quickly faded from his face. "No, I definitely don't want that. If I agree, you have to be serious. No joking or waving the gun around. You have to listen to everything I say so you don't get hurt. Okay?"

"Of course. Thank you." I leaned over to give him a quick peck on the lips. "You reek, by the way."

"I love you too," he responded with a roll of his eyes before he sniffed himself and scrunched up his nose in disgust.

After I helped him wrap his arm in a plastic bag so his bandage wouldn't get wet, I left him to shower—only because he refused to let me help him. Instead, I took the opportunity to clean up the bedroom. It had been an adjustment to get used to living here again, and now living here with Dante.

With this Leone situation taking precedence, neither of us had taken much time to talk about what we were doing. Did he want to live here with me? Get a different place? I couldn't help but wonder if he was as haunted by Uncle Michael's presence—or absence—as I was.

The jeans he'd been wearing were tossed onto the bed, and I stuffed my hands in the pockets to make sure there wasn't anything inside before I placed them in the hamper. A loud gasp escaped my lips when my fingers wrapped around a small velvet box. Almost afraid to reveal what I was holding, I whipped around and put my ear to the bathroom door to make sure the shower was still running before I pulled my hand out of his pocket.

Don't jump to conclusions. It could be anything.

My curiosity couldn't be contained. I slowly opened the box which revealed a beautiful ring. The pink-tinted diamond was so radiant, I couldn't stop myself from slipping it on to see how it would glow against my skin.

Holding my hand up to the lamp, I twisted my hand back and forth to watch the light catch every facet. It didn't escape my notice that it was sized perfectly for me. He'd just been carrying it around in his pocket?

"I knew it would look beautiful on you."

His raspy voice coming from behind me made me jump out of my skin, quite literally caught with my hand in the proverbial cookie jar. "Dante! You scared the shit out of me! I-I was just going to put your jeans in the laundry basket, but then I felt something in there...I couldn't help myself."

When I tried to remove the ring, he stopped me. "No, don't."

"But...you obviously didn't mean to give it to me yet. I feel like I'm stealing it."

"I've wanted to give you a ring since the moment I kissed you." He strode closer to me, with just a towel wrapped around his hips. Little droplets of water clung to his hair, and his lips parted when he bent his head to kiss me softly. "I let you get away once, and I'm not letting it happen again. Besides, I was going to give it to you... before all that happened, so I'm late to the game at this point."

"Oh, really? How were you going to do it?"

He sat down on the bed, patting the space next to him. "After dinner and a carriage ride around the city, I planned to take you back to that jazz bar, get on one knee, and ask you for your hand, like a proper gentleman."

Knowing he'd planned a proposal on the night he'd been abducted made my heart ache even more. I couldn't envision how he must have felt afterward, believing he should push me away for my own good—while watching his own dreams for the future slowly die.

"You sweet, sweet man. I can't believe you were going to woo me. I'm sorry I ruined the surprise…"

"Well, we did everything else ass-backwards, so it only makes sense that you would dig into my pants and propose to yourself."

Rolling my eyes at his teasing, I got up from the bed and looked down at my ring again. "It's perfect."

He barely masked the worry behind his eyes. "So?"

"Dante, I love you so much. Yes, I'll marry you."

Chapter Twenty

Dante

My second proposal of marriage couldn't have gone better if I'd planned it. When she opened the box and saw that ring, she must have immediately known it belonged on her finger. In that moment when she thought she was alone, she radiated with genuine love for me. *Me*.

Michael's death and the subsequent encounter with Leone and his goons brought out the nastier side of me, but Liv wasn't afraid. We didn't need grand theatrics— we had enough of that in our daily lives as it was. Somehow, a low-key proposal where one of the participants was naked seemed so perfectly *us*. No pretense, and no playing games. No more push and pull.

After I cuddled her to sleep that night, I left her in the bed with Nero standing guard. I'd slept for too long, and now I was unable to wind down. Glancing down at her with the new ring on her finger, I felt a giddiness I'd never felt before. Previously, I'd thought it unnecessary to give her a ring, but I was glad for it now. Everyone who gave her a second look would know she was mine, and it gave me the purest satisfaction.

Then I thought about Enzo. Some sick part of me wanted him to see her with my ring on her finger and know he never had a chance of taking her away from me. I still wasn't sure what had caused him to become completely fixated on her, to the point he flew all the way to California just to stalk her. Was it just because she was an extension of Michael?

At this moment, I realized he must have been the man in the suspicious car on campus that day. *That explains why he sped away like the devil was chasing him.* He couldn't risk me identifying him. I couldn't fathom why he would choose to stalk her at school himself, rather than sending one of his lackeys. Until my men found something, I wasn't leaving Livia alone.

At breakfast, I tentatively broached the subject. "I have a suggestion."

Fork halfway up to her mouth, she set her suspicious glare on me. "Okay…What is it?"

Not a great start, but okay. "I want one of my guys with you at all times—"

"But they already are! They wait for me outside of work and everywhere else I go. How much closer can they get?"

"They can't stop Enzo from buying a ticket for a museum tour, then going inside to harass you. He's kept his distance from you so far, but I'm not willing to take the chance he won't try to get closer now that he thinks he's getting somewhere."

She sighed and put down her fork. "I already took several days off, and now I'm going back with a bodyguard? It's a nice place, Dante. They're not going to be okay with me having a suited man tailing me while I give guided tours. The people who go there aren't like us; they'll be unnerved."

A small part of me wanted to cheer in victory when she referred to *us*. But I hated that in order to accept this life, she had to accept the constant risk that came with it.

I reached across the table to take her hand, urging her to look at me. "Is working at the museum more important than your life? I'm not too proud to admit Enzo worries me. He's unpredictable, and I can't stand to think of what I would do if I lost you now...after everything we've been through."

My words seem to hit a chord with her, and her tense shoulders relaxed. "Fine, I'll let Carlo come in with me, but he has to blend in. And I want to go to the shooting range today."

"Fair deal. Have I told you how much I love you?" I crooned, trying to ease the sting of our disagreement.

The flush rising in her cheeks never failed to weaken my knees. "Yes...but I wouldn't mind hearing it again."

Her eyes glazed over as I stroked the pad of my finger across her engagement ring. "I love you so much, my beautiful, sweet, stubborn wife-to-be..."

As per our deal, after breakfast, we got dressed and headed to the shooting range. Heeding my advice, she selected a standard nine-millimeter pistol for her first time. I figured that would be as good a place as any to start; I had several of them, and I figured once she was more comfortable handling a gun, I could give her one to keep on her at all times. The last thing I wanted to do was treat her the same way Michael did. If she showed me she could handle herself, then I could afford to loosen the reins a little.

"I'll go first," I offered, stepping up to the window.

Livia flashed me a concerned look. "I thought you were just going to instruct me...can you..."

"Good thing I'm ambidextrous. I wish I had known it would come in handy someday. I would have practiced more." Keeping my right arm hidden away in the sling under my jacket, I got into my stance. I raised my left arm, flexing my fingers before I picked up the pistol. "Put your earmuffs on, baby. This is going to be loud."

Once I took aim, and rapid fired. Partially to show off, and partially to test myself to see if I was still as good as I thought I was. When the clip was empty, the target sheet came forward to showcase my results. Attempting to hide my cocky grin, I watched as Livia studied the sheet, confused. "Where did they go?"

"I put four through each eye and a few in the chest. I only missed one," I pointed to the hole near the side of the torso on the sheet. "Not a kill shot, but not too bad."

She gave me an incredulous look. "*Not bad?* That's amazing. Show me how to do that!"

I chuckled and positioned her in front of me, giving her a fresh clip and the pistol. After I directed her on how to load it, I watched as her nimble fingers managed it with no issue. Next came the fun part. "Okay, before you even fire the gun, I need to show you the proper stance so that you don't hurt yourself. The recoil on a nine-millimeter isn't that bad, but for someone who isn't used to it, it can be jarring." I placed a hand on her shoulder and directed her to stand in front of a fresh target. "Put your feet shoulder-width apart, the right foot slightly in front, since you're right-handed." I took the opportunity to bend over and adjust her leg, even though it was already perfectly positioned.

"Like this?" She glanced down at me with a hopeful look on her face as I stroked her calf from my crouched position.

It was impossible to keep from constantly touching her. Pink blossomed on her cheeks when I winked at her. "Yes, perfect. Now flex your knees slightly. Don't ever lock your knees, or the recoil might cause you to stagger back and miss your target or fall. See how that feels?"

"Yeah, I definitely feel steadier."

Once she was in place, I showed her how to hold the pistol. "Always keep your finger next to the trigger, never resting on it directly. When you shoot, you have to mean it. You can't take it back—never forget that."

She nodded, and I pressed a quick peck to her temple. "A kiss for luck?"

"You don't need luck, Liv. You have everything you need in that sharp mind of yours. Take a deep breath and exhale as you aim. Fire when you're ready." Taking a few steps back, I awkwardly placed my earmuffs over my ears and waited for her to start. I didn't know if her spatial awareness would translate from her art to shooting, but I watched quietly as she emptied her clip.

When the sheet came up, she scoffed. "I missed three shots! Goddamn it."

I could hardly hide my pride. "Yeah, but you got several kill shots. That's pretty damn good for a beginner. For intermediate even."

Her frown faded, and she leaned into me, running her long nails gently up and down my abdomen. "Good thing I have an expert teacher. Can I make this up with some extra credit?"

The sparks that fizzed all over my body surprised me. I'd barely felt horny in days, being too distracted by the aching in my arm and the stress of hunting Enzo down. Just the lilt to her voice sent me straight down the path to arousal, and I tried hard to ignore it. "We'll make up for it with a few more tries."

I'd have to be dead to stop touching her, but the idea of giving her any false hope made me feel guilty. Though we'd slept together, we hadn't had sex in weeks. As much as she'd seen me at my most needy at the hospital, I was afraid to let her see me raw and exposed in our home setting. Wearing my trauma on my sleeve, as if to mock me for the sin of ever touching her in the first place. *Happy now, Michael?*

Livia still missed two shots, but she was getting closer with every try, and I had to admit it impressed me. "You know, you're a very stubborn girl, but you're an excellent student."

"I can't believe that was ever in question. You had to have seen my report cards on the fridge over the years," she retorted.

I put my left hand over my heart. "Stop reminding me I'm an old man."

That only made her giggle more. "For an old man, you have an amazing amount of stamina, though." My heart nearly dropped out of my chest when she fucking winked at me. *Devil woman.*

Liv let me drive with no argument. I assumed she was trying to humor me, but the way she kept flicking yearning looks at me told me she was incapable of keeping her eyes on the road. It was very reminiscent of the way she acted all those months ago in California, when she finally resigned herself to our insane connection. It would be useless trying to ward off her affections when I wanted her with every fiber of my being.

I let out a breath of relief when we reached the house and I climbed out, then rounded the car to open the door for her. She took my offered hand as I led her to the house. Maybe I wasn't a full-on gentleman, but I had my moments.

We were barely inside before Livia whipped around to face me, placing her hands on my shoulders and nudging me back toward the door. "It got me so hot watching you shoot," she whispered against my neck, planting sweet kisses against my throbbing pulse.

Pressing myself against her body, I couldn't stand to touch her with anything less than all of me. I hated myself for my hesitation when all I wanted to do was rip her clothes off and be inside of her again. "I...don't know if I can do this, baby..."

"I know what you're worried about, *caro*. But you don't need to do anything but let me love you," she whispered back as she sucked on my lower lip, lightly grazing it with her hot tongue.

"What if I can't please you the way I used to?" My vulnerability emerged before I had the chance to push it down again.

Livia stayed silent for a few minutes as she trailed her lips up and down my neck. I felt myself stiffening in my pants as she pressed her body to mine. "All you need to do is look at me with those reverent eyes. The way you show me your love with every look gives me so much pleasure."

She slid her hands up under my shirt to softly stroke my stomach in little circles, and I let out a defeated groan. *I can't resist her.* I fisted my hand in the hair at her nape, pulling her head back to devour her mouth. I growled into the kiss, "Take me, *tesoro*. I'm yours."

Chapter Twenty-One

Livia

The low light of my bedside lamp illuminated the bedroom in a soft amber glow, further intensifying the passion in Dante's eyes as he watched me undress. He leaned against the bedroom door, almost like he was in a trance.

When I approached to help him out of his shirt, I didn't avoid looking at his wrist, but I made sure not to linger too long. More than anything, I wanted to make him comfortable, and show him he was still irresistible to me. Pressing soft kisses onto his bare chest as I unbuckled his pants, I felt Dante's hand stroking up my back to cup my head, holding me to him. As his hand shook, I felt the need pouring from him with every touch.

"I almost forgot how amazing your body feels against mine." He lowered his mouth to mine, nibbling and sucking on my lip with hunger. When we broke apart, he uttered softly, "I love you so goddamned much. Thank you for giving me another chance."

Our tongues stroked together and I let a whimper out into his mouth. My skin felt like it was on fire, and my core ached for him. *We both need this*. "Go lie down."

"So fucking bossy." Gazing back at me with hooded eyes, he licked his lips slowly, then strode over to the bed and lay on his back, as leisurely as he could. I shot him a smirk and followed him over, straddling myself on his thighs, his shaft resting against my stomach.

As I sat on top of him, I leaned down and trailed kisses down his chest and abdomen, alternating with soft lashes of my tongue. "Feel good yet?"

"Liv…" he moaned low in his throat, lightly bucking his hips at me.

I took that as a cue, giving the tip of his cock a teasing lick. His hand flew up to my hair, urging me to take more. My tongue slid down the length, then I took him in my mouth. It felt so good to be able to please him like this again. Dante bucked against me, and I sucked on him eagerly.

"Oh fuck…stop. I don't want to come until I'm inside you." With his hand in my hair, he tugged lightly.

Quickly shifting myself forward, he rested his hand on my hip to gently guide me down. As he filled me, warmth washed over me. Nothing felt more right than being connected this way.

"Oh, Jesus," he rasped as he closed his eyes for a moment, absorbing the pleasure I was bringing him.

My fingers clutched at his shoulders, and I circled my hips. "Do you like this?"

His head fell back against the pillow, his left hand gripping me tighter. "*Yes*. Keep going, baby."

He thrust his hips up at me, making me cry out loudly. I didn't care if anyone heard us—he needed to know how good he made me feel, and how much I needed him. His frantic pulse hammered against my lips, and I whispered against his throat, "Nobody has ever made me feel so needed. And I'm just as desperate for you. Never pull away from me again. Promise me."

"I promise," he whispered into my ear as we

continued our rhythmic motions together. "Let's get married tomorrow. No more fucking around. You're mine, Livia Rossi, and I want the world to know it."

I wasn't sure if he was serious, but he wasn't the type to say things he didn't mean, even during sex. As I continued to slowly ride him, I rested my palm over his heart. "I'll honor you for the rest of my life."

With a gentle grasp on his bicep, I bent my head down to lay the lightest kiss possible right above his bandage. Dante needed to know I loved him for who he was before, who he was now, and whoever he'd become in the future. We'd change together and love each other more for it.

His eyes shimmered. "Come here."

We resumed our passionate embrace, our lips and tongues tangling together constantly as we swallowed each other's fervent moans of pleasure. Feeling the wide base of his cock rubbing at exactly the right place sent me into oblivion. I couldn't hold back my cries as I exploded, my legs shaking. "*Oh, Dante, yes...*"

"That's it, come with me. God, it feels so fucking good..." he groaned into my ear, our sweaty bodies slipping together while we rode out the waves of our mind-shattering climax. My name came out like a prayer when he emptied himself inside me.

Eventually, I lifted myself and laid beside him. There was a hint of a contented smile on his lips as he traced small circles in the palm of my hand. Neither of us said anything for a while, just appreciating each other's touch, and soon I heard the deep, even breaths telling me he was asleep. He seemed years younger, completely relaxed in his slumber. I didn't have the heart to disturb him, so I lay back down with my head on his chest and listened to his steady heartbeat.

Minutes after I'd dozed off, Dante jolted.

"What is it? Phantom pains again?" Without hesitation, I sat up in bed and flicked the light on. "Do you want to try the mirror thing the doctor talked about?"

Dante lay on his back, and he glanced up at me in confusion, then down to his wrist, as if he'd forgotten for a moment. He shook his head and asked, "Do you have a white dress?"

There wasn't any reason to be nervous, yet I was. No one else alive could have loved and cared for me as much as he did. Everything he did, he did for me. My heart hammered in my chest as I attempted to act unaffected. "Yes. Nothing fancy though."

"It doesn't have to be. You look beautiful in anything you wear. Besides, I'll be too captivated by those soft brown eyes to notice."

****

In a way, it was like I'd stepped through a portal when I came back to New York. A few months ago I was in college with one friend and no desire for a relationship whatsoever. Then Dante reappeared and started my surreal journey deeper into a life I'd lived, but never really known. Now I was at the courthouse, getting ready to marry my fiancé, the boss of the Rossi family. I wasn't sure what I believed in terms of fate or karma, but someone had to be getting a laugh out of the roller coaster that was my life.

"Isn't there a twenty-four-hour waiting period after you get the marriage license?" I asked him as we waited for the clerk to help us; his eagerness to get this done so quickly rubbed off on me.

Dante flashed me a wicked grin. "Did you forget

who you're marrying, beautiful?"

"Never. I know exactly who you are. You are a loving, passionate, and loyal man. And I love you so much."

A brief emotional moment caught me off-guard when I thought about my uncle, and I sagged in the little plastic chair I sat in. Dante noticed the shift in my mood immediately and reached out for me. "Are you nervous?"

"No. I want this." Hesitating for a moment, I muttered, "I'm just sorry my uncle can't be here."

"I know. I am too." When the tears rimmed my eyes, he hauled me into his arms. "We can't replace what was—we can only rebuild. That's why we're doing this. We'll be a family, *tesoro*."

The clerk at the front cleared her throat, interrupting our heartfelt moment and giving us paperwork to fill out. The entire process seemed kind of clinical at first, but the smile on Dante's face when he eyed my forms made me giddy again. "Livia Castellano. I like how that sounds."

He wore a dark gray three-piece suit for the occasion, paired with a silver tie. The monochrome made his hazel eyes pop even more. He looked dark and dangerous, but I understood the gentleman underneath, and loved him for all of it. His promise for the future assured me I was doing the right thing.

We were only waiting a few minutes before it was our turn. Giovanni Gallo was the only one Dante told about our plans, and he offered to come as our witness. He followed behind us and sat at one of the benches near the front, also acting as our ring bearer.

The officiant stood in front of a lectern and instructed Dante and me to join hands. I held his left in both of mine, feeling the growing heat between us.

Everything beyond us was a blur when I met his loving gaze.

"If you would like to say a few words now, you may," the officiant said as he gestured in our direction.

It was clear he was nervous, but he cleared his throat and spoke. "Livia, falling for you was the best and most unexpected thing that ever happened to me. I want to spend the rest of my life treasuring you the way you deserve. Every hour. Every minute. Even after my last breath."

Had he just come up with that on the spot? The way he stroked his thumb over the back of my hand gave me tingles, and my declaration poured out of me. "I think the reason I never met anyone else was because you were still in Manhattan waiting for me. And now that I've been out there, I know what I really want. You're the most loyal, fascinating man I've ever known, and I love you so much, Dante."

I didn't miss the welling of his eyes as the officiant instructed us to kiss. He cracked a grin I thought might split his face, then dipped me for a passionate kiss in front of Gio and several other waiting couples. I held onto him tightly, ignoring several wolf whistles that came from the back of the room.

When we left the courthouse, Gio acted like a proud papa, clapping Dante on the back approvingly. "*Congratulazioni!* I've never seen two people better matched than you."

"Thank you, Gio," I said, pulling him in for a hug. "I feel bad that Carlo and Marcella don't know yet, though. They're our friends too."

Dante kissed the top of my head. "We'll invite them over soon and tell them everything. There just wasn't time to make a plan, and we shouldn't be making waves right now, with everything going on."

As much as I hated that Enzo was putting a damper on my life even after all these years, I agreed that rubbing our marriage in his face would only be pouring fuel into the fire.

Maybe it wasn't romantic to the outside observer, but to me it was the most romantic thing ever—knowing how eager Dante was to be my husband, that he couldn't possibly wait another minute to make it happen. With everything we had been through in the past few weeks, it seemed like the clouds were finally beginning to part, and God knew we both needed them to.

Chapter Twenty-Two

Dante

If I didn't know any better, I would have said Enzo Leone was acting paranoid, like he knew we were coming for him. He increased the guard's presence around his house two-fold, and he spent less time socializing in public. It was extremely suspicious for him since he had a reputation for being a party guy. *Any opportunity for him to paw unsuspecting women.*

I never respected the Leones, but now? Enzo signed his death warrant the minute Livia revealed who the cufflink belonged to. It meant that not only did he have a grudge with me, but he also wanted my wife. That was not fucking happening, and I wasn't going to fully relax until he was six feet under.

Better yet, in multiple graves all over the shittiest places in New York, just so he could finally feel at home.

On one hand, I was happy to have a small get-together to celebrate our marriage with some of our closest friends. On the other, I was dreading it. Everyone knew about my hand by now, but I wasn't looking forward to watching everyone's eyes as they vehemently tried not to look at it. I wasn't even comfortable with it yet. Somehow, I wasn't concerned about Livia's feelings about it anymore. She had more than proven that she loved me unconditionally, and she felt no different about me now than she had before *the incident*.

My new bride stepped out of the bathroom with her chestnut waves piled artfully on top of her head and wearing a simple fitted dress in crimson. My jaw dropped when she sauntered over to me as she slipped dangly earrings in her ears. She caught me ogling her and her cheeks quickly flushed as red as her dress. "What?"

"I'm just thinking how lucky I am. I have a beautiful wife." I cupped her face and brushed my lips across hers between each word. "She's irresistible, sweet, and all mine."

Her nimble fingers pushed my hair out of my face. Even such a simple affectionate touch from her made my heart skip a beat. "Have you seen my husband, though? He's tall, dark, and handsome as all hell."

Flashing her a smirk, I rasped, "No, can't say I've had the pleasure. Is he here, or will he object to me pinning you up against that wall right now?"

"Oh, he would," she teased, backing away slowly as she played along. Her eyes twinkled, and I relished in the sight of her happiness. "He's *very* possessive. He'll carry me away into the night, and you'll never see me again."

The grin she flashed made me curl my arm around her waist and pull her close again. That night was burned into my memory. I remembered carrying her in my arms, startled by the wayward thoughts that cropped up. That sexy way she scowled at me, and her intoxicating scent. I'd never been so close to her before, and it felt good— too good.

Goddamn it, I was hard already just from feeling her warmth through our clothes. "Yes, I am. I can and *will* throw you over my shoulder and carry you away from anyone who ever tries to take you from me. That's how precious you are."

Liv leaned in to whisper in my ear, "I happen to like your beast side…"

Suppressing the growl crawling up my throat, I quickly rushed her downstairs before we ended up tangled in bed together again.

Neither of us were religious, and Christmas had come and gone while I was in recovery from my incident, but keeping those we cared about close was all part of the plan we'd made. Livia made her choice when she married me, and I'd made mine long ago. This was our family now.

Livia had laid out a spread that included meatballs, pastas, and roasted vegetables, as well as her now-famous macaroni salad. I thought of Michael immediately, and a quick glance her way told me she had, too. Maybe making one of his favorites was her way of honoring him, but I was sure it was more of a positive memory for her than for me.

All I could think about was that day at my house in upstate, and the look of pure betrayal on his face. It was obvious he resigned himself, knowing he couldn't stop me from being with Livia. But I wasn't stupid enough to think he approved, or that he forgave me. With time, he could have. Michael would have seen how happy we were together, and how we brought out the best in each other. Now we'd never get the chance to show him we could stand the test of time, the trials of our world, and everything else. It stung every bit as much as knowing you lost your father's respect.

I forced the grief from my mind and stood at the table, reaching down to clink a butter knife against my water glass. "Liv and I want to make an announcement."

Marcella's head shot up to look at me quizzically. "*Dios Mio*, don't tell me you guys are having a baby before me and Carlo! I'll slap you silly, I don't care that you're the boss."

Livia choked on the sip of water she was drinking and turned red as a beet. "No, definitely not pregnant!"

I chuckled at her explosive reaction, but when I opened my mouth to continue, Gio joked, "I've never seen this guy so uptight until he brought her home. If she were pregnant…forget about it."

My mood took a nosedive, and Stefano only made it worse. Nodding eagerly, he agreed. "They'll be the safest kids in Manhattan, with wise guys escorting them to preschool."

"Will everyone shut up so I can say it?" I grimaced when I saw the embarrassed smile fade off of Livia's face, replaced by worry. Unable to ask her about it without everyone getting another good laugh out of us, I blurted out the announcement. "Livia and I got married earlier this week. Now you know—you're welcome."

After my rushed delivery of the news, I slumped down in my seat, everyone's eyes fixed on me and Liv. A moment or two of silence passed before the room seemed to explode with excitement. "That's great, boss. I'm happy for you," Carlo said with a genuine smile. "You two are good for each other."

Marcella beamed proudly at Livia and immediately grabbed at her left hand to look at her ring. "How did I not notice this rock?"

She relaxed in her seat a little, but she still looked uncomfortable. "You were too absorbed in changing up my recipes to notice!"

"I only added a little red pepper. Spice is an

aphrodisiac, you know." She rolled her eyes playfully, then flashed me a genuine smile. "But seriously, I'm thrilled for you two! Why didn't you invite us, though?"

"It was a spontaneous decision and we wanted to do it quietly. We thought it best to involve as few people as possible, but we needed a witness," I said, hoping that would excuse her from further embarrassment by her friend.

"That's all I am to you? I have to say, I'm a little offended!" Gio teased.

Obviously, I hadn't expected everyone to be pleased that we had eloped without telling them, but I definitely hadn't expected them to roast us in our own home. It wouldn't have bothered me so much if it weren't for the blank look on Livia's face through the rest of the dinner.

The idea of her carrying a piece of both of us sent a warm wave of bliss through my body. Now I wanted a family with her, and her sudden shitty mood had me worried. I could have sworn she expressed an interest in having kids someday, so why did she look like someone had punched her in the gut? As soon as everyone left, I tried to talk to her about it.

She was loading up the dishwasher when I strode up to her and snaked my arm around her waist. "Leave that. I'll do it."

"I'm almost finished. You helped enough earlier with cooking the meat," she said without looking up.

Taking the last plate out of her hand and placing it in the dishwasher, I nudged the dishwasher closed with my foot. "Something is bothering you. Just talk to me."

Livia quickly shook her head and attempted to convince me with a forced smile. "I think that went pretty well, considering we snubbed everyone at our wedding. Don't you?"

Her quick subject change didn't convince me she was fine. Not one bit. "Yes, it did. But that's obviously not the reason you've been quiet all night. Tell me."

In a quiet voice, she uttered, "It...it was just Stefano's comment."

Thinking back, I tried to remember what he said that could have pissed her off, but came up empty. "What did he do? I'll talk to him and make sure he apologizes."

The expression she gave me made it clear she wasn't angry with him, but me instead. "No! I mean it's pretty clear he doesn't like me, but it's not that. It was after Marcella asked me if I was pregnant."

"Oh..." The involuntary frown crept up onto my face. "Is that not what you want?"

Sighing heavily, she touched my arm. "Look, you know I love that you're protective of me, but Stefano got me thinking..." she trailed off, desperately hoping I'd get where she was going with this so she wouldn't have to voice it.

Luckily, I knew her better than anyone. I took her hand in mine and brought it up to my face, and as I brushed my lips across her knuckles, she gradually relaxed. "I won't keep our children in a gilded cage. Michael loved you, and he meant well, but I intend to learn from his mistakes. Don't worry about that."

Her shoulders instantly sagged. "Thank you."

"For a second, I thought you were about to tell me you *are* pregnant," I said with a chuckle, which turned into a full belly laugh when Livia's face turned horrified.

"After the year we've had? Oh, God. No. This is the one thing we're not going to rush, Dante Castellano." She tilted back her head to kiss me, letting me know we were okay, then she took my hand to lead me out of the kitchen. "I do have a belated Christmas gift for you, though. I wasn't sure how you would feel about it, which is why I wanted to wait for everyone to leave."

"You already gave me the best gift when you said 'I do.' I don't need anything else."

Liv blushed slightly but didn't relent as she led me toward Michael's office. I had yet to see her step a foot in there, and neither had I. Following her, we stood quietly while she watched me take everything in. It felt like years since I had been here.

"Right after we got back together, my uncle's lawyer came by to talk to me about his estate. He left everything to me, except for one thing," she announced, pacing to Michael's desk with purpose.

I raised an eyebrow in confusion when I watched her pull a long rectangular box out from underneath. "What is it?"

She hesitated for a moment, as if trying to gauge how I was going to react. When I laid eyes on the item, it became clear why she was nervous. "I wanted to give it to you, but then…"

I stared down at the violin case, frozen to the spot as she watched me with trepidation, likely expecting me to explode at any moment. Feeling defeated, I shrugged. "I can't play it, Liv. What would be the point?"

"You can't *yet*," she corrected me gently. "I've seen so many videos of people with prosthetics who are able to play instruments. You love the violin, and you don't have to give it up if you don't want to. My uncle wanted you to have it."

Livia put the case down on the desk and padded over to me, where I stood in the center of the room. She wrapped her arms around my waist and tucked her head between my neck and my shoulder, letting me breathe in the scent of her hair. She always knew how to calm me.

When she let go, I finally regained enough feeling in my legs to carry me over to the desk. The smooth leather felt like butter underneath my touch, and clicking open the lock on the side, I opened it carefully. All the breath left my lungs when I laid eyes on the priceless violin inside. "Holy shit, Michael."

Livia cocked her head at me in bemusement. "What? Is there something wrong with it?"

"I don't know who he had to kill to get his hands on one of these, but…I can't fucking believe it." I was almost afraid to touch it, but I had to. To anyone else, it was just a violin. To me, it was one of the seven wonders. "One of these goes for millions of dollars. There are only a few hundred like it."

"Whoa, really? Do you like it? I mean, I didn't technically get it for you, but…I don't know. I was trying to wait for the right time to give it to you. I hope you're not upset with me," Livia babbled nervously, waiting for my reaction.

As I stroked the silky wood, I could only imagine how it would feel to play a violin that produced a sound unmatched by modern standards. Once I swallowed the frog in my throat, I closed the case again and hauled Livia into my arms, while ignoring the pain of my right arm colliding with her back. "Someday, I'm going to play it for you so you can appreciate it as much as I do."

She let out an audible sigh of relief. "Thank you for accepting it."

My voice came out broken and hoarse. "Thank you for giving me the second-best gift of my life." I clung to her, willing myself to absorb some of her unabashed confidence in me.

"It's a beautiful violin."

"Not the violin, Liv." I met her confused stare and swept a tendril of hair out of her face. "For giving me hope."

Chapter Twenty-Three

Livia

After gifting the violin to Dante, I'd nearly forgotten about the tidbit Marcella had shared with me earlier in the evening. While we prepared the appetizers, she informed me a friend of hers was looking for a fresh artist to show in his gallery and immediately suggested me. It surprised me, since she'd only been in my studio a few times, but she seemed genuinely impressed with my paintings.

I had to wonder if her friend truly wanted to show a nobody in his gallery, or if he had no choice. More often than not, when opportunities fell into my lap over the years, there was always someone on the other end who owed my father or my uncle a favor. Positive that no one would give me the truth, I decided to roll with it.

Once our quickie wedding was old news, we fell into a peaceful haze that almost made me forget the potential danger we were under. When Dante wasn't with me, someone else was. At work, either Carlo or Stefano were there, alternating every day to avoid suspicion. One of them would come in plain clothed and unarmed, then blend in among the other patrons while keeping close to me. I hated knowing they were all fussing over me, but I had to admit it was a smart idea.

Now that we knew who was behind this, they could

plan what to do next with Enzo Leone.

If I closed my eyes, I could still feel him running the cold steel of his pistol down my neck, his predatory gaze burning like fire into every inch of exposed skin. His smarmy face disgusted me, and I was grateful when my tears blurred my vision enough that I didn't have to see it anymore. At that moment, I swore I'd left my body and blacked out until I was on the street again, barely having gotten dressed again.

It bothered me that these men were never punished, and that half of the Leones knew what I looked like naked. It made me feel dirty, but I rarely let myself think about it before. It was inescapable now. The last thing I wanted was for Dante to lose himself in his relentless plot for revenge, so for the next few days, I took every opportunity to distract him from the confrontation ahead.

****

For a moment, I almost couldn't believe what I was seeing. As I leaned against the alcove leading into the kitchen, I watched Dante standing at the stove, stirring something in a pan. During my brief time at his apartment, I'd attempted to teach him a few simple recipes, but in no way did I think he was ready to be left unsupervised in the kitchen.

Alerting him to my presence, I crooned, "Well, well. Look at you, handsome."

He glanced up and flashed me a wide grin. "If all I need to do is cook to make you look at me like that, I have to get a lot better at it, and fast."

I sauntered over to him to investigate. After I rose on the tips of my toes to press a kiss to his cheek, I took a wary peek into the pan. "Oh, stop it. You caught me off-guard is all. What are you making?"

"It's supposed to be mushroom risotto. We'll see."

"Do you need help?" I didn't want to make Dante feel like he wasn't as capable as he was before, but I wanted him to know that he could ask me if he needed it.

"I made one of the guys chop mushrooms for me already. I managed most of this on my own."

Admittedly impressed, I got to work lighting candles on the table while Dante served us our food. It surprised me that he would attempt something as tricky as risotto, but it smelled great, so I had high hopes. With a heaping mouthful, my eyes widened. "This is…actually pretty good."

"You sound surprised. I can learn new skills," he said, feigning offense. "I'm not decrepit yet."

Giggling, I took another bite. "Where did you find the recipe?"

His boyish smirk told me he was glad I asked, and he leaned over to pick up a book that had been sitting on the counter. "It's basically the old menu from the restaurant. They're all my mother's recipes."

He handed me the thick notebook, the pages worn and half falling out. Sticky notes stuck out from the pages, marking them as chicken or beef recipes, and other categories. As I carefully turned it over in my hands, I smiled when I saw his mom's handwriting scrawled all over it. "You kept it all these years?"

"I always wanted to taste her cooking again someday. This way I can, and I can share it with you. Does it taste familiar?"

Thinking back to times I ate at Castellano's over the years, it definitely brought back familiar feelings. "Yes, it does. This is so sweet of you, *caro*."

He beamed and stretched his arm across the table to

hold my hand. "I love you, Livia Castellano..." He trailed off with a dreamy haze in his eyes. "God, I love saying that."

The pride in his voice made me smile. It hadn't been very long since he lost his hand, but he refused to let it hold him back. Not only was he determined to do what he had always done in the past, but he was picking up new things as well. I wished I could scream to the heavens and tell my uncle that he didn't have to worry about us, and that we were happy. We'd been dealt blow after blow, but we would always help each other back up. *You'll see, Uncle Michael.*

"I love hearing you say it." With the haste of our nuptials, I almost forgot that anything had changed between us, but every time Dante proudly referred to me as his wife, I remembered. I supposed all the fanfare was what made it feel real, but none of that stuff mattered to me. All I cared about was both of us being alive and well, together. There was one tradition, however, I wasn't willing to part with. I dared him to deny me this. "As soon as things settle down, we need a proper honeymoon."

He chuckled and scooped some risotto into his mouth. "Agreed. We'll go to an island and immerse ourselves in each other, eating coconuts, or whatever the hell they have growing there. Just me, you, and maybe Nero."

I let out a gasp. "Of course, Nero is coming. He probably misses all the palm trees, and he would be pissed if he had to miss out."

"If he ever calls me 'dude,' I'm blaming you."

"Fair enough—" I started, but the sharp, sudden ring of the doorbell made me jump. "Who's that?"

"It's Stefano. I asked him to come when he was finished for the day… He says he has news." The look of contentment slowly faded from his face. "Do you want to stay to hear it?"

"Yes."

He seemed a little disappointed at the lack of hesitation in my response, but I knew he wouldn't hide anything from me—as much as he may have wanted to. While he took Stefano inside to the living room, I loaded the dishwasher. The longer I waited to join them, the longer I could delay whatever was about to ruin our peaceful night.

After I finished, I found Dante sitting on the edge of his seat while Stefano set down a large box on the coffee table. "What's that?"

Both men jumped at the sudden interruption. "It's…um…stuff of yours," Dante answered in as he tentatively reached inside the box to pick through the items. "Stefano found them at Enzo's."

I reared back in surprise. How had he gotten my things? From where? "Wait, you found my stuff in Enzo's house? You managed to get in?"

Stefano chuckled with pride when I gaped at him. "I had to hack the security cameras, but I figured it out."

"You what? You can do that?" I was starting to realize there was a lot I didn't know about Dante's business, and I wasn't sure I even wanted to.

He answered with a scoff. "How did you think Dante knew where you were when you ran off?"

It made me mildly annoyed that he hadn't told me he tracked me on my phone, and that even Stefano knew about it. No wonder he thought I was irresponsible. I turned back to chastise my husband, but his enraged face sent my train of thought off the rails. "Hey, what's—"

"That disgusting prick!" Dante shot up from the couch with a lacy pair of underwear—my underwear—balled up in his fist.

"How did he get those?" The words came out in a shrill tone as I ripped the panties from his hand. I stomped over to the coffee table and rifled through the box myself. Just the idea of him being in a space I regularly occupied made my skin crawl. At least Enzo hadn't been inside my apartment while I was still living there. That I knew of. *Oh, God...* "He's the one who broke into my apartment after I left. This is all stuff I didn't take."

Dante continued to rifle through the box, picking up and examining each item before he put it aside. He pulled out several more pairs of panties, which I had thought were the most disturbing thing he found, until the items became less sexual and more...obsessive. There were several of my paintbrushes in there, one of my candles, and even a used tissue.

Dante's face twisted up in disgust and rage, and I had to close my eyes again. I sank onto the couch, no longer caring that I clutched panties in my hands while Stefano stared at me with concern. He crouched in front of me and rested his hand on my arm. "Livia? Are you all right?"

"I don't understand why he would do all of this."

With a bit of tenderness in his voice, he responded, "I don't know. But we're going to figure this out and take care of it. Don't you worry."

His uncharacteristic gentleness soothed me, despite his icy blue-eyed stare. It was then I realized Dante hadn't said a word since he saw the panties, and I peered around Stefano's back to see what he was doing. He stared down at a bunch of photos in his hand, then laid them out on the table, remaining speechless. "Dante? What's wrong?"

Curiosity forced me to approach him, even though I was terrified to see what they were. His shaking hand clutched the photo, and when I looked down at it, I was instantly transported back in time. It was me in a sundress, with a big floppy hat on. It was taken one of the last times my uncle and I hung out together before he was arrested; I'd just graduated high school, and he'd taken me out to spend the day in Times Square.

It was bittersweet to see this photo, but there was something about it that looked...off. "How did he get this picture? I didn't have a copy of it anywhere."

He reached into his pocket and handed me his wallet. "Pull out the picture behind my ID."

When he got calm like this, I could tell he was raging inside. This was the same quiet storm I witnessed before he snapped Augustine Lombardi's neck under his boot. I flipped open the wallet and pulled out the photo nestled behind his identification card and held them side-by-side.

Stefano peeked over my shoulder for a quick glance. "Someone else took the picture Enzo had. Different angles, but he was close."

"So he was stalking me even before I met him?"

Dante turned his penetrating gaze on me. He looked furious, but his voice remained steady when he finally spoke. "Is it possible that you did meet him somewhere, and you just don't remember?"

"I guess it's possible. But I would have remembered if I had talked to him for any length of time."

Stefano nudged Dante, and they shared a secret look which had me on alert instantly. He turned to me again and kissed the top of my head. Since he was fuming just a second earlier, his sudden affection made me suspicious. "I have something to discuss with Stefano. Do you mind if we use the office?"

My stomach flipped, but I relented. I didn't think I could take any more bombshells tonight. "Of course not. It's your home now too."

"Go lie down, and I'll be in soon. I love you." Dante didn't wait for me to respond before he stalked off with Stefano in tow.

Chapter Twenty-Four

Dante

I saw a hint of worry in Stefano's eyes when he silently suggested we talk alone. Whatever he wanted to say concerned Livia; my shoulders tensed as I led him to the office. I trusted his judgment, but he clearly thought she couldn't handle it at the moment. She'd obviously been shaking when I sent her upstairs to lie down.

How could it get much worse than finding your panties in some pervert's house? And knowing that he had been stalking her for four years, possibly longer? At that moment, I was almost glad Stefano had pulled me aside. I couldn't control the incendiary response to a threat against Livia, and she didn't need to see me like this before I was able to calm down. Since being with her, I had punched several walls and broken doors. The last thing I wanted was to frighten her, or dishonor Michael by tearing up his house in anger.

Taking a few deep breaths, I slumped into the desk chair and glanced up at Stefano. "Tell me."

Instead of sitting down across from me, he rounded the desk, hand outstretched. He passed me a flash drive. "I didn't think you'd want to watch this in front of Livia."

"*Watch* it?" A shiver ran through my body. "What is it?"

"Security footage of a meeting with Enzo and Michael here." Stefano nodded toward Livia's mother's painting above the fireplace. "You knew about the cameras, didn't you?"

I nodded brusquely. It had never occurred to me to check, seeing as Michael wasn't any more a fan of Enzo's than I was. A part of me held resentment toward him for keeping his enemies so close, believing they were allies. He hadn't seen Augustine for what he was, either. And now I found out he'd entertained the man who assaulted his niece, in her own home. Seething, I urged Stefano to get on with it.

"I spent days scrubbing through the old footage. I don't know what I expected to find, but I have to admit it surprised me to see Enzo in a clip from almost five years ago. Here"—he pushed the flash drive into the port—"just watch."

"I'm not going to like this, am I?"

He knew I was a ticking time bomb already, but he wouldn't lie to me. "No."

I opened the file titled *Michael/Enzo.* The moment I pressed the play button and saw my mentor as I remembered him, the wave of emotion overcame me. He sat behind his desk, smoking a cigar as Enzo walked into the room. He looked odd without his trademark scowl.

Michael looked up, and his lips pursed slightly as if to show displeasure for his guest. "Take a seat. What can I help you with, Don Leone?"

Enzo tentatively sat across from him, crossing his leg over his knee in an effort to feign confidence, but his words sounded rehearsed. "I came here as a sign of respect for you as the head of your family. I have a proposition."

Michael raised a wary brow and waved his hand to get him talking. "Yes, and?"

"Well—" He cleared his throat. "—I wanted to inquire about your niece. She's a lovely girl, and I thought we could try to bring our two families together. A sort of merger, if you will."

Michael's mouth dropped open. "I certainly will not. How do you even know my niece?"

Enzo leaned back in his chair, trying to appear as self-assured as possible, but even through the partially grainy footage, I could see the desperation in his eyes. "I've seen her around the city. I'm not trying to step on any toes, but I'll be perfectly honest with you. I want her."

Michael stared blankly at him. "Do you honestly think if I was going to let her date someone from our business, that my first choice would be you? I'd sooner give her to my *consigliere*." When the words left his mouth, I flinched, but kept my gaze on the screen. Michael punctuated his little joke with a jovial laugh at Enzo's expense—and mine.

I guess that's as close to a blessing as I'll ever get.

Enzo struggled to find his words, but Michael didn't give him the chance. "You've been dealing with the cartels, and I don't want them coming after Livia when you inevitably piss them off. No." He then snuffed out his cigar so hard, the paper holding in the tobacco busted at the seams.

So, Michael had known more about his drug dealings than he let on, and yet he'd let it slide. With no time to unpack the revelation, my attention focused on Enzo's face as his surprise quickly turned to irritation. He continued to grovel. "I would treat her well, and I wouldn't let anything happen to her. Just consider it."

"Absolutely not. Business is one thing, but this is family." Michael folded his hands over the desk, his face resolute. Then he pushed back in his chair to get up. "Is that all?"

Enzo rose from his seat and rounded the desk, getting closer to Michael. Not many people knew him as well as I did, but his subtle body language told me he was on high alert. "Be reasonable. I would do a lot of things to make this happen. If I have to renounce my family and join with yours, I will."

With a genuinely puzzled expression, Michael blurted, "Why would you do that?"

"I'm in love with her."

My blood instantly turned to ice in my veins when I heard his declaration. It took immeasurable effort for me to stay in the chair and not punt the computer across the room, but I didn't want to miss a single word.

Michael had never looked more furious than he did when he sneered at Enzo. "That's ridiculous. You don't know the first thing about her. You've never even—" He suddenly halted as if he came to a realization, then he let out a gasp. "I know what this is about…You sick bastard. Get the fuck out of my office."

Without the need for pretense, his scowl broke free. "This was just a courtesy, Michael. I only wanted to give you the chance to make the right choice."

After Enzo stomped out of his office, slamming the door behind him, Michael stood frozen at his desk. Ashen and vibrating with rage, he suddenly rushed to the phone as the clip ended. Not that it mattered; I knew who he'd called right after that happened, but I'd never gotten an explanation for his frantic state back then. Now I did.

It all made sense now.

All those years ago, I had thought Michael was insane for insisting on so much security for her. He had me following her in the city, without knowing I was protecting her from the very man who slipped past me and cornered her anyway. Didn't Michael think it would have helped me protect her from this motherfucker if I'd known? Or was he too worried I'd not be able to resist the urge to kill him myself, sanctioned or not? There were certain things that could never—and should never—be forgiven, whether you were the boss or not.

The regrets and questions repeated over and over in my mind as I hit replay and watched the entire clip again. A small part of me hoped there would be more context hidden somewhere. Anything to help me understand.

Stefano stood by, waiting for the inevitable explosion. "Boss, don't sweat this bastard. The video isn't telling us much that we didn't already know. He's obsessed with Livia, that was pretty obvious from the get-go."

"Doesn't it?" I asked, not bothering to cover the fury in my tone. "He told Michael. This makes his alliance with Augustine make even more sense. But this puts more things into question now."

"What do you mean?"

"This happened almost five years ago. Isn't it strange that Enzo asked Michael for something, and when he refused to give him what he wanted, he gets arrested soon after? He seemed to know exactly why Enzo was so set on her, and conveniently, he's not here for me to ask what the fuck he got his niece into." I brushed my hair back from my eyes and took a few deep breaths.

Why didn't he warn me?

Stefano tentatively laid his hand on my shoulder, eager to calm me down. "We're only seeing one interaction. There could've been more. Maybe he threatened her safety if he told anyone. All I know is, Michael would never have endangered her unless he had no choice."

"You're right. It's just...*fuck*."

"If Enzo really did this, his own people would take him down for it. Once you rat someone out, even an enemy, everyone will know they can't trust you for shit anymore."

Shaking my head, I launched myself out of my seat. "I'm not willing to wait around for them to mete out justice amongst themselves. Leone's brother swore they'd handled it, but that was just another lie. I want Livia to have a life, and I know she's going to resent being under lock and key twenty-four-seven. I want this over."

Usually stone-faced, he didn't often appear worried, but he was now. "What do you want to do then, boss?"

Everyone was still feeling the sting of loss after Michael's death. If we suffered another hit so soon after, I didn't know if our family would be able to recover. We needed to do this carefully. "I need to see the heads of the other three families separately. Tell Gio and split the work between the two of you. No one else hears a word of this."

"This is war, then."

"Helen of Troy, remember? He fucked with me, which was already suicide. But to find out this same man has terrorized Livia for years? He's going to *beg* for death. Knowing he took Michael from us all on top of everything else—"

"We don't know that for sure."

The adrenaline rushing through my veins made my hand shake as I clenched my fist. "I do. He and Augustine were cut from the same cloth. I knew they were sniveling weasels for years! I could have prevented all of this if I had only trusted my own instincts all those years ago. Once this is done, we're not repeating this mistake again. No fucking mercy."

A momentary flash of fear crossed his face at that moment, and rather than feeling guilty about it, I found myself even more energized. "Yes, boss."

"Go. Thank you for your loyalty."

Before he left the office, he nodded to me. "Always."

The only way Livia would be safe would be for Enzo to die, or for us to run—the former being the more favorable option. We were on the run just a few months ago, and I didn't want to do that to her or *us* again. Ever since we'd put down roots here, we'd only grown closer, we'd made friends, and built the beginning of a life together. This wasn't the time for running. It was time to fight.

The idea of telling Livia about the security footage made me dread going up to bed, but after twenty minutes of staring into the fireplace trying to calm down, I finally dragged myself upstairs. With just her lamp on, Liv was fast asleep with one of my books splayed across her chest. I felt guilty for being relieved, but I wanted to avoid distressing her as much as possible.

Determination pushed away negative thoughts as I slipped into bed. I leaned over to press a kiss to Liv's cheek. "I will always protect you, *tesoro*."

****

When I woke, Liv was already clanging around the kitchen downstairs. So it was to be breakfast and interrogation. *My favorite*.

There was little benefit to her knowing Enzo had tried to arrange some kind of twisted arranged marriage via Michael, but I'd promised to keep her informed on all things that involved her. She wasn't just involved anymore—this was all about her.

I tried to decide whether to voice my suspicion about him being behind Michael's arrest. If it turned out that it wasn't about the drugs, but about his disdain for Michael after his rejection, I didn't know how she would take it. If I knew Liv as well as I thought I did, she would blame herself for the whole thing. How could it be her fault that she was so damn desirable that men would break alliances for her? And Enzo didn't even know her as I did. If he truly knew the woman who haunted my every waking thought, he would have gone to any lengths to possess her. Even in the not-so-clear security footage, I could see the lust and need plain on his face.

In a way, it was fate that our paths crossed. If I hadn't been with her, how long would it have been before Enzo succeeded in taking her? Without me or Michael to look after her, she would have been completely unaware of the danger lurking behind every corner. A desperate man like Enzo, with no obstacles in his way? The thought made me shudder.

Livia poked her head out of the alcove. "Why are you just standing in the hall?"

I jumped at the sound of her voice. "I was thinking."

"Well, you can do that while you eat. Come on."

She was the only woman aside from my mother who

could order me around and actually get results. Once I settled down at the table in front of a plate of peppers and eggs, I met her shifty gaze with a raised brow. "You're buttering me up again."

She knew she was shit at being sneaky and sagged in defeat. "If I have to cook all day to get you to cooperate, then so be it. Although I'm beginning to suspect that you're doing it on purpose."

The anxiety I felt in my groggy state slowly began to melt away at her playful tone. Whatever plagued me, she always made it bearable. "I plead the fifth, my beautiful wife."

"Yeah, yeah. Get talking, Mr. Tough Guy. I want to know what Stefano told you. Don't think I didn't know you waited around for me to fall asleep before you came upstairs."

"You always go right for the jugular, don't you?" I stalled by taking a bite of my food, my eyes rolling back when the flavors hit my tongue. "This is delicious."

"Can you blame me? I'm married to the don. I have to be a little cutthroat to deal with your stubborn self."

"Touché, my vicious girl. Touché."

Chapter Twenty-Five

Livia

It was difficult for me to be angry with Dante for keeping me out of things with Stefano the night before. I was shaken after seeing the things Enzo had taken from my apartment in California. But after a night's sleep, I just wanted everything out in the open.

I peered at him from across the table, stretching out my hand to take his. "Just get it out, and then we'll figure out what to do. How much worse can it get?" Dante's jaw ticked when the question came out of my mouth, wiping the smile right off my face. "Oh, God. What?"

"Stefano showed me some security footage—"

My hands clapped over my ears before he could get out another word. "Please tell me it's not what I think…"

The idea of Dante watching me being humiliated was revolting. I couldn't decide what scared me more— his rage at actually witnessing it, or letting him see me in my most vulnerable state.

He quickly cut in when he saw the panic on my face. "Not that one. I know what I can and can't handle, and you being hurt is one thing I can't see without going feral." When my face finally relaxed, he explained, "I had Stefano erase all the old footage from the club. As soon as this is done, we'll make sure he doesn't have any copies lying around."

It warmed my heart knowing he did that to avoid further humiliation on my part. I couldn't blame him for being enraged about all of this, but it only validated my worries. More than ever, we needed to keep our wits about us—especially Dante. The last thing we needed was for him to act out in a fit of rage and let logic fly out of the window. I didn't want anyone else I loved behind bars or underground.

The tension sat heavily in my stomach, chasing away my appetite in record time. My fork landed on the plate with a loud clink. "Then what was it?"

Dante frowned at me and followed suit, pushing aside his food. Suddenly, it didn't seem like such a good idea to have this discussion over breakfast. "It was a video of a meeting between Enzo and Michael, not long before he was arrested. Apparently, Enzo had seen you out and about and became obsessed. He set up a meeting with Michael to ask him for permission to date you."

With a scoff, I spat out, "What kind of person does that? Did he bring a goat with him to sweeten the deal?"

"Old-fashioned mob mentality." Dante shrugged and scratched his bearded chin. "It was…strange to see him that way. He was begging him to consider it, but obviously, Michael said absolutely not."

"Well, this is one time where I'm really glad he chased a man away from me. I know almost nothing about this Enzo, except that he's crazy. It makes sense now why my uncle was so protective…"

There was a hint of uncertainty in his eyes that confused me. "What I'm left with now is to determine just how unhinged he is. After Michael rejected his proposal, Enzo's entire demeanor changed, and he subtly threatened him. When the video ended, Stefano and I came to a conclusion, but I truly hope I'm wrong."

I assumed once my uncle was gone, he took his chance because he knew he would get away with it. What else was there to determine? "About what?"

Dante took a deep breath and grabbed my hand, squeezing it. "I think he didn't take the rejection well, and he retaliated by ratting on Michael."

The room seemed to shrink as all the air left my lungs. *It can't be.* "*No*…Please don't tell me he did all this over a goddamned crush!"

"Liv, think about it. Michael and Enzo were allies, but over the years, as Augustine rose up in the ranks and started dealing drugs with him, Michael kept a tight leash on them. That was strike one, but then you came along. It all makes perfect sense."

"Clearly, I'm missing something here. There might be a motive, but how do we know for sure?"

Dante squeezed my hand comfortingly, as if he dreaded telling me more. "I had a suspicion that someone ratted him out years ago. I thought it was strange that he was the only one implicated." I furrowed my brows, prompting him to explain, "Usually, when these busts happen, they take down several guys, or even an entire crew. He had to have been behind it. Who else had the most to gain from him being gone?"

Only one other name came to mind. "Augustine. But if it were him, he would have relished the opportunity to brag about it. So, it couldn't have been."

"Exactly. Augustine got exactly what he wanted, and with your uncle out of the way, Enzo knew he would have an easier time getting to you."

"What are we going to do now?"

He reared his head back and gave me a critical look.

"We? You are not going to do anything. Whatever I plan, I want you as far as humanly possible from the fallout."

"Excuse me? Look at everything he's done! I want to know what's going to happen to him. Maybe even talk to—"

"Absolutely fucking not. The things I'm going to do to Enzo...I don't want those thoughts in your head. He ruined Michael's life, violated you, stalked you...and took my motherfucking hand!"—Dante shoved his arm up in the air for me to see—"Do you seriously think I'm willing to risk you in any way?" His rage bubbled up to the surface, his face growing redder with every second I kept my determined stare fixed on him.

I shoved my chair out from under the table and stood up. "Good job not treating me like my uncle used to." As I stomped out of the kitchen, I was well aware I was overreacting, but I couldn't stop myself. It was almost preferable to risk myself than be seen as a victim again.

As I grabbed my purse and fled out the front door, Dante called out to me. "I know I can't shield you from everything, Liv. But that doesn't mean I need to expose you to everything, either. Not when it's dangerous. This shit changes you!"

When I ignored him and flung open the door to my uncle's car, Dante stood in the doorway with an expression of pure panic on his face. "Come back, baby. Let's talk about this."

I faced him for a moment but didn't give him a chance to coax me back into the house. "I'm not leaving for good, just for a while so I can clear my head. You infuriate me sometimes, Dante."

His relief was obvious when I closed the door behind me and sped out of the driveway. Carlo would be following behind me any minute now, but I didn't care anymore. I needed to talk to someone other than my husband—someone who had been through something similar.

Maybe I was being a brat, but I didn't like the idea of Dante making a plan for revenge and leaving me completely out of it. I wondered if anyone aside from my uncle had ever protected *him*. But Dante was right about one thing. Enzo was dangerous, and I wasn't sure what I wanted from him. I only knew I wasn't going to allow myself to be put in a cage again. Not for anyone or any reason.

It wasn't long before I checked the rearview mirror and saw Carlo's car trailing behind me. He wasn't even trying to hide it. He gave me an apologetic wave, and when I arrived at my destination, I chuckled to myself—I bet he never expected to tail me to his own house.

Once I got out of the car, he joined me at the front door with a grin. "If you had told me you were coming here, I wouldn't have followed you."

"Dante still would have made you, and you know that." An uncomfortable thought came to mind, and I frowned again. "He doesn't trust me."

"With everything that's happened, he's worried. You went missing just taking the dog for a walk. That's enough to make any man paranoid, but it doesn't mean he doesn't trust you." Carlo patted my arm comfortingly and opened the door to usher me inside. "Marcella is here. Go ahead and spend some time with her. I'll tell Dante you're here and to let you be for a while, okay?"

"I expect he'll be here in ten minutes regardless of what you say, but thank you for trying. You're a good man, Carlo." Overcome with emotion, I threw my arms around him and hugged him tightly before Marcella rushed out of the kitchen.

"*Cariño*, what's wrong?" Her lilting voice was tinged with concern when she approached us. "Are you okay? What did he do now?"

"Oh, you know me so well already, Marcella. Or you know Dante well, I can't tell which."

"If I've learned anything over the past few years, it's that you Italians are just as passionate as us." She took a firm hold of my hand and half-dragged me into the living room with her. "Out with it."

Twisting my ring around my finger, I sighed. "I don't even know where to start. How much did Carlo tell you about what's been happening the past few days?"

"Not a lot of details, but that we're likely going to war soon because of Enzo Leone…" Marcella seemed to register something in her head, and her hesitant gaze shot to me. "Is he the man who hurt you?"

"Yes. Do you know anything about him?"

With a sympathetic look, she shrugged. "Not much. Carlo keeps me far away from him. He has a reputation for being a predator. I've only seen him a few times, and he gives me the creeps." She took my hand. "When he told me, I had a feeling it had something to do with you. I'm so sorry, Livia."

"I just want to stop living this nightmare, knowing he's out there plotting against us. Dante insists he's dealing with it and that he wants me nowhere near it. But a small, sick part of me almost wants to see him suffer for what he did to me." I accepted the glass of gin that Marcella handed to me and sipped on it. It wasn't my thing, but she must have sensed that I needed something stronger than wine for once.

Marcella sipped her own drink and sat on the couch, turning to face me. "Do you remember what I told you about the cartel leader?"

"The one you fled from in Colombia?"

She tapped her nails on her glass a few times before she finally looked up at me again. "Yes…After I sold my soul to save my brother, he immediately took us with him back to his compound. But he didn't know we already had a plan."

Eager for more details about their escape, I leaned forward. "What did you do?"

Taking a moment to collect herself, she sipped her drink. "The only way to get him alone was to seduce him, and…I did what I had to do, then we ran."

I was stunned. She wasn't saying it directly, but I knew exactly what happened. She killed the cartel leader in order to escape with her and her brother's lives. "Wow…Marcella, I'm so sorry that happened to you."

She looked at me with surprise. "There's a reason I was so afraid of this man. He was known for extorting women this way—eventually, they always disappeared without a trace. I couldn't let myself be next." She inhaled deeply and met my gaze. "Can you honestly tell me what I did was wrong?"

"No," I answered without hesitation.

Before she had a chance to respond, Dante rushed into the living room and practically yanked my arm to get me up from the couch, shooting an accusatory glare at Marcella. "*What are you trying to do?*"

Carlo followed a furious Dante into the living room, stepping between him and his wife. "She's just telling her about her own experience, to give her some perspective—"

"Carlito, I can handle this myself!" she shouted, pushing him aside to face Dante. Carlo flashed me an embarrassed frown but took a few steps back to let his wife have at it. "All due respect, Livia is a strong woman. I perceived that from the second I met her. I'm not saying she should go out and start a brawl for her honor, but she deserves justice. Revenge, even."

Dante took a step back in shock. "But…that's not the kind of woman she is."

With determination, I squared my shoulders and faced him myself. "Maybe it's the kind of woman I need to be if I want to survive in this world. I chose you, which means I chose this life. I'm your wife, not the little girl you're babysitting. Not anymore."

"I—" he started, but I interrupted him before he could say anything else.

"I don't want anyone else dying because of me. I have to know why."

Chapter Twenty-Six

Dante

I could almost see Michael's scowl, cursing me for turning his little girl into a vengeance-seeking monster like me.

"What do you want to do? Interrogate him? You know he's not likely to be wandering around without at least ten guards." I couldn't hide the snark in my tone with my next words. "If he's smart, he's suspicious of us already, now that we've rescued your underwear from his house."

Livia huffed and approached, her glare firmly on me. "Enzo targeted me for a reason. If you kill him now, I'll never know what it was all for." Marcella joined Livia at her side, rubbing her arm to comfort her. As annoyed as I was at the moment, I was glad I'd set them up.

When she nodded enthusiastically, I almost wanted to take back that sentiment. "You deserve closure, *cariño.*"

Carlo shot her a warning glare, but she rolled her eyes at her husband. It was clear to me then who wore the pants in that relationship when he slunk away to avoid being embarrassed again. I was beginning to understand how he felt, because both of us had taken on stubborn women who refused to yield to our judgment.

My shoulders sagged in defeat. Months ago, it became clear to me that Livia and I were more alike than I first thought, and I hadn't realized just how true that assessment was until now. I couldn't say I didn't understand where she was coming from. If someone took away my chance to understand why I had to suffer the things I went through, I wouldn't have taken it lying down either.

This time, I gently coaxed her to the car in silence. I couldn't stand the deadly quiet, and when we hit a red light, I turned to her. "You don't know Enzo. He may look stupid, but he's cunning. You won't be able to trust anything that comes out of his mouth, anyway, and it'll only cause you more grief. I can deal with this quietly, and then you'll never have to see him again."

She ignored me, her famous scowl in place, staring straight ahead. "That was rude, you know. We didn't even say goodbye."

"Livia, baby, don't fucking push me. I'm trying here."

She rolled her eyes. "Fine. Do you have a plan yet, or not? How much has been going on that I know nothing about?"

Rubbing my temple in exasperation, I sighed. "Nothing concrete yet. If we want to take out Enzo, we need to make sure that nobody has hard feelings and tries to retaliate. If we even sense that there might be any dissent, we're nipping it in the bud. No mercy." I didn't want her to see me as a ruthless monster, but I was beginning to realize that after all she'd been through, she might have understood.

I'd thought I changed so much for her, but now I realized that I had an effect on her as well. And I wasn't entirely sure that was a bad thing. Looking at her, shoulders squared and determination painted across her face, she looked like a warrior goddess to me. Not the meek little girl everyone treated her as.

"Well, I don't want to be left in the dark about whatever happens. I deserve to know."

We pulled up to the driveway and I had to close my eyes for a moment and take a few deep breaths. "I promised Michael I would keep you safe and make you happy. I don't want you around these kinds of men, or even knowing about the things they do."

Her hand rested on my leg and with a firm tone, she argued, "I'm no innocent angel, and that's not on you. I was born to this, and neither of us can change that. I either have to adapt or leave."

Livia leaned closer to me and cupped my face in her hands, brushing her lips gently across mine. It was as if she needed to remind me that her soft side was still there. "You're right. When we're together, I can let my guard down, but outside of this, we need hard shells to deal with it all."

"Exactly. I'm still me, and you're still you. Let's go inside and make up. I hate fighting with you," Livia said as we walked up to the front door.

I bent down to plant an affectionate kiss to the top of her head. "It's still like foreplay to me. Get your ass upstairs, and we'll talk game plans after."

****

When Livia went to work the next day, I began phase one of my original plan. Hoping it would set the precedent for my meetings with the heads of the other families, I met with the most old-school of my allies first. Anthony Conti and I got along fairly well, and I had a feeling he would side with me in this situation. Anyone who looked at my condition right now would be insane to say I was in the wrong, especially once I showed them proof of Enzo's betrayal. We were all criminals, but even we had lines we refused to cross. Breaking the law, lying to rivals, murder—fine. However, no one would be able to look past someone giving information to the feds. It was a cardinal sin.

Stefano was my best guy for digging around for information unnoticed. He could have broken into a museum and walked out with the most prized painting there, hacked the cameras, bypassed the guards, and no one would have been the wiser. It was a truly invaluable skill that I came to appreciate and harness. I sent him on a fact-finding mission to find any evidence that Enzo Leone had corresponded with the police in any capacity, and it didn't take long before he hit pay dirt.

Forte had become my temporary HQ, as I was still not quite comfortable enough to use Michael's house as my personal office yet. Livia assured me she didn't mind me using the office, but it felt wrong to me, like I was replacing him.

When I entered the club, Stefano waited eagerly at the bar with a glint of amusement in his eyes. "You have a sixth sense for rats, I have to admit."

I accepted the bottled water from the bartender before I gestured for Stefano to follow me to my office. "I knew it. What did you find?"

He pulled a file out from under his arm and waved it at me. Once I shut the office door behind us, he flipped open the folder and slapped it proudly on the desk. "I leaned on my source pretty hard. Eventually, he coughed up a copy of an affidavit signed by some other guy."

"Who the guy?"

"He's nobody—a shill. I found him, and he informed me that Enzo gave him the information to testify so that it wouldn't blow up in his own face. Fucking coward."

If I had any lingering ounce of respect for Enzo, it was dead and gone now. The police hadn't even been after him—it wasn't as if he needed to throw Michael under the bus. Not that it would have been an acceptable excuse, but it would have been an excuse nonetheless. Enzo was a spoiled child who threw tantrums when he didn't get what he wanted, and he sang like a canary just days after the meeting with Michael. The worst part was, he didn't even do it on his own.

"I don't know how it's possible, but I'm shocked. He has some goddamned balls."

"Not for long…" he trailed off for a minute as if trying to figure out where my head was at, slumping down into a chair. "Did you tell Livia about the video?"

Trying to ignore the disappointment that it wasn't vodka, I swigged my water. "Of course I did. You know her well enough by now to know that she never lets things go. She wants justice for all of it. Michael, me, herself. This piece of shit has tormented her for long enough, so I can't even blame her."

It didn't help that there was a fully stocked bar not fifteen feet from where I sat. I'd been doing well up until the incident, but now the stress of the situation made the cravings harder to ignore. If anything happened to her, it would be the end of me.

"I think it's dangerous to let her get involved, Don Castellano. All due respect," he added on at the end as if that would curb my temper.

"I don't disagree. But she's not like other women. If I ever thought for a second she would be a demure mob wife, I would have been not just delusional, but plain fucking stupid."

The only reason I wasn't putting him in his place was because he was right—but so was Livia. I wanted to respect her wishes while protecting her, but I wasn't sure it was possible to do both. If I tried to control her, it would only push her away again.

"You've got your work cut out for you."

His statement made me smile. Even though I hated to be questioned, I appreciated that my men had a soft spot for my wife. How could they not? Most of them had known her since she was a child. She was strong, intelligent, kind, but fierce. I could have her pinned underneath me, mewing like a cat in heat one minute, and then be faced with her razor-sharp claws the next.

"That's what Michael said when he first sent me to watch after her," I said with a laugh. "If only I had known how true it was."

Chapter Twenty-Seven

Livia

One of the things I loved most about my friendship with Marcella was knowing someone else understood my position without judgment. Even though I'd been ushered out of the house like an unruly two-year-old, she was completely unfazed by our rushed departure.

She grinned at me and clinked her wineglass to mine. "If I had a dime for how many times Carlito dragged me away from someplace, I would be richer than you, *cariño.*"

After Dante told me he'd be busy all day in meetings with the heads of the families, I couldn't pass up this opportunity to spend some time with her, and also grant myself a much-needed distraction. "You wouldn't be so blasé about it if you knew how many times Dante has interrupted me during a conversation to drag me away. Usually with men, though, so this was a first for me."

Pursing her lips slightly, she surprised me when she said, "To be honest...I can kind of see where he's coming from. He's only trying to protect you."

"You were ready to kick his ass yesterday, and now you're on his side?" I sputtered in disbelief, placing my glass down on the table.

"I'm not switching sides. I definitely don't agree with him keeping things from you, but can you blame him for being a little overprotective, with everything that's happened since you came back?"

"No, of course not." I gazed down at my ring glinting in the remaining sunlight coming through the window and sighed. "Dante is all hard edges to the outside world, but with me he's different. I have to toughen up too, but sometimes I wonder if he would prefer me to stay innocent and helpless. Doesn't he know I won't make it here that way?"

With a comforting smile, she patted my arm. "Oh, Livia…I've seen the way that man looks at you. Not to mention the pure torture on his face every day you two were broken up. I'm sure this is more about him than you."

"I'm sure it is. He's said it since the beginning—he thinks he's corrupting me." Then why did he marry me? Was our pull so strong he couldn't deny himself any more than I could? "He still feels guilty because my uncle didn't approve of our relationship. We could've smoothed things over eventually…I know we could have, but we ran out of time."

I felt Marcella's hand rubbing my back soothingly. "You're still grieving—give yourself some slack. Both of you just need some time to catch up to all these changes. And I know Dante would do anything to avoid losing you again."

"You're right. He would."

My phone rang again—specifically, Dante's ringtone. Shaking her head, she gestured for me to take the call and went to refill our drinks.

"Hey, is everything okay?"

His gruff tone barked at me from the other end. "Where are you?"

"With Marcella. I told you, I'm not occupying an extra guard to come to Carlo's house when they can be better used elsewhere."

Dante grunted into the phone. "I thought once I married you, you'd stop being such a stubborn *principessa*..."

With a hint of snark, I asked, "Did you actually think that?"

After a moment's pause, he chuckled. "No. And I love you too much to ask you to change."

When I hung up the phone, Marcella arrived with refreshments and a smirk. "What was it this time?"

"He was checking on me again. Luckily, I didn't get chewed out this time for not bringing a guard with me."

"See? He's loosening up already. I told you, things will get better over time. He took you shooting too. That was a big deal. Carlo still won't even let me touch his guns."

There must have been some kind of protective gene ingrained into these men. In spite of that, it felt good to know Dante and I were slowly finding our way to a balance between protection and suffocation. "I'll tell you one thing... You say spice is an aphrodisiac? Try going to the range with a sexy man."

The roars of laughter that followed felt strange to me—but in a good way. It had been so long since I'd had a friend to talk to this easily. My life in California had been peaceful, an experience I wouldn't take back for anything. Now everything was much more complicated, but I didn't miss my old life. Here, I was my genuine self, and the people who loved me actually knew me. My artist side, my Mafia *principessa* side, my stubborn side—all of it.

My text notification chimed, and I laughed out loud. "Why am I not surprised? Now Dante wants me to come to the club."

"I'm sure there's a good reason. If not, tell him off and come back here. We can find ways to entertain ourselves while he stews."

She clearly enjoyed ruffling the feathers of these men, maybe even more than I did. "That sounds like a plan. I guess I'll head over there now and see what my indecisive husband wants."

Was he really so worried he didn't trust me to be in a house with Marcella and Carlo? It wasn't as if they didn't keep guns in the house, and now that I'd trained a bit, I knew how to use one. "He calls me stubborn. He needs to look in the mirror," I muttered to myself as I drove toward Forte.

While stuck in traffic, my phone rang again. I didn't bother to look before I answered and put it on speaker, tossing it on the passenger seat. I already knew who it was. "Yes, *dear?*"

Dante's voice boomed in the car. "Where are you going now?"

Seriously? "Dante, this is starting to feel a lot like California. I'm literally on my way to you right now."

"Then why are you going the other way? I'm at home."

I gripped the wheel of my uncle's car in frustration. "What are you talking about? You sent me a text and asked me to meet you at Forte, so that's where I'm headed."

The seconds-long silence after my statement was deafening, and a wave of fear washed over me when I heard the panic in his voice. "That wasn't me. Turn around and come home. Now. I'm sending Carlo to make sure no one follows you." He let out a nasty string of curses into the phone before I heard him yell, "Stefano, find out how she got that text!"

My heart constricted in my chest. I wanted to be angry about Dante tracking my every move, but if he hadn't, who knows what would have happened to me? I couldn't hide the shakiness in my voice. "D-do you think it was Enzo?"

"I'm positive it is. It's a trap, and you almost walked right into it. Goddamn it, Livia."

"How was I supposed to know he could send a fake text from your phone number?"

He sighed into the phone. "I'm sorry. You couldn't have known. But now that he's making contact directly, it's only a matter of time before he pushes even further. I need to end this. The others are in agreement, but I won't walk into a trap again. We need a plan."

Enzo was much too paranoid to leave himself out in the open for Dante to hunt him down again…not like he was right now. I thought for a moment, then inhaled deeply. He wasn't going to like this, but we were running out of options and time. "What if this is our chance to turn his tricks around on him?"

"What?"

"He thinks I'm coming to meet you. Wouldn't it be surprising if I showed up, and then you and your men appear?"

His response was immediate. "*Use you as bait? You're out of your fucking mind if you think I'll allow that!*"

My hackles rose, and I whispered my reply into the phone, sure it would cause Dante's detonation. "I'm already a block away."

"Turn the car around! I'm not playing games."

Cringing when his angry curses filled the car, I silently waited for him to finish his tirade before I calmly said, "No. This will work. He thinks he has me, but he doesn't."

I envisioned him running his fingers through his hair in frustration. "Stefano! Pull the car around. We're going." I kept the phone clutched to my ear as I listened to his heavy breathing, trying to calm himself down. A car door slammed, and his roughened voice startled me. "We're coming now. You *do not* pull in until I have eyes on you."

I hadn't expected him to give in, and I was relieved—until I realized I'd just argued to walk straight into Enzo's arms. A cold chill came over me, and my voice came out in a squeak. "Okay."

As furious as he was, he desperately tried not to show it, responding in a soothing voice, "Don't be scared. I'm here and I won't let anything happen to you. Keeping you safe *is* self-preservation for me. Do you understand?"

He believed he would die without me, and he would do anything, go anywhere, or kill anyone to keep me. "Yes, Dante. I understand."

"I love you, Livia."

"I love you too."

The car idled in the alley a block away from the club, waiting for him to give me the go-ahead. After a few minutes of chilled silence, the fear in his voice was evident. "I see your car. Go ahead. We're going to wait five minutes and head in through the back. No longer."

My hands shook when I let myself out of the car and

walked across the nearly abandoned parking lot, pausing for a moment when I reached the threshold. Behind that door, I would be confronted with the face that haunted my nightmares for the past four years. I forced myself to hold my head high and go inside.

It took my eyes a moment to adjust to the lower lighting inside the club, and once I scanned the room, I found it totally empty. No one behind the bar, on the dance floor, or occupying any of the plush velvet chairs. It looked strange in the daylight and with no music to break up the eerie silence.

As far as whoever sent that text, I still wasn't a hundred percent sure. Whoever it was intended for me to believe they were my husband. In the interest of playing along with the ruse, I called out, "Dante? You cleared the place out for us?"

My voice echoed off the walls of the empty bar, followed by a deafening silence. I spun around, scanning for movement in any dark corners, or behind the bar, but still saw nothing. Despite the sick feeling in my stomach, I knew Dante would be coming in five minutes, and all I had to do was stay vigilant until then.

The hair on my nape stood on end when I sensed someone behind me. Too terrified to turn around, I asked, "Who's there?"

"Oh, baby girl, I've been dying to hear that voice again."

The raspy drawl sent a shiver down my spine. I whirled around to face him. Lorenzo Leone, better known as Enzo, came out through the swinging kitchen door, prowling, as if readying to chase me. My heart pounded in my chest, but I forced myself to speak. "You…Why did you trick me into meeting you here?"

"So, you do remember me. I knew it. You left a lasting impression on me, as well," he crooned, his dark gaze roving up and down my body. The way he looked at me made me feel naked even though I was fully covered. He'd seen it all, and he was probably picturing it as his lascivious gaze lingered on my chest. "I've done away with every obstacle. Surely, you must have seen by now how far I'll go to have you to myself."

He hadn't directly admitted to what Dante and I both knew, but him subtly throwing it in my face made my blood boil. Before I could think twice, I spat, "In what universe does assaulting a woman lead to a romantic love story?"

He chuckled awkwardly as he scrubbed his hands down his cheeks. "I admit the way I approached you back then was a little harsh, but I was understandably upset after your uncle said I wasn't good enough for you. It was ballsy of him, seeing as he was fine with dipping his pen in *my* company ink…"

"*What?* You're lying!" Even as the words left my mouth, I knew he wasn't. My uncle's worst nightmare was being sent to prison where he would be unable to protect me from Enzo. Finding out he'd taken drug money when he was always vehemently against it was a shock, but I didn't have time to think about it now.

"And then when I saw you stumble into the club a few months later…it was like divine providence. I only wanted to humble Michael a bit. I swear I wouldn't have let anyone touch you."

There was nothing he could do to convince me he didn't enjoy the fear in my eyes, then or now. He fed off of it, growing more excited the more afraid I became. His skewed logic made no sense to me, and I continued to stare blankly at him, trembling, with no idea how to respond.

As if to pretend he cared about reassuring me, he added, "But it wouldn't be like that this time. I can take better care of you than Castellano, that's for damn sure."

"You don't even know me!"

Enzo sauntered closer, stopping only two feet away from me. "You're aware I've been watching you, so you know that's not true. I know everything about you…and now that you're here, we can start over."

Chapter Twenty-Eight

Dante

Having gotten the go-ahead from the other families, I would have been free to make a plan for getting to Enzo. However, rather than allowing me time to come up with a safe solution, my *principessa* chose to walk into the unknown. I refused to leave anything else to chance. I wanted to kill him with every fiber of my being, but not more than I wanted to get Livia the fuck out of here.

As long as she lived, whether he died today or tomorrow didn't matter one bit to me, because I knew he would, eventually. I would make sure of it.

My heart was in my throat as I watched Livia go inside the club. There was only one flashy car in the parking lot, which meant he'd probably come and paid everyone else to clear out. I didn't appreciate him fucking with my business. It was neutral territory, but him choosing this place was a deliberate move. He wanted to lure her back to the place where he humiliated her. Even shit faced, I could never be that cruel to her.

Although he was a sick, desperate man, I believed in some disturbed way, he actually loved her. How he could love her while taunting her was beyond me, but if it meant her life wasn't in danger, I would take it. And as I waited in the car with Stefano, the only shred of hope I held on to was my unsure assessment of an insane man.

Thankfully, Stefano happened to be with me when Livia went rogue, and I put him on security camera duty. If Enzo had gone to the trouble of clearing out the place, he'd likely locked us out of the cameras too. He pulled his tiny computer out of his bag and started typing away. As he worked, he darted a hesitant gaze toward me every few seconds.

At first, I ignored it, because I had enough problems already, but eventually it got on my nerves, and I glared at him. "If you're going to fidget the entire time we sit here, I don't think I'm going to make it. Spit it out."

"Sorry, boss," he sputtered quickly. "I just wonder if we should bother with this at all. Why wait when we can go get him right now? That's your wife in there."

"Believe me, it's taking everything in me not to rush in there and put a bullet in his skull for what he did to her. But she made her decision, and as much as I hate it, I have to let her do this. We're waiting. You just worry about those cameras."

It was starting to get on my nerves that everyone in my life questioned my ability to look after Livia. If I tried to stop her, I'd only be pushing her away again. She wouldn't have seen it as me protecting her. She would have seen it as me not trusting her, and that was the last thing I wanted. With my fists clenched on my lap, I silently seethed beside Stefano while I waited the most agonizing five minutes of my life.

"Got it," he announced proudly and angled the laptop toward me so we could both watch the events playing out before us. We watched as Livia entered the empty club, then she walked around, looking for any sign of people inside. She called out to me, playing Enzo's game. *My beautiful, smart girl.*

When I heard his sleazy tone, I felt a sudden ache in my right wrist. It took great strength to hold in my growl as I watched him unabashedly ogle her, and Livia's body stiffening under his perverse gaze. All I wanted to do was go inside and rip him to shreds.

In fact, I am going to do that. With my mind made up, I moved to open my car door.

"Boss, don't. Get back in."

"Excuse me?" I barked back at him. "Didn't you just say this was a waste and to just go get him?"

He didn't speak; he only pointed toward the front door of the bar, where several armed men had taken point outside. They hadn't seen me yet, and I quickly darted back inside the car, closing the door as quietly as possible.

"What's going on in there?" I croaked, trying to relax, knowing she was trapped with Enzo in my club. Again. I'd hoped he was desperate enough to get near her that he would have left himself vulnerable, but that was my mistake. *He'd had backup last time, too... What have I done?*

As soon as he turned the video toward me and I laid eyes on it, the feed cut out. "Shit," he mumbled as he continued tapping away.

"What did you do?"

"They must have cut the security system."

I pounded my fist into the steering wheel. "Fuck! I never should have let her do this. Goddamn it, if he hurts her again…"

Once he'd put his computer away, he pulled open his jacket to show me his holster. "Then we go in blind. I can only see two guys. They haven't seen us yet; we can take them."

With a nod, we got out and darted down the alley two blocks away from the club. We circled around until we found a good vantage point of the more secluded back entrance, where three more armed men stood outside, guarding the door.

This trap was only meant for her.

As we huddled so close, yet unable to reach Livia, it infuriated me. I wasn't sure if I was cursing myself more for loosening the reins, or just for choosing this particular time to give in to her stubborn ways. Due to Enzo's obsessive infatuation with her, I didn't think he had it in him to seriously harm her, but I could have been wrong. I'd read dozens of books about serial killers who murdered the object of their affection, and I wished I hadn't taken the gamble on a snake like Enzo Leone.

Good job, Castellano. He could be doing anything to her in there, and you just let her go.

The way the guards stood eerily still reminded me of Liv's description of Michael's guys back in the day— gargoyle-like. If I found them intimidating, I could only imagine how she felt.

Imagination was all we had to go on, because aside from ambient city noise, we heard nothing to indicate what was happening inside. Was it more calming to hear a commotion or deadly silence? It had been at least ten minutes since she'd gone inside, and I glanced down to check my watch for the hundredth time.

"It's been too long. We need—"

I swore I could feel the reverberation before I heard the bang, and everyone's heads—including the guards'—collectively snapped up in alarm. *Livia...*

Stefano's hand landed on my shoulder as I bolted up

from my crouched position. "What do you want to do?"

I brushed his hand away, then reached into my jacket for my pistol. "We take care of the guards and get my wife the fuck out of there."

He paused at my side, giving me that quizzical look again. "And Enzo?"

"If he's not dead already, he's going to be. I don't care if he's in there confessing his sins and begging her forgiveness. Some things can't and shouldn't ever be forgiven."

Chapter Twenty-Nine

Livia

The last time Enzo had me in his grasp, he had the upper hand. Back then, a clueless version of me walked into the club, an invisible spotlight set on me from the moment I stepped over the threshold. After all was said and done, I was shaken to my core. For the next four years, I looked over my shoulder constantly, waiting for the moment the nameless man would reappear. I'd never planned for the day I finally had the chance to confront him, because I was too busy running away from my past to face it.

In this moment, I vowed that no man or building would turn me into a victim again. Every one of my lingering ghosts was tied to this man, so it wasn't just about me anymore. Grief for all the people I'd lost filled me, and he had the nerve to stand before me and sweep it all under the rug. The hatred poured out of me as I stared him down.

"Start over? After you humiliated me in front of a dozen men? After you got my uncle arrested? Or after you harassed my best friend to take disgusting pictures of me? What about Dante's hand? I wouldn't do these things to my worst enemy!"

"Someone is doing her research." Enzo clicked his tongue in approval before he stepped closer. "Doesn't it feel better knowing it was a friend and not a stranger? I did that for you, baby girl. Michael wanted to stop this, and I couldn't let him do that. And judging by your runaway stunt, it seemed like he was in your way too."

His words made my buried guilt jump up into my throat. Sure, I'd complained many times about my uncle's overprotective nature, but never in a million years did I prefer a world without him in it. Panic coursed through my veins every second I remained here. It had definitely been longer than five minutes. *Where is Dante?*

I willed my voice to stay steady when I responded, "You're wrong."

"If Michael had just approved, none of this would have had to happen. You could've been Mrs. Leone. And what do you have now? Nothing. No family. Just a boyfriend with a stump pretending to be the boss."

This man was truly deluded. My stomach turned at the idea of him touching me again, but determination flowed through me. Enzo wasn't going to get the better of me. Using my left hand, I brushed some tendrils of hair out of my face, showing him my ring. "I have plenty left to fight for."

The sight of it caused his eyes to flash with anger, giving me some satisfaction that I managed to shock *him*. "You married that prick? Livia, you were supposed to be mine!" Enzo's jaw clenched, his furious gaze glued to the engagement and wedding bands on my finger.

Feeling brazen in the moment, I leaned in until my face was inches away from his. "*You're* the reason I left Manhattan. Dante is the only reason I came back, and I *ran* to the altar to marry him." I wanted to cut him as deep as he'd cut me, and I spat, "If he had no hands, he would still be more of a man than you are."

It was at that moment something shifted, and rather than give me a snarky retort, Enzo fell silent as if he'd actually been hurt by what I said. Stumbling back on his feet, he took a few deep inhales, then reached over the bar for a bottle of whiskey. After he took a generous swig, his dark eyes met mine again. "You don't know what you're saying."

It was startling to see him regarding me with his wounded gaze, but I forced myself to speak. If I didn't get answers, then this would have all been for nothing. "I just want to know why. Why me, Enzo?"

A long silence followed, where he stood directly in front of me, not touching me—just watching me carefully. His face went through a barrage of different emotions I couldn't figure out as he studied my face. It wasn't the same way he'd looked at me when he first came in, but it made me feel just as exposed. My skin broke out in goosebumps, willing him to finish his inspection quickly, but I wouldn't allow him to intimidate me into looking away.

Light wrinkles formed near the corners of his dark eyes as we studied each other. He had to be in his fifties. His brows were bold and darker than the rest of his hair, which—as I looked closer—had streaks of silver. If he were anyone else, I would have thought he was handsome. But everything he'd done made him hideous to me. Evil from the inside out.

Enzo's soft mutter startled me. "I think those eyes are what first captured me." He cocked his brow in amusement, which only confused me more. "You're the spitting image of your mother. So beautiful."

That was the absolute last thing I expected him to

say, and I struggled to find my words. My voice cracked when I answered, "What?"

He chuckled lightly with a faraway look in his eyes. "I thought I was seeing a ghost when I spotted you in Times Square. Those same shimmering waves, those chocolate eyes, the full lips…it brought back so many memories I'd buried. I knew Nicola and Angelo had a daughter, but he was so protective of you—as was Michael—I never got a good look until that day. I was floored."

The blows kept coming as I struggled to put everything together. "You…you were in love with my mother?"

When he caught the shock on my face, he grinned, but there was a hint of pain in his eyes that caught me off guard. "Seeing as we dated, yes. She left me for that *disgraziato* you call a father. She chose her side and look where it fucking got her." Anger rose in his voice with every word, his irises barely visible anymore. "You were my second chance. You're so much like her…"

The previous confidence I felt was shredding to pieces with every revelation, and I staggered back on my feet. "I didn't know…"

"Of course you didn't! No one did." As he took a step closer, his chest practically touched mine. "I was her dirty little secret before she settled down with the man her father wanted her to marry. But she left her mark on me, that one. Little did I know she'd leave behind a carbon copy of herself, just for me."

It sickened me when I met his gaze again and saw the adoration behind it. "You've been screwing with my family for over a decade because you got your heart broken? You're deranged."

Enzo shrugged casually. "I prefer to see myself as extremely…determined. I'll do *anything* to get what I want."

In a feeble attempt to stop myself from slapping him, I repeatedly clenched and unclenched my fists at my sides. "Are you the reason Augustine killed them? You couldn't have her, so no one else could? What else have you done to ruin my family?"

He looked offended. "Don't be stupid. When I found out what Augustine did, I was devastated. I would never have hurt Nicola. He was climbing the ranks, and I couldn't touch him. So, I used him as a pawn, knowing that either Michael or Dante would take him out for me eventually. I just had to wait for it all to play out."

Grabbing a nearby chair to brace myself, I tried to process everything I'd heard. My life was a tangled web, entwined with other people's stories from before I'd even been a thought to my parents. The revelation blasted away any illusion that I was ever in control of my fate. "My God…"

"You asked for answers, so now you're getting them. Don't complain, sweetheart."

When the word left his mouth, I couldn't hide my recoil. Knowing I'd never hear my uncle call me sweetie or sweetheart again only hardened my resolve to make it out of here. "Do *not* call me that."

He shrugged, likely unaware of the wound he'd just poured salt in. I glanced down and saw a healing wound on his right hand, and the moment the realization came to me, it sent me over the edge. That was how he'd lost the cufflink. Nero had only been defending himself. Little did he know, he gave us the evidence we needed to finally put a name to the nameless man.

I turned my back to him in order to compose myself. Once my heart rate finally slowed, I cleared my throat and faced him again. "You hurt Dante, and you violated me. You're the reason my uncle is dead! Let me make it perfectly clear to you. I will never be yours, Enzo. You're nothing but a monster to me."

As he approached me with cool determination, he seemed completely unperturbed by my refusal, and my utter disgust for him. "Maybe I need an angel to tame me. Walk out of here with me right now, and I won't dismember your husband."

His cruel promise delivered in such a casual tone sent shivers all over my body. "I won't let you near Dante, or anyone else I love again."

I can't let him get close enough to touch me. Never again.

"Then your solution is very simple. Come home with me. At least give me a little preview of what I've been missing…" he suggested as he prowled closer, extending his arms toward me. "I still remember how soft your skin was, and I'm itching to see if it tastes as good as it feels."

Willing myself not to shake, I held out my hand to stop him from getting any closer, my hand inches away from his chest. When I felt his fingers curling into the hair at the nape of my neck, coaxing me closer, I smelled the familiar scent of his cologne—the images that flashed through my mind revolted me. On a suppressed whimper, I pleaded, "Please, don't…"

A fire ignited inside me, and almost involuntarily, my knee shot up between his legs. Enzo stumbled back a few feet, snarling at me, "You think that deters me? I love a challenge, if you haven't noticed yet."

I reached into my back pocket and felt the cold steel of the pistol I'd taken from Dante's stash. Before I could think about it and change my mind, I brought it out and pointed it directly at Enzo. "Get back, asshole."

His gaze fell to the snub-nosed pistol in my hand, and then he had the nerve to grin at me. "You won't kill me. Not with that tin can, not with anything."

"I don't want you! Doesn't that matter to you in the least?" I took careful steps away from him, trying to keep my hand from shaking as I gripped the handle.

If I didn't hate the sound of his laugh before, I did now. "You will learn to love me back, Livia. I'll spoil you to your heart's content. And don't let my age fool you—I can fuck you so good you'll forget Castellano in a week. I'll have you begging for more, I promise you…"

He continued his approach, and when I felt my back hit the wall, my breathing became erratic. Dante wasn't coming for me, and I was out of time. Enzo's eyes were frenzied as he reached out to grab the pistol from my hands. I didn't know if his pseudo-love for me would prevent him from hurting me, but I wasn't ready to take the chance. When his hand rested over mine, I had no options left.

I curled my finger to rest on the trigger and pulled.

Without the protection of the earmuffs, the boom was much louder than I'd expected. And the kickback was surprising for such a small gun. The moment I fired, the tiny pistol fell from my hands like a dead weight. My vision had glazed over, and I forced myself to refocus on Enzo staggering in front of me.

"Baby girl, that was not very fucking nice," he heaved, clutching his stomach.

Frozen, I watched as all the color drained from his

face; blood spurted from his belly, soaking his hands and through the fabric of his suit. For a few moments, he stared straight through me before he went down. A stool from the bar went with him when he fell. As the pain set in, he writhed on the floor, groaning in agony.

Trying to block his cries of pain from my head, my hands shook as I reached into my bag for my phone. I hadn't heard from Dante in over twenty minutes, and I worried what was going on outside. I rang both him and Stefano, with no answer from either. If they hadn't come in yet, then it had to mean something was wrong. I didn't want to risk going outside and walking right into a firefight.

Letting my back hit the wall, I slid down until I was sitting on the floor, my knees scrunched up to my chest. When I glanced down again at Enzo on the tile floor, he was motionless. Some part of me expected to feel overwhelming guilt, or relief in this moment, but I felt neither of those things. I felt nothing.

Chapter Thirty

Dante

The dead quiet that followed the boom of Livia's gun chilled me to the bone. I'd never put down five men so fast in my life, and running on pure adrenalin, we barreled inside Forte. While I went in search of Liv, Stefano veered off to my left to check for anyone who may have been hiding. The first thing I saw was bright, fresh blood pooling across the dance floor.

Dread hit me like a punch to the gut. Relief came a moment later when I heard a small whimper to my right. Looking down, I found Livia crumpled against the wall. I crashed to my knees beside her, but she gave no reaction, just stared straight through me.

"Talk to me, tell me what happened." Running my hand over her body, I quickly checked her for injuries, and gasped when I saw blood on my palm. "*No*...where are you hurt?"

"I'm not, but he is," she answered in a monotone, pointing to a fallen barstool and the motionless heap formerly known as Enzo Leone, beside the bar.

Seeing his bloody form splayed out on the floor, and Livia's stoic state brought back flashes of memories from eighteen years ago. In her blank eyes, I saw myself, and I'd have been lying if I said it didn't take me aback.

"He was never going to stop hunting me."

Until Stefano recovered the security footage, that was enough for me. If I could save her the stress of having to talk about it, I would. Admittedly, a small part of me didn't want to see what she'd done. What *I'd* stained her with. I'd brought her back here and practically thrown her into her tormentor's arms, then forced her to kill to protect herself because I wasn't there.

Spit on Michael's grave, why don't you?

Livia continued to be unfazed by my presence while I led her to my office, which thankfully had a full bathroom. Her arm flopped lifelessly at her side once I let go. "Take off everything you're wearing and take a shower."

"Why?"

Maybe it hadn't sunk in yet, since she was used to being splattered with paint. I gestured to her sweater and jeans—that sweater definitely used to be blue, but the blood had spread, turning it a sickening shade of violet.

When her eyes finally cleared and she realized where she was, her words came out barely above a whisper. "Oh…my God."

"It's going to be fine. Just go wash up. Then I'm taking you home."

Without any regard for the open door of my office, she tore off everything as if Enzo's DNA burned her. She stood naked in front of me in three seconds, looking down at her body to see the blood had seeped through her clothes and stained her skin. "I don't want anything of his touching me ever again."

Stefano entered, and his eyes widened when he saw Liv naked beside me. She didn't move, and I quickly spun her around to shield her with my body as he whipped his face to the side. "Oh, shit! I'm so sorry, Livia."

"What the fuck, man?" I barked. "Give us a second."

It was the quickest I'd ever seen him move. He turned his back and waited for Livia to scurry into the bathroom. I resisted the urge to punch him while I got out a t-shirt and pair of sweatpants with the club's branding on it. I slipped inside the bathroom to leave it for her before coming back to the office.

He still had his back turned when I sat down at the desk and snorted. "You can turn around now. She's in the bathroom."

"Sorry, boss. I really didn't mean to—"

I waved him off. "Don't. It's fine. I don't think she even noticed you were there... I'm worried about her."

With clear relief on his face, he relaxed. "It'll sink in eventually. It's good for her to be numb right now while you take care of her." He took the bloodied clothes and turned to leave, then paused. "I'm sure you remember your first. It's nothing to us now, but the first time is memorable."

Everything I saw in Livia now reminded me of myself back then. What had I expected? For her to break down and feel guilty? She rid the world of a scumbag who never deserved to breathe the same air as her. Just like I had. Maybe it was fate that he lured her back here.

Enzo was meant to die in the same place where he assaulted her, and I gave Stefano the task of making it so nobody would ever find him. The footage he managed to recover from the backup cameras turned out to be both illuminating and disturbing. As much as I didn't want to see my beautiful girl's hands stained with blood, I forced myself to sit down and watch it all the way through.

The pieces fell together in my mind with every confession the spineless prick uttered. Enzo was twisted, but I never expected the bombshells he dropped. It was almost as if he was dying to get his story out, anything to get Livia to somehow sympathize with his sob story.

Finding out that Michael had been taking drug money explained his reasons for not telling me about the threat. Michael truly thought he was the only one who could protect her, and I didn't know whether to feel more offended or betrayed by his actions. After what I'd been through with Augustine, he'd been on the take? I understood why he'd never told me, but that didn't make it any easier to swallow. And not only had he lied about that, but he'd known about Enzo's history with Livia's mother.

Enzo's grief over losing Nicola obviously sent him off the deep end. I'd met Livia's parents before, and I definitely saw the resemblance between Livia and Nicola, but enough to latch onto this obsession for so long? Was there some magic in her family line that beguiled men until they lost their fucking minds? Sometimes I felt crazy too, but I was lucky enough that she loved me back as she proudly declared, flashing her ring right in his face. God, I loved her snarky *principessa* side. *Suck on that, Enzo.*

I never imagined when I let her walk in there that she would have actually fired a shot. A big part of me—bigger than I wanted to admit—was damn proud of her. She thought she pulled one over on me by swiping that pistol. I had noticed the day it was gone, but I let it go. If I'd have taken it back, then she'd have been defenseless when all of this went down. My only solace was knowing I'd given her the tools to protect herself, unlike Michael.

Sometimes I still heard his disapproving voice in my ear, but it didn't deter me anymore, because I was determined to prove him wrong. Livia and I would bend, but we would never break.

****

After all that happened at my apartment, neither Liv nor I wanted to step one foot inside the place. I terminated the lease and moved the rest of my stuff into the house. No more bachelor pad, alone with my dog and a bottle of vodka in the freezer to keep me company. Livia confessed she felt haunted in this house, but neither of us had the energy to think about sorting through Michael's belongings just yet.

The only family she had was gone. All that was left was me, and I never wanted her to feel like she was lacking while I was around.

After the night at Forte, Marcella invited her friend to come see Livia's work, and he promptly requested ten paintings to display in his gallery. The pure joy on her face was infectious, and instead of being overwhelmed by the mountain of work, she relished it with a smile. I'd found someone who was like me in all the ways that mattered, and unlike me in all the ways I needed.

Not being afraid of hard work either, I threw myself into my position as the head of our family. Heeding Livia's fears, I began to invest in a few legit businesses in Manhattan. I didn't think I would ever be a nice nine-to-five white-collar man, but I didn't plan on being the boss forever, either. I kept hearing her words in my head. *Either prison or death.* I was determined to one day be the exception to the rule, but until then, I was going to proceed with as much caution as possible to avoid both.

The events of the past few weeks seemed to put the

fear of God in everyone. Even my most staunch haters felt sympathy for what Livia had gone through and didn't want a repeat in their own families. The people who needed a reminder had seen how ruthless I could be, and the streets had been quiet in the days since. Once word got out that Enzo had ratted on Michael to the feds and subsequently disappeared, people slowly started to disassociate themselves with the Leones, which turned out to be a benefit for us.

During my rage of finding out the nameless man's identity, I'd sworn to strike down anyone in the way, but I couldn't do that now. I realized the only way to ensure I didn't corrupt Livia as I feared was to be creative about my solutions from now on. Risking prison was never a concern for me with Michael's team of lawyers on standby. Risking death had never mattered because I didn't have anything to live for. But the one thing I was not going to do was destroy the one ray of light in my life with my darkness.

By offering an olive branch and advocating for Luca to take the lead of the Leone family, I'd made an unlikely and hesitant ally.

Ally may be a strong word. I still didn't trust him, but he was at a disadvantage. By me offering a hand in friendship, not only could I ensure he was indebted to me, I could also keep a close eye on him. After all was said and done, I hosted a get-together at my club in congratulations. My subtle way of saying, *Yes, we're going to dance on your figurative grave, Enzo.*

It wasn't my intention at first to bring Livia along, but in the back of my mind, I admitted I was curious if seeing her would get a reaction out of Luca—something to indicate how much he knew, or what his intentions were. I'd thought she would have been too traumatized to ever step foot here again, but she insisted.

"I want to meet him. That way, I'll know who I'm looking for over my shoulder."

I wasn't sure I liked her having that mindset, but if it meant she wouldn't do anything reckless again, I'd take it. With my hand resting on the small of her back, I led her inside the packed club. Her muscles tensed the moment we entered, and I leaned down to whisper in her ear, "I'm right here. If you want to go at any point, just say the word, and we'll go."

"No, I'll be okay," she assured me, straightening her back and jutting out her chin. "Is that him there?"

Even I felt a bit of pity for Luca as he stood alone by the bar with a cocktail in his hand, swirling it around in the glass. His relief was evident when his gaze locked on me, and he let loose a warm smile. "Dante, hey. Thanks for doing this for me." After glancing at the empty stools on either side of him, he frowned. "As you can see there hasn't been much support as of yet."

I nodded brusquely. "It's a show of good faith. Give it time."

When Luca finally spotted Livia beside me, his expression morphed into one of surprise. "And this must be Livia." He reached out to shake her hand, and after a few moments of deliberation, she took his hand in hers. "I'm Luca Leone. It's an honor to meet you."

Her voice came out slightly shaky, but she refused to look away from him. "It's nice to meet you too. Congratulations."

Luca squeezed her hand before letting it go. "Thank you. That's very kind of you to say."

Once she had sufficiently memorized Luca's face

for her nightmares, we slipped into my office to have a chat where we would be safe from prying ears or cameras. When the door clicked shut behind me, Luca turned to me and bobbed his head approvingly. "She's a sweet girl."

I doubted anyone could blame me for being protective when it came to her, but the clipped reply came out anyway. "Yes. She is."

"Tough cookie, too. I admire that."

"As do I. But we're not here to talk about my wife," I said, enunciating the word *wife,* just in case an obsession for Rossi women was genetic, I didn't want him getting any ideas.

"Remember, there's a cost for my alliance, Luca. Few are willing to look past what your brother did, as you can plainly see by the attendance in your vicinity. I, however, see a potential ally, and I prefer not to judge someone based on who they have the misfortune of being related to." It was no secret there was no love lost between Enzo and me, but I didn't want to arouse suspicion with Luca, either.

He gave a somber frown. "I know. I appreciate that, and I won't forget it. For the record, I always tried to convince him to stop with the drugs. It was killing him. And now who knows what hole he got himself in."

Or more accurately—holes.

Even though his drug abuse provided more explanation for his psychosis, it was still no more of an excuse. "I'm glad you see it that way, because the families are in agreement on this. We don't want any more unnecessary violence, and having leaders fucked up on coke makes for bad decision-making."

"I agree completely."

I wasn't sure whether I could trust his effortless agreement, but for now, I was placated. "We'll talk, Luca."

I'd have made friends with the devil himself if it meant I'd never have to know the pain of losing Livia again.

Chapter Thirty-One

Livia, a few months later.

Every time we even whispered the word *vacation* or *honeymoon*, the real world crashed down on us, as if to remind us we hadn't earned a break yet. Whether it was a work crisis on Dante's behalf, or mine, there was always something.

After Marcella's friend had shown my work in his gallery, I'd caught the eye of a few big-name socialites who loved my work and spread the word. It felt like my dream was finally coming true, and I put in my notice at the museum. Many sleepless but happy nights were spent painting commissions until my wrist grew sore.

On the nights where Dante hadn't been working late, he'd come home and keep me company while I painted. He had a vast collection of old classical music records he'd play for me—to inspire creativity. The records were for me, according to him, but every time the record player was on, he was in my studio, listening. Maybe in some small way, it helped fill the void the loss of his ability to play music left behind.

Even now that he'd gotten the hang of his new prosthetic hand, he hadn't touched the violin my uncle left him, but I didn't say a word about it. Whether he picked it up again or not made no difference to me. He saw his music as his worth, but I saw it only as the catalyst that made me look at him more deeply for the first time. Everything else I learned, and everything else I felt after that was all due to him. Just him. Once Dante finally learned I had given him my heart whether he wanted it or not, he came to a kind of catharsis.

When he'd seen the state of me after the altercation with Enzo, he seethed with a fury I had never seen before—he looked ready to set the world on fire, but he managed to rein himself in. I was proud of him for that. Every ruthless act made it easier to let yourself snap, and if me pulling the trigger on Enzo saved Dante from chipping away more of his humanity—I was willing to put my own on the line, because I knew he wouldn't have stopped at just one bullet.

Despite the history with Enzo's younger brother, who my uncle and Dante had interrogated when I went missing, Dante decided to leave him to take Enzo's place as boss of the Leone family. He saw it as a *keep your enemies close* type of thing, and I couldn't disagree with his decision. Especially after all I had seen, and what I'd done, I couldn't let myself become jaded to death. It wouldn't have been right to ruin more lives in fear of what they may or may not do in the future. The last thing Dante wanted was to turn Manhattan into a bloodbath.

I didn't know Luca well, but I knew he had Leone blood running through his veins, and that meant I would never be able to completely relax around him. There was no way he didn't have at least the smallest suspicion toward us, with Enzo's obsession with my mother, and his sudden "disappearance."

Knowing what I did now, I wondered how Enzo managed to keep his history with my mom secret. Unless he was as secretive as she was, Luca must have been around when they were together at least once or twice. And when he found out, would he understand what I'd done, or would he be coming for us next?

If it had been anyone else, I would have been sorry for what I'd done. But everything I had heard and experienced of Enzo told me he was a raving lunatic, and a predator. I knew I was guilty, but I didn't feel it. Whether I had pulled the trigger or not, he'd signed his death warrant already. How many more lives had been saved because he was gone? I was sure a lot of guys were breathing easy when they realized they didn't have to pay him back a loan, or worry about getting their legs broken.

I didn't want what happened to change me, but I kept the same suspicious eye on Luca as Dante did. The question in the back of my mind was always, *friend or foe?* Being suspicious of people came natural to me, but now even a mannequin would have gotten a second glance from me.

And now that we'd been married for a while, some antiquated status shift occurred, and I quickly became accustomed to endless charity functions and *family* weddings with Dante and his associates and their wives. This was something I'd usually been spared from during my childhood; my parents and my uncle strived to keep me as far from their associates as possible. I'd asked him to involve me in the community, and this was the result.

The surprising part was realizing just how much the criminal line blurred. It felt strange to bump shoulders with the same people who were outwardly against everything we stood for. Police chiefs, congressmen, and I'd even met a senator during one of the Contis' daughters' weddings. Dante and he had talked about the upcoming election as if they weren't two people on opposite sides of the law.

These events were infamous for being boring, and now I knew that was true. Here I sat at yet another banquet, which was basically a convention for rich men to exchange money for favors, or maybe pass a hidden note in a handshake.

Luca was usually in attendance as well, and his presence never failed to bring a twinge of nervousness. He was never impolite, and he always greeted me with respect, but I didn't know if I could trust his charm. Occasionally, I'd look up from our table and spot him across the banquet hall, and sometimes he'd already been looking at me.

I turned my attention back to our table. It felt normal to me now, when my entire life I'd been so intimidated by these men. But as I sat at the glossy mahogany table, covered in fancy placemats, china, and gorgeous floral centerpieces, I felt at home with these men—even Stefano. He'd been concerned about me being a liability for Dante, and he made it no secret he disapproved of nearly everything I did, but his concerns had been dashed after the night at Forte. Of course, he still thought I was reckless for walking headfirst into a trap, but I would have preferred to be anything over weak.

Dante leaned into me and pressed a soft kiss to the top of my head. "I wrote a check already, so we don't need to hang around. Are you ready to go?"

"Ready to be alone with you? With no one around for miles? Yes, please."

With the dust finally settled, we decided to take that honeymoon. Just me, Dante, and Nero for a few weeks at his house upstate. It wasn't too far to prevent us from coming back to the city in case of an emergency, but it was far enough it was unlikely anyone would be popping in. Those days in the house with Dante had been bliss, and I was looking forward to making even better memories with him in what I hoped would eventually be our permanent home.

As we bid our goodbyes to everyone, Dante made a big show of telling everyone that just because we were staying in the state, that didn't mean they should call unless someone was in peril. Gio found it humorous that he was acting like a concerned dad, telling his kids not to get too rowdy while we were out of town. "I think I can hold down the fort for a while, boss. If I shit my pants, I won't bother you."

"Good, because I'm not changing diapers for anyone I haven't had a hand in bringing to life." He grinned and flashed me a hinting look, causing me to blush an ungodly shade of red.

I shot him a halfhearted scowl and elbowed Dante in the ribs. "Thank you for that, Gio."

"Hey, I'm not the one who spurned this fatherly instinct," he retorted, holding his hands up in surrender.

I knew what Dante was going to say before he opened his mouth, but I kept my mouth shut and smiled up at him, waiting for it.

"Only yourself to blame, my love."

From the function, we immediately headed home to pack before anything stopped us from leaving. After hurriedly changing our clothes, we loaded up the car, Dante putting his prosthetic hand to work. As proud as I was, I couldn't help but feel a little bit concerned for him. I wanted to tell him to take it easy without making him feel like he couldn't handle himself. "I can help, *caro*."

"No!"

For a moment, I wasn't sure if he was being stubborn or if he was hiding something from me as he carefully stacked our luggage to his liking. Or maybe he was only eager to get on the road before his phone went off again.

My worries soon fell away the farther we got from Manhattan. This was our time now. The traffic began to thin out as we got closer, and we wound down the windows to enjoy the breeze. I peered into the backseat to see Nero's ears flapping in the wind as he stuck his head out of the window. He'd never looked happier.

My smile widened when Dante rested his hand on my leg, running it up and down slowly. "I like that I can do this again."

His happiness was clear on his face, making him more handsome than ever. I couldn't help but beam back at him. "Me too."

My relief didn't last long, because the closer we got to the house, the more fidgety Dante became. If he was worried about how things were going back at home already, it didn't bode well for the next few weeks. Now that we had finally carved out some time for ourselves, I didn't want reality rearing its ugly head. Dante wouldn't easily give up the reins to anyone, even his underboss. He was comfortable with his position, and I doubted he planned on giving it up anytime soon. Not that I even expected it anymore.

Even I was fidgety by the time we got to the house and settled in. In an attempt to distract myself from the sudden energy, I whipped up a quick meal for us.

During dinner, he was oddly quiet still, and I couldn't take it anymore. "What's going on with you?

You were so happy when we left, and now you look like you're going to the gallows."

In the space of five minutes, he'd wolfed down his food incredibly fast while I still had half of mine unfinished on the plate. "It's nothing bad. I'm just nervous about my surprise."

"What do you mean? What surprise?" *Oh, thank God.* I attempted to hide my relief that it wasn't about work, my stress replaced with giddiness.

Confusion came over me when he pushed back his chair and left the room without a word. I stayed at the table and waited. After several minutes, I started to wonder if he was coming back at all, and I called out, "Dante?"

Another agonizing few seconds passed, and then I heard the familiar sound. Goosebumps rose on my skin in an instant. It was faint at first, but it grew louder as I watched Dante emerge from the bedroom with my uncle's violin in position. My mouth dropped open, and it took several moments before I could say a word. "You're doing it, *caro mio.*"

The proud smile on his face took my breath away. As he walked closer to me, his eyes slid closed and the melodious notes filled the entire room. I became enthralled watching his graceful movements and the expression of utter satisfaction on his face. It was a pure, unabashed contentment I only got to see when he looked at me, or when he played music. Enzo may have taken his hand, but Dante was never more whole until this moment.

When he insisted this violin was priceless for a reason, he was right. The music it created was almost otherworldly compared to anything I'd heard before.

He finished the end of the piece and opened his eyes; they were shining with pride. "The prosthetist had an attachment made so I could play again. I wanted to surprise you."

The hope in his voice made my chest tighten, and I got up from the table to inspect his hand. "So, that's why you were being so shifty. When did this happen?"

As if he were looking to me for approval, his cheeks colored slightly. "A few weeks ago. I needed to practice. It's not the same, but with time I'll be able to play as well as I used to."

"You did so well. I'm proud of you."

"Are you falling in love with me again?" he retorted with a wolfish grin.

Wrapping my arms around his neck, I giggled and rose to my tiptoes and pressed my lips to his. "I fall in love with you every morning when I wake up and see you beside me. Anything else is just a bonus after that."

Dante seemed pleased by my answer, granting me with a warm smile before he brought the violin back to position. With reverence in his eyes, he crooned, "This next one is for you, my beautiful girl."

A word about the author...

Rose is an avid reader and hopeless romantic with a twist. When she isn't penning gritty stories and morally ambiguous characters, she can be found mingling with the book community on social media or enjoying a cup of tea while daydreaming about the next story. Rose resides in South Florida.

She can be reached at: www.rosethorgaard.com